MAX

C.J. PETIT

C.J. PETIT

Printed in the United States of America

First Printing, 2017

ISBN: 9781075991585

TABLE OF CONTENTS

C.J. PETIT

CHAPTER 1

May 12, 1878
Burden, Kansas

Max had the door to his shop wide open on that beautiful May morning as he needed the extra light whenever he worked on delicate jobs. Besides, he liked to be able to watch the traffic and just greet folks as they passed by his workshop. On cloudy days, or when he was working by lamplight, he'd work on the bigger equipment that needed repair.

He had a thriving business in his hometown and a reputation for doing exceptional work that kept him busy. If it moved and it was broken, Max could fix it. Ever since he was very young, he enjoyed discovering how things worked, but it was more than just enjoyable, Max had a unique talent to innately understand why things did what they did and the intelligence to not only put things back together but to improve their functionality.

It began when he was just five when simple toys were disassembled and reassembled, although not always successfully. As he grew older, he learned from those very early failures, moved on to increasingly more complex mechanisms, and became the bane of his parents when he started on household items.

When, at the age of eight, he completely dismantled the grandmother clock in the parlor, Max was close to the end of his young existence. Luckily, he had it reassembled and working correctly before his father returned home from running a shipment out to a neighboring town. His father did notice that the clock's chime had started working again, and his mother had suggested that perhaps it had started again when she had accidentally bumped into it. He owed his mother for covering for him, as she always did.

Like most boys, Max was far from a young saint in other aspects of his childhood, but his transgressions were limited to the occasional swiped cookie or the almost required stolen school days when the fish were biting. His worst offense was when he told the butcher, Mister Horace Schooner, that he was a poop-head. The butcher had loudly complained to his father as Max stood nearby with his head down, expecting his well-earned spanking. His mother's intervention wasn't necessary for the Poop-head Incident when, after the butcher's vitriolic accusations, Max's father had confirmed his son's assessment of the butcher and told him that he was, indeed, a poop-head.

After the war, Max expanded his work to include firearms, because so many had filtered into the civilian market. He finally moved up to repairing the large steam engines that had started to appear on local farms and mills. Too often, the farmers and mill operators would fall victim to salesmen who pitched their products as reliable, low-maintenance machines. When they discovered otherwise, they called Max.

This morning, he was working on a wall clock for the Peters. For a tall young man, Max had amazing manual dexterity, which was critical for exacting jobs like this. Amanda Peters had brought the clock in the day earlier, almost secretively dropping it off with barely a word.

He had always liked Amanda, even when they were in school together. She was a happy, friendly girl and not bad on the eyes, either. Amanda was one of those girls that would become the focus of a schoolboy crush by every boy in the school and Max was no exception. Now, she was a handsome, likable young woman and still earned a soft spot in Max's heart.

6

MAX

Last year, she married Johann Peters, who was a year older than Max and two years older than Amanda. Max never did understand why she had chosen Johann. He was a good-looking young man and many of the young women in Burden had set their caps on him, but he wasn't highly regarded by the male side of the populace. He didn't like to work, and he was known to bend the rules. Johann was basically considered a poor excuse for a man, by the other men, at least. But Johann seemed to tolerate them all despite their low opinion of him, with the lone exception being Max.

Johann openly despised Max and always had. Why he had his deep dislike for him, Max hadn't a clue, but he didn't deal with Johann that often as he was out of town a lot in his new job as a drummer for farm equipment. He assumed that Amanda had dropped the clock off for repair while he was out of town, knowing that her husband wouldn't approve of her seeing Max even on a strictly business basis.

He had told Amanda that the clock would be ready for pickup today. Normally, there was about a three-day wait before he could start on a job, but he had to get Amanda's done quickly so Johann wouldn't notice its absence. There would be no charge for the repair either, but it wasn't because it was for Amanda, well, mostly it wasn't.

It was just how Max ran his business because he had the flexibility to do so. His fees ranged wildly, and if someone could afford a steam engine, they'd pay well enough, so he could afford to not charge some of his customers at all. He knew that many of his customers couldn't spare that extra fifty cents or a dollar for a repair, and he'd do the job for just the satisfaction of seeing the broken item working again. None of his well-to-do customers complained because they needed his services and his rates were still fair. As a result of those charges, he had a decent bank account, which covered his meager expenses and allowed him to do the pro bono work. Naturally, his pricing structure led to a steady flow of work to his shop.

He was just about finished with the Peters clock when he heard banging against the common wall to the east that his shop shared with an abandoned stagecoach office. He didn't pay it any mind for the first few seconds, but it continued, and his curiosity got the better of him. So, he put down his tools and walked out the back door of his shop through his living area. He turned right and noticed that the back door of the old stagecoach office was ajar, and as he reached the door, could hear the banging, but he heard other sounds…human sounds.

He yanked open the door and was stunned to see Mary Preston, her blouse open and her skirt pulled up, pressed against the wall by Walt Emerson. They both turned and saw Max with his mouth agape.

Suddenly, Mary slapped Walt and shouted, "Max! Get him off me! He's trying to rape me!"

Max needed no more incentive as he took two long strides forward, grabbed Walt by the collar, then hurled him across the back room. Walt stumbled backward until he slammed into the far wall and hastily pulled up his britches, incensed with Max's intervention. He charged back as Max stalked towards him then suddenly stopped and kicked at Max's right knee, trying to put him down. The kick struck higher than the knee, and only buckled Max, but left Walt's boot high. Max grabbed Walt's foot and yanked it up, dropping Walt to the floor. Walt then scrabbled along the floor and head-butted Max in the stomach. When Max crashed with his back against the wall, he kneed Walt in the chest, then as his head was coming up, Walt caught Max flush on the jaw with an uppercut with his left fist. But there wasn't much force behind it and Max threw a hard right to the left of Walt's face. Walt took the blow, spun, and hit Max's chest with a solid left.

8

MAX

Meanwhile, Mary buttoned her blouse and smoothed her skirt as she watched the two young men pummel each other. Max was slightly smaller than Walt, but a lot stronger. Max took some ineffective punches, but Max finally landed a sharp uppercut to Walt's chin. He toppled backward and hit the back of his head against an old hardwood table. There was a loud crack and Walt dropped to the floor and lay still.

Max, breathing hard, ran over to Walt and placed his hand on his chest, but felt no heartbeat. Max stood slowly and looked down at Walt, stunned that a simple fistfight had resulted in him killing a man.

Mary walked up quietly behind Max and put her hand on his shoulder.

"Is he dead?" she asked quietly.

Max just nodded, and the room remained silent for another thirty seconds when suddenly, there was a loud banging at the front door. Both quickly turned their faces in that direction. The ruckus must have attracted attention.

Mary begged, "Max, thank you for saving me. I owe you so much, but I can't let anyone know about this. My reputation will be ruined, Max. Everyone will think I'm a whore."

Max turned to the lovely, distraught Mary and said, "I'll tell them it was just a fight. You go ahead and leave."

She smiled and whispered, "No matter what happens, I'll be here for you, Max."

She leaned over and kissed him softly before scurrying out the back door. Max waited until she had gone and then walked to the front office and unlocked the front door.

City Marshal Emil Becker was at the door with Paul Schneider, the owner of the general store on the other side of the abandoned depot, who must have heard the commotion.

Max said, "You'd better come in, Emil. Walt Emerson is dead."

The marshal shot past Max and into the back room as Max and Mister Schneider followed.

"What happened, Max?" the marshal asked as he knelt over Walt's still-warm body.

"I was working in my shop and heard some banging from the far wall, so I came over to find out what it was and found Walt pounding on the wall. It made no sense at all, so I asked him what he was doing. He turned and told me it was none of my business, and I told him it was annoying me, and he didn't like that. He seemed upset about something, so he walked over and took a swing at me, and it turned into a brawl. After we traded punches, I hit him, and he fell backward, hitting his head on that oak table over there."

The marshal stood and said, "I'll get the doc in here to determine the cause of death, but I'm going to have to arrest you, Max."

That surprised Max. Usually, fights between two men were nothing more than a spectacle.

"Why? It was a fair fight."

"Because no one saw it, Max, and it resulted in a death. Don't worry about it too much. It probably won't amount to anything."

"Alright," he replied.

MAX

"Let's go to the jail, Max," the marshal said as he turned and walked out of the office with Max trailing behind.

Mister Schneider remained behind to wait for the doctor.

Once they were outside, Max asked, "Marshal, before I get put in the jail, can I finish the clock I was working on for Amanda Peters? It's almost done, and it won't take five minutes."

Emil nodded and replied, "Go ahead. Just come over to the jail when you're done. I've got to go and see the doc."

Max said, "Thanks, Emil," then returned to his shop to complete the clock repair.

He let his hands do the simple finishing work that remained as he thought about what had just happened.

Mary Preston had been one of his four girlfriends as he progressed through his school years. She was number three when he was fifteen. She was a pretty, brown-haired, blue-eyed girl with a quick laugh, and was something special to Max for one reason; she was his first kiss. But like most teenage romances, it had faded away. They had remained friends, and as Mary had reached her older teens, she had blossomed into quite an attractive, well-formed young woman. Max guessed it was those well-developed curves that had attracted Walt's eye.

Walt Emerson was somewhat of a mystery to him. He knew Walt for a couple of years in school, but he had dropped out of the fourth grade to work on the family farm and was the only son of Jerome and Emily Emerson. His mother had died when he was ten, so his father raised him and his two sisters. Max had only seen Walt sporadically over the years since school, whenever he came to town to pick up supplies, but usually, his father did that. His sisters were much younger. They were both teenagers and still in school. Patty must be fifteen and her younger sister, Colleen, was a year younger and were both pretty young girls. He imagined it must be hard for them to go to school and take care of the household as well.

But he and Walt had never had a problem before, and his death weighed heavily on him as he finished the work on the clock and set it near the front of his shop with a note for Amanda telling her it was repaired and there was no charge.

He left the door to his shop open, walked across the street to the jail then went inside. There was no one in the office, so he walked to the back and put himself into a cell but left the door open. If the marshal wanted to close the door later, he would.

He sat on the cot in the cell and just dwelled on what had happened. *Why hadn't Mary screamed when Walt had first started his attack?* Her blouse was already open and her skirts were already pulled up. *Why didn't she scream? Was she so worried about her reputation that she would rather be raped than let anyone know what was happening?* But fair fight or not, he had killed Walt Emerson and maybe he should go to prison. The Bible said 'thou shalt not kill', and he had killed.

After he'd spent another twenty minutes pondering that question, the marshal finally walked through the door.

"See you made it, Max. I'm gonna need a statement from you."

"Alright. Do you want me to write it now?" Max asked.

"Go ahead. Use the small room across from the cell."

Max nodded, then walked out of the cell and into the small room that was little more than a closet with a chair and a table. There were sheets of paper and pencils on the small table, so he pulled out a sheet and began to write.

He was torn between telling the truth or fulfilling his promise to Mary. He chose to keep the promise and wrote exactly what he had told the marshal when he had first explained what had happened. Part of the reason was to keep his promise, the other was to accept the blame for what he had done.

Once he decided to leave Mary out of the statement, it didn't take long to write, and just ten minutes later, he stood, left the room, then strode across the office to Marshal Becker and handed him the sheet.

"Did you want me to go back to the cell now, Emil?" he asked.

"Go ahead. I'll leave the door open, though."

"Thanks."

Max returned to the cell and stretched out on the cot. The cell was just a holding cell that was used to house drunks and serious prisoners that needed to be taken to the county courthouse for trial. He had never been in a cell in his twenty years and he didn't like the feeling of being there.

He spent another two hours just ruminating over what had happened and the possible consequences that awaited him. *Why did he even go over there?* It wasn't his business at all. But if he had ignored it, Mary would have been ruined and her life would have been filled with pain. No, he finally decided, he had done the right thing but was still shaken by having killed Walt, despite what he was trying to do to Mary.

The marshal finished writing his own report for the county sheriff, then stood and entered the open cell.

Max looked up at him as he said, "Max, why don't you head on down to Sunny's for lunch? Tell them the town will pick up the tab because you're a prisoner."

Max rose from the cot, replied, "Yes, sir," then stepped out of the cell and left the jail. He'd pay for his food himself and wasn't about to tell anyone that he was a prisoner.

When he walked into the diner, he felt as if he was naked as everyone just stared at him, the rumors of Walt's death followed by his arrest and incarceration having already made the gossip circuit. He sat down and waited for what seemed like an hour, but was probably only a minute, before Nancy Whitaker, the waitress. came to his table.

"What happened, Max?" she asked quietly.

"It was just a stupid fight, Nancy. I have no idea why he was even in there. He got mad when I asked him what he was doing. We threw a few punches, and when I hit him, he fell and hit his head on an oak table and must've broken his neck."

"Are you going to prison?" she asked with concern.

"I don't know. Maybe I deserve to go."

"Everyone here likes you, Max. If they send you to prison, it wouldn't be right."

"Thank you, Nancy. Could I get some lunch, please?" he asked.

"Oh, Of course. What would you like?"

"Just bring me the special and some coffee."

"Coming right up," she said with an awkward smile.

MAX

He had finished his lunch of beef stew, biscuits, and coffee, paid for the food and was returning to the jail when he saw Jerome Emerson leaving the jail and climbing onto his wagon. He glared at Max as he turned the wagon around and headed east.

Max had intended to approach him and apologize for what had happened, but after seeing his face, he didn't think that would be possible and didn't blame Walt's father one bit. He continued walking and then reached the marshal's office and stepped inside.

No sooner had his right foot crossed the threshold than Marshal Becker said, "Max, Jerome Emerson was just here."

"I noticed. I was going to talk to him to explain what happened, but he just gave me a dirty look and drove away."

"He's pressing charges, Max."

Max stopped dead in his tracks and stared at the marshal before asking, "For what?"

"Manslaughter."

Max was stunned for a few seconds and then just nodded, his stomach threatening to leave his lunch on the jail floor. It seemed as if he was about to really enter the justice system.

Emil said, "No one was there, Max. If it was up to me, I'd let it go, but I can't do that if he's pressing charges. I'm going to have to send you to the county jail and they'll hold you for trial. It'll probably be in a couple of days, but don't worry about it. I'm sure the prosecutor won't bother filing charges."

Max took a few more steps into the office and sat down hard in the chair next to the marshal's desk.

"What will happen, Emil?" he asked quietly.

"It depends. If the charge is involuntary manslaughter, which it probably will be if the prosecutor decides to go to trial, the maximum sentence is ten years. But you have a clean record and a good standing in the community, so it won't be that, even if they find you guilty."

"Is that likely?"

"I don't know, Max. I really don't know. I think it's highly unlikely that it will even get that far, but if it's one thing I've learned over the years, predicting what will happen once someone's been charged is a waste of time."

Max exhaled, then asked, "Can you have someone tell my parents?"

"I'll tell you what, Max. Why don't you go and talk to them? I'll need you back here soon, though. I've already notified the county, and they'll probably send someone either later today or early tomorrow morning."

"Alright, I'll be back in a few minutes," Max replied as he stood.

Max was almost in a trance as he left the marshal's office and walked east across the boardwalk and then cut diagonally across the main road and continued eastward before turning down a side street. He finally reached his parents' house, stepped up to the porch, opened the door, and went inside.

"Mama?" he shouted.

He knew his father would be at work at this time of day. He owned and operated a freight company and usually was out of town delivering heavy shipments during the day.

MAX

"Max, in here," his mother shouted from the kitchen.

Max walked quickly to the kitchen and found his mother doing laundry.

"Mama, I need you to sit down because I don't have a lot of time."

His mother could see the stress on his face and dried her hands on her skirt as she walked to the kitchen table and sat down.

"Max, what's wrong?" she asked.

Max sat across the table from his mother and replied, "Mama, I've been arrested and they're taking me to the county courthouse for trial either today or tomorrow."

Elsa Wagner was shocked. *Her only child had been arrested?* This was far beyond stealing an occasional cookie, which she always knew was the worst thing he'd ever done.

"Max, what happened?"

"I got into a fight with Walt Emerson. I hit him, and he fell and hit his head against a table, then he died. I've been charged with involuntary manslaughter."

"Why did you get into a fight?" she asked, even that fact had surprised her.

"I heard banging from the abandoned stagecoach office next door and went to find out what was causing the noise. I found Walt banging on the wall, and then we got into a fight over it."

Elsa knew her son better than anyone else did and asked, "Max, you're not telling me all of it. What really happened?"

Max sighed. He could never get anything past his mother.

"Mama, if I tell you, you can't let anyone know. I made a promise."

His mother's face grew stern as she said, "I'm not going to promise anything of the sort, young man. Now, you'll tell me the truth and you'll tell me now."

Max sighed again, then replied, "I found Walt pressing Mary Preston against the wall. Her blouse was open, and her skirts were pulled up. When I saw them, she slapped Walt and shouted that he was raping her. I pulled him off and then we had the fight. Mary asked me not to say anything about it because she was worried about her reputation and everyone calling her a whore. So, I told her I wouldn't."

Elsa shook her head as she said, "Max, you have to tell them. You could go to prison for doing exactly what you should have done."

"I know, Mama. But it's too late because I already wrote my statement and I can't change it now. If I did, then they could call me a liar and that I was just looking for an excuse."

"But surely, Mary wouldn't let you go to prison just for her reputation."

"Mama, you know what a value most girls put on their reputations. If it got out that she was about to be ruined, then half the boys in the area would descend on her."

Elsa sighed, then said, "But still, Max, being assaulted isn't the same thing as being caught just giving yourself away."

"But it's too late anyway. Maybe she'll come forward if I get found guilty. She said before she left that she'd be there for me."

"I wouldn't put your trust in her, Max. You have always been too naïve when it comes to girls. You never could see past the pretty faces. But all I can do is just hope that nothing comes of this. I'll tell your father when he comes home."

"Mama, regardless of the reason, I did kill Walt Emerson. The cause is almost irrelevant. I deserve to be punished for what I did because I broke the commandment about killing."

Elsa was stunned by his admission, but still proud of him for being the man she knew he would become even when he was just a small boy.

"Will you be over at the jail with Emil?"

"Until they come and get me. Mama, I want you to take the key to my shop. I need it locked up after Amanda Peters takes her clock back. If I do go to prison, can you see that it's kept clean?"

His mother could only nod as the possibility of her son being sentenced to prison finally struck home and she lowered her head and began to sob.

Max placed the key on the table, then stood, walked around to the other side, and gently lifted his shaking mother from her chair, wrapped his arms around her, and kissed her softly on her forehead.

As he held her close, he said softly, "I love you, Mama. Tell papa that I love him, too."

Elsa sniffed and whispered, "I will. We love you, Max."

"I know, Mama," he said before releasing her, then turning and leaving the kitchen.

Max then walked down the hallway, through the parlor, and out the front door, then returned to his new temporary house in the jail. As he crossed the street, he saw Amanda Peters walking back to her house, clutching her clock. She looked at Max and began to say something, then changed her mind and hurriedly trotted down the street.

Max took that as a sign of things to come. He may have been popular before, but he wouldn't be any longer. Amanda wouldn't even say a simple 'thank you' or 'hello', and he doubted if anyone else would either.

He watched Amanda retreat to her home, then turned and continued to walk to the marshal's office, reached the jail, and walked inside. The office door had been left open and there was no one there as he returned to his cell and sat down. He believed that he had no options left, and besides, when it came right down to it, he felt that he was guilty. He had killed Walt Emerson, and now he had to pay the consequences for what he had done.

The marshal returned twenty minutes later carrying a telegram in his right hand and saw Max sitting on the cot.

"The county sheriff is sending a deputy to come and pick you up in a little while, Max."

Max just nodded as the marshal sat down at his desk, and Max could see that he was almost as troubled as he was himself.

After an hour and a half of silence, the door to the jail opened and a tall, thin man wearing a badge entered the office.

"Got a prisoner for me, Emil?" he asked.

"Afternoon, John," he replied and then turned to Max. "Max, Deputy Crawford is here for you."

Max didn't reply, but just walked out of the cell to the front of the office and presented his wrists to the deputy, who just tilted his head and looked at him. Max assumed that it wasn't typical behavior for a criminal. Then the deputy shrugged and snapped a pair of handcuffs on him.

Max was correct in his assumption as John Crawford wasn't used to having such compliant prisoners.

"Catch you later, Emil," the deputy said as he nudged Max toward the door.

"Bye, John," an almost guilty-looking Marshal Becker replied.

Max walked out the door followed by the tall deputy.

Once they were on the boardwalk, he said, "Go ahead and get on the horse to the left. Don't try runnin'. It ain't a good idea."

Max just nodded and stepped up on the horse as the deputy untied his horse, mounted, then turned left and rode east out of town, trailing the prisoner transport horse with a handcuffed Max in the saddle.

Several residents stopped and watched Max being led off, but Max kept his eyes straight ahead. He had already made his decision about what would happen when they reached the county seat. He would plead guilty, as he knew he was, and then, he would serve his penance, not his sentence.

Forty-five minutes later, the deputy and Max arrived at the county jail in Winfield. It was a lot larger than Burden's one-cell facility, but Max didn't care. He knew he wasn't going to be there very long before he'd be sent to the Kansas State Prison. The deputy stepped down and advised Max to dismount. He complied, and the deputy tied off his horse and led Max into the county jail.

"Whatcha got, John?" asked the deputy sheriff at the desk as they entered.

"Manslaughter from Burden."

"Cell four."

"Come on," John said as he motioned to Max.

Max followed the deputy down a hallway to the back of the large office where the cells were located, and when he reached cell number four, the deputy nudged him inside with a hand on his shoulder, closed the door and locked it, then told Max to put his hands between the bars so he could take off the handcuffs.

After the cuffs were removed, the deputy turned, leaving Max alone in the cell. There were two other occupied cells. Max guessed them to be cells one and two. The occupants were both sleeping, which seemed to be the only thing to do, so he stretched out on the cot and soon fell asleep.

————

He was awakened by a loud clanging on the bars and Max thought it might be dinner time, but he was wrong. He sat up and saw a short, dark man in a suit carrying a satchel standing outside the cell door.

"Are you Max Wagner?" he asked.

Max simply looked at him and nodded.

"I'm Henry Talbot, the prosecuting attorney for the county. You've been charged with involuntary manslaughter. Do you have an attorney?"

Max shook his head.

"Do you want an attorney assigned to you?"

Again, Max shook his head.

The prosecutor was somewhat surprised and asked, "How do you intend to plead?"

Max spoke the first word he had uttered in four hours when he replied, "Guilty."

Now the prosecutor was even more surprised. He'd read the prisoner's short statement and the doctor's report and was close to not even prosecuting the case because it was going to be a difficult case to win. It was nothing more than a fistfight that resulted in an accidental death.

"Are you going to waive your rights to a jury trial?" he asked, his eyebrows peaked.

"Yes."

"Well, it makes my job easier," he said before he turned and walked to the front office.

"Deputy Bannister, can you unlock this cell for me, please? I'll need the prisoner escorted across the street to the courthouse."

Deputy Bannister looked at him with a bit of surprise. The prisoner had just arrived, and he was curious about what had just happened, so he figured he'd go along to find out.

"I'll do it. John Crawford is on the way back from the privy."

He walked over to the far wall and took the ring of keys, then walked back to the cells with the prosecutor. After unlocking the cell, he entered, snapped on the handcuffs, then he and Max followed the prosecutor across the cobblestoned street to the brick courthouse across the street. They walked up the wide stairs and entered the large double doors that had been left open to get some breeze circulating.

The prosecutor turned into his office and sat down at his desk then motioned for the deputy to sit Max in a chair across from him. Max had seen the gesture and sat down before the deputy had a chance to push him into the chair.

"Mr. Wagner, I'm going to give you a form to sign. What is your home address?"

"14 Mission Street, Burden, Kansas," he replied, which was his shop's address. He lived in a room in the back.

He wrote that down along with the date: May 12, 1878. He then wrote, 'I, Max Wagner, plead guilty to the charge of involuntary manslaughter and waive my rights to be represented by an attorney and a trial by jury.'

When he finished, he slid the sheet across the desk to Max and said, "Mr. Wagner, if this is all correct, I need you to sign below this statement and write the date. If you don't agree, don't sign. Realize that in signing, you will be sentenced without trial."

Max nodded and took the offered pen, signed his name followed by the date.

The prosecutor took the paper back and looked at his signature and was surprised at the delicate touch. If he hadn't seen the robust young man sitting across from him, he would have thought a woman had signed his name.

"Mr. Wagner, we'll go and see Judge Andersen in a few minutes, but I have to know something. Why are you being so cooperative? You're facing prison time and not even saying anything."

"Because I'm guilty," was his short response.

The prosecutor said, "Mr. Wagner, I read your statement and the doctor's findings, and I'm somewhat perplexed. I'll be honest with you and tell you that I was close to not even prosecuting the case. It was just a fistfight that turned out badly. Now, having said all that, and knowing that in all likelihood, if I did take this to trial, you'd probably be acquitted, I'll give you one more opportunity to change your mind. I'll rip this up if you want to plead 'not guilty'."

"Sir, I appreciate your honesty, but whatever else, in the end, I killed Walt and I deserve punishment for what I did."

The prosecutor glanced up at the deputy, shrugged, then stood and said, "If you'd escort the prisoner, deputy, we'll go and see the judge."

Max stood without being told and followed the prosecutor into Judge Andersen's chambers with Deputy Bannister walking beside him. They stepped into the dark room, sunlight pouring in from a tall window but failing to brighten the room as much as it should have because of all the dark wood.

Max and the deputy remained standing while the prosecutor went into the judges' chambers to talk to Judge Andersen. Five minutes later the prosecutor returned, stood next to Max and the judge arrived two minutes later in his robes and sat on the bench.

He stared at Max in a curious mix of disbelief and concern as he said, "Max Wagner, you have pled guilty to involuntary manslaughter. Do you have anything to say on your behalf?"

Max replied, "No, Your Honor."

The judge looked at the prosecutor who just raised his eyebrows. He then looked at Max and was as surprised as the prosecutor after listening to what he'd been told. He seemed to be a good young man and seemed genuinely anguished by what he had done, but he had pled guilty and had to be sentenced accordingly, even if it was for the minimum sentence for the crime.

The judge intoned, "Mr. Wagner, I sentence you to a term of five years in the Kansas State Prison. Court adjourned," before smacking his gavel and leaving the courtroom.

The prosecutor was curious about Max's reaction to the sentence and wasn't surprised a bit when Max had no reaction whatsoever. He just waited quietly to be escorted back to his cell, as the deputy took his arm, turned him away from the bench, and led him out of the courtroom, the courthouse, and then across the street to the jail.

———

Back in Burden, Hermann Wagner had arrived home and was given the news by Elsa. He was more than shocked, he was numbed. It took almost a minute for that sensation to be replaced by a deep anger as he told Elsa he'd go and talk to the marshal. She knew he was upset and should try to calm him down first, but she also wanted answers herself, so she let him go.

Forty minutes later, he returned, still angry, and met his wife at the door and they walked to the parlor.

After they sat on the couch, he said, "Elsa, it seems a bit vague. Max and Walt Emerson had a fight. There's no denying that. But there was something else, too. They think a girl may have been involved. When the marshal and the doctor went in to examine the body. They both noticed a lilac scent that was still lingering in the room. Then, when they checked Walt's pockets, there was a note saying to meet him in the old stagecoach building at nine tomorrow morning that was written in a light, feminine hand. Did Max say anything about a girl?"

Elsa replied, "He told me that he heard the banging on the wall and found Mary Preston against the wall with her blouse open and her skirts pulled up and Walt Emerson pressed against her. When Max walked in, she slapped Walt and told Max that Walt was trying to rape her. That's when Max stepped in and they had the fight."

"Then he shouldn't have a problem. Everything that happened was justifiable. He rescued the girl, but why didn't he tell the marshal?"

Elsa sighed and answered, "She had asked him not to say anything to protect her reputation, but I don't think she was in danger. She hadn't screamed or fought until Max saw them. I think she wanted to be there and only reacted that way, so no one knew what a hussy she really was. Our son may be a big, strong young man, but he's still hopelessly naïve when it comes to women. But the problem is that Max told me at the end that the reason for the fight didn't matter. He had killed Walt Emerson and he had to pay his penalty."

"He said that?" asked her astonished husband.

She nodded and said, "I think maybe he's being too hard on himself, Hermann."

"Marshal Becker said he was in the county jail. It's too late to go there today, so I'll go over the first thing tomorrow and see him. We'll get him a lawyer and let the truth come out. I don't want Max having that hanging over his head for the rest of his life."

She hugged her husband before they walked out to the kitchen to eat a delayed dinner.

CHAPTER 2

The next morning, Max was given a tray in his cell with his breakfast. He drank the coffee but left the food as his stomach was still on edge, then laid back down in his cell and waited. An hour later, a deputy arrived at his cell, unlocked it, and had him sit on the cot while he put shackles on his ankles and then on his wrists. Max didn't care anymore. He was beyond caring. He was being punished for what he did, and he deserved it.

The deputy led him outside into the start of a bright May day. Normally, he would have appreciated the beautiful sky and light breeze, but not this morning. He was put into a wagon and transported to the train depot where the deputy pulled Max from the wagon and led him shuffling to the platform. He had a nine-hour train ride in front of him and had never ridden on a train before, so he should be thrilled, but nothing like that mattered anymore.

Forty minutes later, after the train had arrived huffing into the station, he was walked across the platform, and when the train stopped, he was escorted up the steel steps and into the passenger car. He was cuffed to the seat in front of him and sat down. He had just used the chamber pot in the jail before leaving, so he was good for the trip.

The train left Winfield at 9:20 on the 13th of May. His five-year sentence had begun.

———

Hermann Wagner arrived in Winfield twenty-five minutes later and walked into the sheriff's office to see his son. When he was told that Max had pled guilty to the charge and had been sentenced to five years in the Kansas State Prison, he collapsed into the chair next to the front desk and remained sitting for ten minutes without saying anything. He finally stood, turned on his heels, and left the office without saying a word.

––––––

At 7:10 that evening, the train arrived at Lansing, Kansas, home of the Kansas State Prison.

After being escorted from the train, Max was tossed, literally, into a barred wagon for transport to the prison. He was the only one in the wagon, which was either better or worse, depending on how one looked at it. As the wagon bounced along the road, Max was despondent in his condition, but still didn't regret his decision.

It took almost an hour for the wagon to enter the high stone walls of the prison, and once behind those walls and yanked out of the wagon, he was read the rules of the prison and issued his prison wardrobe.

One of the things he was told was that if he chose to work, because he wasn't sentenced to hard labor, he would be paid twenty-five cents a day. If he chose, he could work six days a week, and Max already decided before he took another step toward his permanent cell, that he'd work. It wasn't because of the dollar and a half a week, either, it was because he wanted to work. He needed to sweat and feel the stress of physical labor almost as added penitence for taking Walt's life.

He began his real sentence three days later and was assigned to a road gang. He worked with a sixteen-pound sledgehammer breaking up rocks that would be used for subsurface under the cobblestones in newly constructed roads in Kansas cities and towns.

He learned quickly that he should close his eyes just before the heavy face of the sledge connected with the stone to prevent sharp fragments from ripping into his eyes. His first few days were hard on his arms and back, but he wouldn't give in and kept going out on jobs. When he returned to the prison, he was hosed down to get all the dust and sweat off, and as cold as the water was, he found that he enjoyed it.

Each night, he would delve deeply into the circumstances of his arrest. He was still convinced he was serving his penance, but after the first week, he was beginning to come out of his shell. He still didn't chatter, but he started talking to his fellow inmates. Max was already bigger than most when he arrived, so he wasn't subjected to many of the cruelties that beset the smaller prisoners, and even the more violent ones left him alone.

Two weeks after his arrival, he received a letter from his mother who wrote that she had told his father about Mary and that most of the town supported him.

He wrote back to his parents explaining that he intended to make the most of his incarceration and not do anything to lengthen his sentence. He told them both not to worry and that he loved them very much.

He received regular letters, mostly from his mother, once a month or so after that, and he wrote back within two days after receiving her much-appreciated missives.

As the weeks became months, he continued to work on the road gangs, and never missed a day due to sickness. Even in the harsh winter when the wind would howl down from Canada and drive snow across the plains, he'd work. When there were two feet of snow on the ground, he'd be out there shoveling walkways. His only real days off were Sundays and when it rained so much that no one could do anything. On those days, he read. He found that the prison library was more extensive than he would have expected, and it even could request special books from the Leavenworth City Library. He concentrated on technical and engineering books, but read anything he could find that interested him, although he rarely read novels or fiction. In those few off hours when he wasn't reading, he laid on his bunk with his eyes closed and imagined all sorts of geared contraptions.

One night, in the middle of March 1879, he was sitting on his bunk and listening to a cellmate, R.T. Wyler talking about how he had been caught. They all knew that Max was in the can for manslaughter, but he hadn't gone into the details. When R.T. had finished, he looked over at Max.

"Max, I know you're doin' time for manslaughter, but how'd that happen?"

Max figured it didn't make any difference who knew about Mary this far away from his hometown and they were all in prison anyway, so he decided to provide the details.

"I was working in my shop and heard some banging in the abandoned stagecoach office next door. I went to check and when I pulled open the door, found this girl I knew with her blouse open and her skirts pulled up being pressed against the wall by this guy I knew. She slapped him and shouted that he was raping her, so I grabbed him and pulled him off her. Then we had a fight, and when I hit him, he fell over and hit his head on a thick table. It killed him."

R.T. laughed, and Max was a bit irritated when he asked, "You find that funny, R.T.?"

"It's only funny 'cause you believed her, Max."

"You think a girl is gonna lie about being raped?" he asked in disbelief.

"Let me ask you, Max. If she was being raped, why didn't she scream before you opened the door?"

It was the same question he had asked himself the day it had happened, but he felt he needed to defend his position.

"Maybe she didn't want anyone to know, so her reputation wouldn't be sullied."

R.T. laughed again and shook his head.

"You beat all, do you know that, Max? Alright, let me ask you this, then. Was her blouse ripped open or just unbuttoned?"

Max hadn't even paid it a second thought. He thought back to that day. *It hadn't been ripped!* The buttons were all there because Mary had buttoned them right back up as they fought.

R.T. continued, seeing Max's expression.

"Ah! You see it finally. She wasn't being raped, my friend. She just wanted a little lovin' and you walked in on 'em. She did that whole rape scene just so you wouldn't go and tell everybody that she was a loose girl."

Max collapsed on his bunk and exclaimed, "Good God! I killed Walt for no reason at all!"

"It's not your fault, Max. Blame the girl. If she had just told you to go away to mind your own business, you would have. Right?"

"Yeah."

"So, it's all her fault. I'm surprised she didn't want you to hump her right there, as all excited as she musta been."

Max ignored the comment, but let the realization finally hit him. *How could he have been so naïve?* Of course, Mary wasn't being raped. For the first time, he recalled the look on her face when he first opened the door. She had her eyes closed and her hands around Walt's neck as his head was buried in her chest. *Why hadn't he remembered that?* All he remembered was the slap and then Mary's shout claiming rape.

He was still guilty, but now he was angry. Mary Preston had sent him here as much as he had and hadn't even bothered to tell the marshal or the county sheriff about it. His attitude changed immediately. He'd do his time. He'd work his butt off. But then, he'd return to Burden and take his life back. He wouldn't do anything about Mary, but he wouldn't let it take the rest of his life away, either.

So, with an almost unrecognized urgency, he continued to work out his sentence. He worked a lot harder than any of those lifers assigned to hard labor by the judge and without realizing it, he was gaining bulk and strength with each swing of the heavy sledgehammer.

In addition to his almost demonic level of hard work, he was also a model prisoner, creating no concerns for the guards. He never violated even the smallest rule because he didn't want one hour added to his sentence. He ate the lousy food to keep his weight up and didn't know that his weight was climbing as he continued his labor because they didn't have a scale. By the end of his first year, he had put on almost thirty pounds, yet he retained his manual dexterity, despite the heavy callouses that covered his hands and fingers.

His skills at doing repair work eventually came to the attention of the captain of the guard one Saturday night when one of the guards joked about how mad he was that his watch had stopped.

"Say, Jake," he said to the guard, "tell the captain that I can fix his watch for him. I did a lot of that before I got here."

Jake looked over at Max and asked, "You serious, Max? You were a watchmaker?"

"No, I fixed everything. I've done watches, clocks, steam engines, and farm equipment. You name it, I fixed it."

"I'll mention it to him. You won't be able to use any sharp tools, though."

"For watch repair, I'll need them. But I can do it under close supervision, and it shouldn't take an hour."

"Okay. I'll see what he says."

Max knew that only his reputation as a hard-working, trusted inmate allowed the offer to be passed to the captain.

The next day, Max's only day off, he was escorted from the cell to the prison workshop. Captain Forrest met him there and handed him his watch.

"My father gave me that watch, Max. Don't screw it up."

"No, sir."

Max took the watch to the bench under the scrutiny of the captain, pried off the back cover, and saw the problem immediately. It was a simple repair and it took him five minutes. He put the cover back on, wound the watch, then handed it back to an astonished captain of the guards.

"Jake told me you said you fix anything. Is that right?" he asked as he looked at his ticking timepiece.

"Yes, sir."

"Can you fix a steam engine?" he asked as he looked at Max.

"Yes, sir."

"Okay. You can go back to your cell now."

"Thank you, sir."

Max returned to his cell under the escort of a prison guard wondering why he'd asked about a steam engine.

The next day, he reported for the hard labor detail and was pulled out of line by the captain.

"Come with me, Max."

"Yes, sir."

Max followed but didn't appreciate losing out on a day's work but walked behind the captain until he reached the foreman's shack. The foreman was an employee of the man who had the contract for the prison labor, Henry Trask. Mr. Trask owned a construction company and paid the state fifty cents a day per man. He got the cheap labor he needed to get simple jobs done, and the state made twenty-five cents a day per man.

Captain Forrest talked to the foreman for a few minutes and then waved Max over.

"I'm going to remove your shackles, but you'd better not try anything. Mr. White here will show you the steam engine that's been causing them problems. Just fix it and when you're done, get back to the work detail. Don't make me send a guard over there."

"No, sir."

The foreman looked at the captain, hoping he wasn't being put at risk. The captain was violating all sorts of rules, but he knew no one would report him, and besides, he wanted to be on Mr. Trask's good side. Mr. Trask was a generous man to those he appreciated.

Joe White led Max almost a mile toward a deep pit that was filled with water. There was a hose going into the water and another hose that led to a nearby creek. The recalcitrant steam engine was sitting idle in between the hoses.

"That thing's supposed to pump the water out of the quarry, but it's been a pain in the ass. It runs maybe an hour at the most, then after it dies, we have to let it sit for three or four hours before it'll work again."

"Does the engine stop or does the pump just stop working?"

"The steam engine just slows down and then stops."

"Do you have some tools I can use?" Max asked.

"There's a toolbox that came with the engine. It's mounted on the other side."

"Who's going to watch me?"

"Not me. I need to get back to the foreman's shack. The captain said you could be trusted, so don't make him out to be a liar."

"I won't. I don't want to do anything to extend my sentence."

"Keep that in mind," he said as he left.

Max felt a little queer being alone for the first time in almost a year.

He took in a deep breath and walked to the engine, figuring it had to be a stuck governor or safety valve. If it ran okay for an hour, something was shutting it down. He started a fire in the box and began adding coal until enough pressure had built up, then started the steam engine and engaged the pump.

The water began flowing out of the creek end as he began walking around the engine, checking the different valves and governors. After forty minutes, he noticed that the engine suddenly sped up. The governor kicked in, slowing it down suddenly and the engine died.

For Max, it was child's play after that. He found the sticking valve, removed it from the circuit, disassembled it, cleaned it with kerosene, and then lubricated it. He reassembled it and then put it back into the steam circuit, fired up the steam engine again, and let it run. After an hour, he cleaned up, then headed back to the work gang, but as he passed the foreman's shack, he stuck his head in the door.

"Mr. White, it's fixed now and shouldn't act up again. You had a sticking steam exchange valve. I left it running, but you'll need to have someone add some more coal soon."

The foreman was surprised that the job was already done and suspected that the prisoner hadn't really fixed a damned thing as Max closed the door and returned to his work detail. The captain saw him coming, had one of the guards put his shackles back in place, then Max picked up his sledgehammer and waddled past the captain.

"Is it fixed, Max?" he asked.

"Yes, sir."

The captain nodded, and Max went back to pounding rocks. Probably from that water-filled quarry.

The foreman spent another two hours watching the steam engine run before he finally conceded that Max had indeed fixed the problem. He smiled when he knew that Mr. Trask would be happy with him for getting it repaired at no cost, especially after the repairman from the company that sold him the steam-driven pump had already declared it repaired two weeks ago.

––––––

Then the repair floodgates opened for Max. It started with the guards and soon, even prisoners were bringing him things to repair. Max was surprised at some of the things that prisoners had, one even had a thermometer and barometer board.

He still went out on work details though, and did his repair work on Sundays and weeknights, balancing it with his reading.

In March of '82, after not having received any mail for six months, he finally received a letter, but it was from his father, which had him worried before he even opened it.

It was a short, single-page letter. He apologized for not writing, saying that he had been busy between work and caring for his wife. She had come down with some disease of the stomach which was then complicated by the arrival of pneumonia. His mother, and his father's beloved wife, Elsa, had died on the 27th of February from pneumonia. It was crushing news. He loved both his parents, but his mother had always been special to him, and here he was two hundred miles away, locked in a prison cell, and hadn't even been able to go to her funeral. It was the greatest punishment he could have imagined.

He didn't weep or become despondent. He didn't even let anyone know because this was so personal, but he began attending church services on Sundays, feeling that he owed his mother that at least. She had been trying to get him to attend regularly since he left home to start his business, and now he would.

He didn't receive any more letters from his father after that and thought his father had simply been so distressed by the loss of his wife that he couldn't bear to write a letter to his son in prison.

So, Max pressed on with his routine of working, reading, and repairing.

He had no problems with the other inmates, including those in his cell, until one day, after he had served four years and eighteen days, one of his regular cellmates departed to return to civilian life, and they got a new man. He was a hard man, one who had inhabited cells like this for most of his forty-four years and enjoyed being the top dog in each of his other incarcerations. He was a big man too, taller and heavier than Max, but he was going to fat. He had lived too large in his brief excursions of freedom. His name was Ernie Butler but didn't like anyone calling him Ernie. He preferred his moniker of 'Big Dog' and Max thought it was an insult to the entire canine world. Ernie was a pig of a man, and even in this world of unwashed and unshaven men, Ernie stood out and reveled in it.

Two days after Ernie arrived, he ordered another cellmate, Miles Standish, which was his real name, to give him the book that Miles was reading. Max knew that Ernie couldn't read and was just exercising his authority that he gave himself as top dog.

Miles, who was in for embezzlement, looked at him and made a tactical error when he said, "Ernie, you can't read. Why do you want my book?"

Ernie snarled, "Because, I said so, little man. And you'd better show some respect."

Max had always liked Miles and had acted as the small man's protector in the past but let this go for the moment.

Compounding his error, Miles replied, "Ernie, just leave me alone."

Ernie hopped down, snatched the book, and was getting ready to rip it in half when Max said calmly, but with authority, "Give the book back, Ernie. It's not yours."

Big Dog whirled, glared at Max, and snapped, "I'll do whatever I want."

"No, you won't. If you're going to stay in this prison cell, you'll behave. We all got along before you got here, so either get along or you'll wish you had."

Ernie dropped the book and stepped threateningly toward Max as he growled, "You're gonna be sorry you said that."

Max sat up on his bunk, stared up at Ernie, and said, "Back off, Ernie. You're too close and my eyes are starting to water."

"That's from tears, 'cause you know what's comin'."

"I'm warning you, Ernie. Go lie down and cool off," Max said calmly.

Ernie reached for Max and as soon as he did, Max quickly extended his right leg and smashed the toe of his right boot into

Ernie's groin. Ernie's extended arms were two inches from Max when they suddenly changed direction and reached down to his nether regions before he buckled and went to the ground screaming.

Not fifteen seconds later, one of the guards came rushing to the cell door and shouted, "What's going on in here?"

Max stood as was required when addressing a guard and said, "Sir, this inmate was taking another inmate's property and when I advised him to stop, he threatened me with bodily harm and was preparing to attack me. So, I rendered him unable to do so."

The guard looked at the writhing Ernie, then back at Max and asked, "Kicked him in the nuts, huh?"

"Yes, sir."

"Well, he deserved it, I'm sure. I think I know a better cell for Ernie anyway."

He started snickering and then left. Max had always cultured a good relationship with the guards, and it came in handy tonight.

Two hours later, with Ernie sitting on his bunk glaring at Max, a pair of guards entered the cell and took Ernie away. Max found out later they had put him in a cell with a mean giant that didn't tolerate cellmates that gave him a hard time or refused his offer of close friendship, so Ernie became his new best friend.

After that, things calmed down. The months and seasons of his last year passed. Max never heard a single word from Burden, and without even a word from his father, that final year in prison seemed to last almost as long as the previous four.

His repair workload from the guards and prisoners fell off after a while. He had repaired hundreds of things, including four major repair jobs for Mr. Trask, but his repairs rarely failed, so there was just nothing much left.

He continued to work as hard as ever to pass the time, reading what he could. But mostly if he wasn't working, he was thinking, letting his mind wander sometimes over machines that he had repaired and how to make them better. It was a great mental exercise and could take hours. He could close his eyes and imagine the gears and cogs turning levers and releasing valves to move other cogs and levers.

His sentence was almost over and in two more weeks, he would finish his sentence and be a free man and wondered what he would do. He calculated that he would have over three hundred and fifty dollars coming to him for his work. He had $845 in his bank account in Burden when he left, and they'd provide transportation back to his hometown. Then he'd see what had changed in five years. He knew one thing. He'd never trust another woman. Mary had shown him what happened when he did, and he vowed never to be so naïve again.

He continued to go out on work detail jobs up until three days before his release. It was a Saturday anyway, so he'd begin his 'vacation' from hard labor on Sunday, which meant he'd get one extra day off before his release. Release sounded almost magic like 'abracadabra'. Just one word and he'd be a free man again after spending a quarter of his still young life behind bars.

———

Tuesday morning, he shook hands with Miles Standish, who still had another two years on his sentence, then shook hands with his other cellmate, Red Bristow, who had eight more years to go on his bank robbery sentence. The guard called him out of his cell and Max walked behind the guard down the hallway.

He was directed to a hallway he had never noticed before, and the guard closed the door behind him. Max stopped, then glanced back to find the guard no longer there. He continued and entered a room with a half door leading to a storage area. A guard stood behind the half door.

"You Max Wagner?"

"Yes, sir."

He turned and pulled out a large cardboard box.

"This contains your civilian clothes. You didn't have anything else on you when you arrived. Is that right?"

"Yes, sir."

"Sign here," he said as he handed him a clipboard with a form indicating that he had been returned everything that was due him.

Max signed the sheet and gave the clipboard back to the guard.

"Go through that door," he said, pointing to the right, "The first door on the left after you enter the hallway is a room you can get changed in. Leave your prison clothes in the room. When you're done, go to the room on the right."

"Yes, sir."

Max felt his heart pounding as he accepted the box of clothes, then turned and entered the door, walked down a short hallway, and found the small room. He sat down and pulled off his prison clothes for the last time. He pulled on his underwear, then tried to pull on his pants. They were very tight around the thighs, but he managed to finally squeeze into them before he

44

tried to put on his shirt. That was a disaster when the seams ripped open on the shoulders and the cloth parted in the back, but eventually, he got it on. That was his first true inkling of just how powerful he had become.

He left the uniform, closed the door behind him, then went through the other door and found a guard behind a desk. There was a chair in front of the desk.

"Are you Max Wagner?" he asked.

"Yes, sir."

"Have a seat, Max."

Max sat down, feeling strangely out of place.

"You worked a total of 1551 days since you arrived," the guard said then paused and asked, "You served a five-year sentence and worked all but ten days?"

"Yes, sir."

"Even prisoners assigned to hard labor usually only work a couple of hundred days out of a year."

Max didn't reply, so the guard continued.

"The State of Kansas owes you $387.75. Do you want that all in cash? I wouldn't recommend it."

"No, sir. I'll take $300 in a draft and the rest in cash."

"Wise decision. Give me a minute."

The clerk/guard wrote out a draft, counted out the cash in front of Max, then gave him a thick envelope.

He looked at Max's attire and said, "I'd suggest you invest in a new shirt."

"Yes, sir."

"I also have a letter for you from Mr. Trask," he said as he handed Max a white envelope.

Max put it in the heavy envelope without opening it.

The clerk then slid more papers across the desk to him and said, "Here's the official documentation you need to show any law officer that you completed your full sentence and are not on parole."

Max folded it and slid it into the thick envelope with the cash and draft.

"Finally, here is your train ticket back to Burden. Mr. Wagner, you are no longer a prisoner of the state and are free to go. The door to your right leads to the city of Lansing."

"Thank you, sir."

Max stood and with his heart still pounding, reached for the door's handle, turned it, and when he pulled it open, the bright May sunshine flooded the room and Max left the prison.

It was May 13, 1883.

Somehow, even though Max had felt the same sun on his face when he worked outside on the work details, the heat and light felt different as a free man. Now, he needed to start acting like one.

He was somewhat surprised that he wasn't as bitter as he expected to be. Yes, he had spent five years in prison, but he felt he had come out a wiser and better man. He wasn't as naïve as when he had walked through those doors. He understood the real world more. Living with convicted killers and thieves for five years had broadened his outlook on humanity but the Sunday services had also enriched his soul, which he never could see happening when he'd first entered that gate.

He would return to Burden and see his father, visit his mother's grave and pray for her there as he had prayed for her almost every day. He would miss his mother more than anything else. If there was any reason to be bitter, it was that. But even then, he realized how painful it would have been to watch her die. Being in prison had spared him that agony but felt guilty for being unable to be there for his father as he had to care for his wife and watch her die.

He took in a deep breath and walked into Lansing, then soon found a clothing store and walked inside where he bought a new shirt, a pair of pants, and a belt. He paid for them and then used their changing room to put them on. Before he left, he bought a new Stetson as well, then left the clothing store and then went to the nearest diner for a real meal that he could choose from a menu.

He spotted Martha's Diner two blocks away and quickly walked across the street, having to avoid the traffic, which somehow added to his sense of newfound freedom.

After reaching the eatery, he sat down, and a very pretty waitress bounced to his table and smiled broadly at him. He didn't understand why but ordered a steak and baked potato with coffee. She smiled at him again and said she'd be right back.

She was, too, and brought a pot of coffee and a cup, placed the cup on the table, and filled it with steaming coffee. Again, she smiled at him and left.

Max figured she was angling for a big tip and sipped the coffee. Compared to prison coffee, it was hot nectar.

His train was due to depart in an hour and twenty minutes, so he thought he may as well open the letter from Mr. Trask.

The letter was wrapped around a hundred dollars in cash. In the letter, Mr. Trask told him how much he had saved him in not only repair bills, but lost labor costs. He also said that if Max ever needed a job or a reference to please contact him then thanked him for all his help.

Max tucked the money back into the letter's envelope and then back into the thick envelope, feeling as if he was a wealthy man. But he'd have some expenses when he got back to Burden, too, but not a lot. When he returned, he'd buy a horse and tack, and he'd like some new weapons. The guns he had when he was arrested are probably old and seized up by now. He'd left them cleaned and oiled, but five years is a long time. Besides, he liked some of the new guns.

The waitress brought his steak and potato, complete with sour cream and butter. There were also biscuits…real, fluffy, biscuits. They looked almost better than the steak, so he tried one first and was rewarded after he spread some butter on one and let the flavor spread through his mouth. *Oh, my! Was this good!* He finally cut into the steak and thought he'd pass out from the taste.

But he survived the meal and did leave the smiling waitress a large tip. The food made it worthwhile and she was pleasant to his eyes. He may not trust a woman ever again, but he sure did like to look at them.

After leaving the diner, he had a pleasant stroll to the train station. He already had his ticket and he didn't have any luggage, so when he reached the depot, he stepped onto the platform, took a seat near the bench, then watched the people, the road traffic, and the trains. The train was on time and at 12:40, Max Wagner boarded the train for Burden, Kansas. It was time to go home.

CHAPTER 3

Max slept for most of the trip and was surprisingly bored for most of it. It only began to get exciting when he passed through Grenola, the last stop before Burden. It was already dark, but not too late, so his father should be awake.

The train arrived at 8:40, and before the locomotive brought his car to a stop, Max hopped down onto the platform. He didn't waste any time as he trotted across the platform and onto the quiet streets of Burden. He walked down the main street to the unnamed side street where his father lived, saw the house, and smiled as he continued to jog. When he reached the entrance and put his hand on the fence post to swing onto the walkway, then slowed to a walk as he approached the darkened house. *His father was asleep already?*

He walked onto the porch, turned the doorknob, and found it locked. This was unusual as his parents never locked the door. He walked around the porch to the back door and discovered that it was locked too. Now, he began to worry. *Why would his father lock the doors?*

He thought about going through the window but decided he'd just go to the hotel and get a room for the night. He would have gone to his shop to sleep if he had the key, but he had given it to his mother. He could break the hasp but didn't want to cause a commotion, so he headed for the hotel.

He walked into the hotel and saw the familiar face of Katie Enright at the desk.

"Hello, Katie," he said as he smiled at her.

MAX

She stared for a few seconds before asking, "Max? Is that you?"

"Yes, ma'am."

"My God, Max, you've changed!" she exclaimed as she stared at him.

"I am five years older, Katie."

"I know, but you're so much…more," she said as she smiled at him just as the waitress had.

"Katie, I'm going to need a room for the night. I just got in and my father has the doors locked to the house, so I can't get in."

Her smile evaporated as she said, "Um, Max. I shouldn't be the one to tell you, but your father is dead."

Max almost collapsed and had to grab the desk for support.

"What? How? When did it happen?" he croaked.

"He died about three months ago when one of his freight wagons collapsed on him."

Max simply stood there trying to absorb the loss. No wonder he hadn't gotten any letters. But why had no one even taken the time to let him know? Not even a message. *Not one damned word!*

He was filled with anger and grief, and it was a bad mix. He couldn't find out anything tonight, but he'd sure find out more tomorrow.

Finally, he managed to get both emotions under control and said, "Okay, Katie. I understand. Thank you for telling me."

"I can't believe no one told you, Max. I thought you knew."

"No, I guess it wasn't important enough news to pass along. Could you give me a room for the night, Katie?"

"Oh, sure," she said as she handed him a key.

She didn't ask for the two dollars, but Max gave them to her anyway.

"Thank you, Katie. I'm sorry it had to be you that told me. It's not fair to you."

"It's alright, Max," she replied as she smiled at him, just not as much as before.

He nodded and went to his room, walked inside, and closed the door. He didn't even light the lamp, but just pulled off his boots, stretched out on the bed, and fell asleep.

———

When Max awakened the next morning, he was seriously disoriented. There were no bars, no snoring cellmates, and no guards. His heart raced until he finally remembered that he was in a hotel and was a free man. He sat up in the bed, took a deep breath, then after pulling on his boots, left his room to attend to his morning ritual. He needed to get a bath, a shave, and a haircut, but first, he needed to get something to eat.

He left the hotel, dropping the key off at the unoccupied desk, and walked out into the street. It was early, but not crack-of-dawn early. He guessed it was around seven o'clock. He walked down the street, passing his still locked up shop, wondering what condition the interior was in. He'd find out soon enough.

MAX

He reached Sunny's café and walked inside. The place was already half-full, but he found a table and sat down. The few people that looked his way just glanced and returned to whatever they were doing. He recognized all of them, but maybe they didn't recognize him, or they did and didn't want to have anything to do with an ex-con.

A young waitress that he didn't recognize right away floated to his table and dazzled him with a brilliant smile.

"Hello, could I take your order?" she asked.

"Four eggs over easy, bacon, biscuits, and coffee."

"Coming right up," she replied and gave him another big smile before returning to the kitchen.

He figured waitresses everywhere were learning ways to get bigger tips and smiled to himself.

The waitress returned shortly with his cup and a pot of coffee, put the cup down, and filled it.

"Are you new around here?" she asked.

"Not at all. I grew up here. I've just been away for a while."

"I'm sure I would have remembered you," she said as she smiled again before turning and heading back to the kitchen.

Max wasn't sure, but it sure seemed like she was flirting with him. She couldn't even be twenty years old. Probably only about eighteen. That would have made her only around thirteen when he went off to prison, and he suddenly felt old.

She returned quickly with his order and set it down along with a crock of butter and another one of honey.

"Thank you," he said.

"You are very welcome," she replied.

She left, and Max made short work of the breakfast. The honey for the biscuits was a nice touch. He finished his breakfast and left fifty cents on the table for the twenty-cent breakfast. That should make her smile some more, he thought as he headed for the door.

As he was leaving, a more mature woman of around thirty years of age shot him a giant smile as well. He tipped his hat and left the café. This was getting strange. He wondered what had happened to all the women in the state while he was away. Maybe it was because he needed a shave and haircut.

But first, before he did anything else, he needed to find his parents' resting place and headed for the town's cemetery. It wasn't that large, and he looked for the newer stones. His father only died a few months ago and his mother less than a year earlier and he easily found the two graves. They were next to each other, but their markers were very plain. He would go and talk to John Lambert and have new, proper gravestones made.

He walked to the mortuary and found John Lambert behind his desk.

"Morning, John."

"Max?" he asked with wide eyes and raised eyebrows.

"Yes, sir. I just got back and was wondering if I could get new markers made for my parents."

"I thought you might want some. I had to make them generic because if I added anything else, it wouldn't be right."

"I understand. Let me write out what I'd like. Can we get marble markers?"

"We can, but it will take a week or so to get them done."

"There's no rush."

Max wrote out what he wanted on their markers and paid John the twenty-eight-dollar bill.

"Thanks, John."

"You're welcome, Max. It's good to have you back."

Max smiled, then left to find out what had happened to his father. He figured the best place to start his quest for answers was where he had started the five-year journey, City Marshal Emil Becker's office. He wasn't sure the marshal would be in his office yet because it wasn't quite eight o'clock.

He stepped up onto the boardwalk and passed the general store knowing he'd need to return and buy a lot of items later. He reached the marshal's office and stepped inside, finding Marshal Becker behind his desk.

He looked up quickly and asked, "Can I help you?"

"Emil? I need to find out about my father."

The marshal had the same reaction as the mortician when he asked, "Max? Is that you?"

"Yes, sir."

"I barely recognized you. You've gotten a lot bigger and your face has changed quite a bit, too. It's not so boyish."

"Five years in prison will do that to you."

"I'm sure that it did. Max, you really screwed that up. You should never have gone to prison at all. Why didn't you say anything about a girl?"

"She asked me not to. Besides, it didn't make any difference, I still killed Walt Emerson."

"It would have made a huge difference. She could have told us what happened."

"It doesn't matter, Emil. It's over and done with. I need to find out what happened to my father. No one told me, and I only found out when I found the house locked and had to check in at the hotel and Katie Enright told me."

"Have a seat, Max."

Max sat down and waited for the story.

"We found your father crushed under one of his freight wagons. He must have been changing an axle by the looks of it."

"Marshal, that doesn't make any sense to me at all. My father used to lecture me about the dangers of not supporting a wagon when you're changing a wheel or an axle. If he changed a wheel, he used two jacks. If he was changing an axle, he used four. The man was meticulous when it came to maintenance."

"All I can tell you is what we found."

"Who reported the accident?"

"John Lambert."

"The undertaker?"

"He was driving his hearse over to your father to have him look at his front axle. John always had your father work on his hearses. He didn't like to get his hands dirty."

"What did the autopsy show?"

"They didn't do one."

"Why not? I thought they required an autopsy for a suspicious death."

"This wasn't suspicious. They found him crushed, Max. It wasn't like he was murdered."

"I'm not so sure. If he had been hit by a falling tree, or even a crazy bull, it wouldn't have bothered me. But for my father to be caught under one of his freight wagons doesn't make any sense to me."

"Well, it's over, Max. I'm really sorry for you to have to come home to find both of your parents gone."

"Emil, why didn't anyone let me know my father had died?"

"That's a good question. Usually, there is another family member to send out notices. But in this case, I guess everyone thought someone else was going to do it."

Max just sighed and asked, "How can I get into my father's house?"

"Go and see Jim Garson. He's handling your father's estate."

"Alright. I'll do that."

"Max, it really is good to have you back."

Max stood, shook his hand, and left the office, no less perplexed than when he had entered.

He knew where Garson's office was, so he headed that way. It was the only truly fancy office in town. Even Doc McKenna didn't have as nice an office.

He stepped up to the office door and went inside. James Garson had his back to the door and was filing some papers when Max walked in.

He turned and asked the now expected, "Can I help you?"

"Mr. Garson, I've come to see you about my father's estate."

His eyes grew wide as he asked, "Max? Is that really you?"

"Last time I checked."

Garson offered his hand and Max shook it before taking the seat that Garson indicated.

"Max, before we get started, I really need to chew you out for what happened five years ago. You should have contacted me. You didn't need to go to prison."

"So, the marshal says. But I did and I'm out now."

"Max, the one question that everyone seems to want to know is who the girl was in the stagecoach office. It's common knowledge that there was one."

"How did it become common knowledge?"

"There was the lilac scent in the office and then the marshal found a note in Walt's shirt pocket in a woman's handwriting saying to meet him there at nine o'clock."

Max hadn't heard that before. So, it was just a tryst, like R.T. Wyler had said it was. He felt like a bigger fool than he had before but didn't see any reason for saying it.

"It doesn't matter. There's no sense in embarrassing her."

"Max, she's the reason you were even arrested."

"It really doesn't matter anymore. I'm just going to get on with my life."

"I understand. Sorry for asking. It's just the gossipmonger in me. Let me pull your father's file."

He stood and turned to the same filing cabinet he was using when Max had entered, pulled a file, and sat down at his desk.

"Your father did have a new will made after your mother died, but it's very simple. You get everything, including the house, the freight business, and his bank account. While you were away, as executor, I've used that account to pay for weekly maintenance of the house, but it didn't affect the balance that much. The interest payments covered the cost of cleaning. Here's the deed to the house, with two keys, the paperwork on the freight business, which includes the warehouse, the four wagons, the eight teams of horses, and the bank book with a balance of $6,437.22."

"What do I do with the freight business? I have no intention of running it."

"Since your father's death, it's been operated by Simon Whitley."

"Simon's a good man."

"He expressed an interest in buying the business, and he'd like to talk to you if you want to stop by the warehouse. He should be in today."

"I'll do that."

"I'll need you to sign for all the things I've given you. I also have a letter to the bank telling them that you are the sole inheritor of the account."

Max signed where it was indicated and slid the receipt back to James Garson.

"I appreciate your help, Mr. Garson."

"Call me Jim, Max. You're not a youngster anymore. You may be the most man I've ever seen."

"Jim, before I go, can I ask you something that has me puzzled?"

"Sure."

"Since I've been out, every place I go, I get these giant smiles from women that I don't even know. Have women changed that much in five years, or do I need a haircut that badly?"

"You do need a haircut, but you really have no idea?"

"Not a clue."

"At the risk of sounding less manly, Max, you are an imposing figure of a man. When you were here last, you were tall and reasonably big. You were also a handsome young man. But now, you're, well, you're what we all wish we could be. Does that give you the right idea?"

"Really? I knew I'd put on some weight."

"It's more than that, Max. It's your face, too. It's not so boyish anymore. You look like some poster or a face on one of those dime novel heroes."

"Now I'm just embarrassed. I can't help it, though. To be honest, I don't think I'll ever be able to trust a woman again after what happened five years ago."

"Don't go to that extreme, Max. I've been married for eighteen years now and I'd trust my wife with anything."

"Maybe I'll find one who I can trust, but I'm not going to go beating the bushes looking for her."

"She'll find you one of these days, Max."

"Maybe."

He shook the attorney's hand and left the office. His next stop was the bank to get rid of some of the cash in the thick envelope and the bank draft, then take care of the bank account change.

He walked two buildings down the boardwalk to the bank in just a couple of minutes. Like most small-town banks, it wasn't heavily staffed or guarded. So, when he walked in, several heads swiveled in his direction. His lack of a firearm must have put them at ease because they all went back to what they were doing.

He approached the desk of the only clerk, Ed Smith.

"Morning, Ed. I need to get some things done."

Ed looked up and asked the expected, "Max? Is that you?"

"Yes, sir. Mind if I sit down?"

"Oh. Sure, go ahead. What can I do for you?"

"I have a letter from Jim Garson about my father's account. I need to transfer that balance to my existing account. I had around $840 in there before I left. I also need to make some deposits."

"Sure. Not a problem. Do you have the letter?"

Max gave him the letter and pulled out the thick envelope from inside his shirt.

"I'll be right back with the forms and balance sheet," he said before standing and walking behind the cashier's window.

After he left, Max opened the thick envelope and took out the three-hundred-dollar draft, and counted out fifty dollars in cash. That would leave him around two hundred in cash, which should last him for quite a while. But then he figured he'd need a horse and saddle, weapons, food, clothes, and probably some things he hadn't thought of, then changed his mind and kept all the cash with him and wondered if it would be enough.

Ed Smith returned with some papers and sat down.

"Okay. First, your beginning balance was $1072.42. You forgot about the interest."

Max took a pen and endorsed the three-hundred-dollar draft.

"Now, I see you've already got a draft to deposit. I'll give you a receipt then I'll get a new total after we close your father's account and transfer the money to your account."

"Ed, I'm going to have a lot of expenses the next few days. Let me have another hundred in cash, will you?"

"I'll do that."

MAX

When the clerk finally finished all the paperwork and slid the new account balance to Max along with the hundred dollars in cash. The adjusted amount was $8,122.74, Max assumed the difference was for an interest payment that was made since Jim Garson had the balance calculated.

"I'll just need you to sign the receipt. I've given you ten blank drafts for the account. That should last you a while."

Max signed the receipt and shook Ed's hand.

"Thanks, Ed. I appreciate the help."

"Not a problem, Max. It's good to have you back."

Max felt he should go and get a bath, haircut, and shave, but felt the pull to go to the house and see what memories awaited him. But even before he visited the house, he had to stop at his father's warehouse and see Simon Whitley. He needed to get out of the freight business as he had no interest at all in that line of work.

The warehouse was on the opposite side of town from the house, so he turned that way. It was almost a half mile away, but he didn't notice as his long strides ate up the distance and he still had a lot on his mind.

He hoped Simon Whitley recognized him and wasn't sure if he should be amused or annoyed by the constant, 'Max, is that you?', introductions.

He reached the warehouse, seeing the large Wagner Freight sign. He remembered how proud his father had been when the new sign had been hung on the building. He recalled that as the sign was being hoisted into position, his father had told him the almost required, 'Son, someday this will all be yours'. Well, now it was his and he didn't want it.

He stepped into the small office in the warehouse and found Simon sitting at the desk, writing.

"Morning, Simon."

"Max! Welcome back!" he shouted and jumped up from behind the desk.

He tried to give Max a bear hug but couldn't quite wrap his arms around Max.

"Good God, Max! You're huge!" he exclaimed as he stepped back.

Max smiled and said, "I'm just impressed that someone recognized me."

"I wouldn't have if you hadn't spoken first. Your voice is a little deeper, but it's still you. You have changed a helluva lot in just five years, Max. I suppose everyone is giving you grief for just pleading guilty."

"They are. So, what's going on here, Simon?"

"When your father died, I kinda took over because I wanted it to be the same first-class operation when you returned that it was when you left."

"It seems to be. But I'll be honest with you, Simon, I'm not a freighter."

"I know. I told Jim Garson that I wanted to buy the business from you. I don't have a lot of money, though, Max. I can give you a thousand dollars now and then make monthly payments out of the profits, say a hundred dollars a month for three years. Can you let me do that?"

"Will that put you and Emily in a financial bind, Simon?"

"Not at all. I've been saving up, so we'll be fine."

"If it's not going to hurt you, then that's fine with me. I don't want you to have a financial burden, Simon."

"I appreciate the concern, Max, but the business is doing really well, so it won't be a problem at all."

"Did you want to have Jim Garson draw up the contract?" Max asked.

"I'll go and see him. I kind of asked him if he could draw one up just in case. He just needs to fill in the numbers. Can we do it later this afternoon? Is that okay?"

"That's fine. Simon, about the accident. Did it make any sense to you at all?"

Simon blew out his breath and answered, "Not a lick. You know how your father was about safety when it came to those heavy wagons. Why would he get under a wagon to change an axle with only two jacks?"

"There were only two jacks?"

"That's what got me to wondering. When John told us of the accident, we went running out there and found him under the wagon. He was a bloody mess, so we got the wagon lifted and found just two jacks. I pointed them out to Emil, but he said it was just an accident. It was, but I still wonder about it."

"So, do I. Well, I've got to get to the house. I haven't been there since I've been back. Did you know that no one told me about my father's death? I found out when Katie at the hotel told me."

"That's terrible! Nobody sent you a message?"

"I guess everyone thought someone else would do it."

"It's still a crappy way of doing things."

"You've got that right. Well, I've got to go, Simon. I'll see you later."

They shook hands and Max left the warehouse to finally go to the house.

He walked quickly down the street, passing his workshop. As he walked, he thought about his father's accident. Maybe he should just let it go as the accident everyone seemed to think it was. Maybe it was just that and it was his constantly rubbing shoulders with murderers and other violent men for five years that was tilting his perspective.

He reached the house and pulled the key out of his pocket, unlocked the door, and stepped inside. He half expected to see his mother in the kitchen, smiling at him. She always smiled when she saw him, and he would always smile back at her. He was ashamed to admit he missed his mother more than his father. He loved his father dearly, but his mother was like life to him.

He sighed and closed the door behind him. *Where to start?* He walked to his mother's kitchen and noticed the empty larder, as it should have been. He'd have to restock the food supply soon but needed to find the key to his workshop first, so he went into his parents' bedroom.

Everything was neat and tidy inside and in the rest of the house, too. He began with the drawers and all he found were clothes. He'd arrange to give them to the local charity when he got around to it. He noticed that his mother's clothes were still there.

He picked up one of her dresses and started to smile and wondered why they were all in such good condition. Most looked almost new. He imagined that his father was buying her new clothes to make her feel better. She always liked nice clothes. It was her biggest weakness.

He smiled at the thought of seeing his mother beaming, looking at the new dresses his father would bring her, even if she knew she would never wear them. He replaced the dress and then went through the other drawers. His father had one drawer of clothes and his mother had eight. His father spoiled her with her one minor flaw, and he didn't blame him, either. He had contributed on a few occasions but had to have his father get the right size. His mother was an extraordinary woman. He closed the last drawer and left his parents' bedroom.

He tried his bedroom next and found the key on the dresser, then went through his drawers and found his old clothes. Except for the underwear and socks, the rest would go to charity.

He walked into the bathroom, found his father's razor, shaving brush, and mug, and thought he might as well put them to use. He stropped the razor until it was sharp, then he set it aside and walked to the kitchen. He found some wood and started a fire in the cook stove and had to prime the pump to get the water flowing. He rinsed out a pot and then filled it halfway with water before placing it on the cookstove.

He needed to think of what he needed to buy over the next few days. His most pressing need was food for the house, more clothes, then he'd need a horse and tack. Depending on the condition of his weapons in his shop, he may need to buy a new rifle and pistol rig.

By the time the water was warm, which was all he needed, he carried it into the bathroom and filled the sink, removed his only shirt, and soaped up his face. Then, he finally shaved off the two-day stubble and felt clean. He'd take a bath tomorrow. He was walking out of the bathroom, drying his face when he heard the door open. He wasn't armed, so all he could do is look, and was more than mildly surprised to see Amanda Peters staring at him.

"Who are you and what are you doing in this house?" she demanded.

"I live here, Amanda," he replied as he smiled at her.

She squinted and stared for a few seconds before she asked softly, "Max? It can't be."

"Sorry to disappoint you, Amanda."

"No, I didn't mean that. I mean, you look so different."

Max could tell she was flustered and said, "So, everyone keeps telling me. What are you doing here?"

"I was hired to keep the house clean until you returned. I forgot you were coming back so soon."

"It didn't seem too soon to me, Amanda."

"Oh, I'm sorry again. It seems like I can't get my head working."

"Would you do better if I put my shirt back on? I wasn't expecting anyone."

"I suppose that might make things easier."

MAX

Max went back into the bathroom, pulled his shirt off the hook on the door, slid his arms through the sleeves, and was buttoning the front as he returned to the hallway.

Amanda was still flushed after seeing Max. She had never seen any man who looked like that, even with a shirt on. Without a shirt, it was almost frightening.

Max was still buttoning his shirt as he walked back into the front room and approached Amanda.

"Amanda, why are you cleaning houses?" he asked.

"Honestly? I need the money. I also take in some sewing."

"What happened with Johann?"

"Oh, he's at home. He's just having a hard time finding a job."

"When was the last time he worked?"

"I don't remember. I think it was about a year and a half ago."

"If you'd like, I can talk to Simon over at the freight company. They're always looking for workers."

"I think he already turned that idea down. He's looking for something more to his liking."

"Work is work, Amanda. When I was in prison, I signed up for the hard labor details just to feel useful. I missed nine days in five years. If he wants to support you, he can find work."

"You just need to understand Johann. He's just different."

"If you're okay with that, Amanda, that's all that matters."

69

"So, you won't be needing my services any longer?" she asked.

"If you're uncomfortable coming over here, then I'd understand, but if you want to continue, that's fine, too."

"You wouldn't mind?" she asked, somewhat surprised.

"I'm not really keen on the idea of keeping the house clean, but I also am not too sure that you'd want to continue. It might start tongues wagging, Amanda."

"If you're in your shop, it shouldn't matter. Are you going to go back to work in your shop?"

"I am. But it's going to take me a while to get settled. How often do you stop by?"

"Once a week. I usually come on Wednesday afternoons."

"That's fine. How much have they been giving you?"

"Five dollars a month."

"That's not enough, Amanda. Make it ten and if you're comfortable with it, you can keep showing up on Wednesday afternoons."

"Are you sure, Max? Ten dollars is a lot for a part-time cleaning woman."

"It's all right."

She smiled and began to walk into the house.

"Amanda, why don't you take the day off. It won't affect your pay. I just think my presence would put you in a bad situation."

"Oh. That's right. Okay. I'll be back next Wednesday."

"Fine. I'll leave your monthly pay on the kitchen table on the first of every month. Okay?"

"Thank you, Max," she said as she smiled and then left the house.

After she had gone, Max sat down and wondered what had happened to Amanda. She was always one of the brightest students in school and was very popular as well. She was the whole package. Pretty, smart and had a nice figure. *What had happened after she married Johann Peters? Now, he's not working for a year and a half and she says it's okay because he's different? She's cleaning houses and taking in sewing so he doesn't have to work, and doesn't think that's wrong?* He shook his head. He'd never understand women.

––––––

Amanda was ecstatic. An extra five dollars a month and no additional work. She was so glad that Max was back but was still stunned by his appearance. He was the same Max, but he had turned into the kind of man that could melt a woman's heart by just smiling at her. She was still bouncing along when she reached her house, trotted up the steps, and opened the door.

She was about to step over the threshold when she heard giggling inside, and it certainly wasn't from Johann. She could feel jealousy trigger her anger and wanted to go in and confront the woman but changed her mind, then abruptly turned and walked back down the stairs, leaving the front door open. She walked across the street and into the alley across from the house, where she set down her bag and waited.

Twenty minutes later, her patience was rewarded when she saw Johann arrive at the front door with…Alice Roth! He kissed her and grabbed her behind, then Amanda heard the same giggle she had heard earlier. She was torn by what she was seeing. She loved Johann, despite his faults, and thought she knew all of them. But now, seeing him fondle another woman, she still didn't know whether to cry or confront him. She watched Alice take one last kiss, then look up and down the street before she popped out of the house, scampered down the stairs, and quickly walked down the street.

Amanda turned back down into the alley and started crying. She had such wonderful news and now this. She cried for five minutes before she steadied herself and dried her eyes. She knew that Johann would be expecting her home in fifteen minutes and expected her to make his dinner. She took a deep breath, and finally accepted that she must not be satisfying his needs and would do more to make Johann happy. It was what was expected of her as his wife. She must be the problem.

―――

Max left the house and headed for his shop after the disconcerting Amanda episode, wondering if he did the right thing in letting her continue. But she obviously needed the money, he just hated the idea of supporting that bastard husband of hers.

When he arrived, he unlocked the door and found it almost exactly as he left it, albeit with a thick coat of dust. The first things he inspected were his two guns. He pulled his Winchester '66 Yellowboy off the wall and blew off the dust. He held off moving anything and checked the barrel, finding it reasonably clear of rust before he cycled the lever. It was very stiff, so he then checked the breech. The gun probably still worked but knew he wouldn't trust it until he disassembled it and cleaned every piece and coated them with oil.

Next, he pulled out the Colt 1873 model from his holster. The leather on the holster was cracked and beyond salvaging. The pistol wasn't as bad as the Winchester, though. He still thought he'd buy a new pistol and gunbelt and toyed with the idea of a two-gun rig. He already knew he could shoot with both hands with only a slight edge to his right. But that was five years ago, and he'd have to practice if he wanted to regain that level of proficiency. But for now, the shop would require some serious cleaning.

He left the front shop and walked to his living area in back. It was deeply covered in dust as well, as he expected, then he unlocked and opened the back door. The small corral and barn that he had built were in working order, but he'd need more hay and oats for the new horse.

He locked the back door again and left the living area, crossed through the shop and once outside, locked the front door, then decided to have some lunch and headed for Sunny's. He was greeted with the same giant smile from the same young waitress and wondered if the smile would diminish after she'd gotten used to his being in town.

He sat down and when she flounced over to ask what he would like, he ordered the ubiquitous special, whatever it may be. It turned out to be some very good pork chops and gravy with boiled potatoes. He paid the fifty-cent bill with three quarters and smiled at the waitress as he left. She may be young, but she was very pretty, and it had been a long time for Max, more than five years for some reason. He hated to admit it to anyone, but it had been longer than five years…a lot longer. Twenty-five years, in fact, and he needed to change that.

After leaving the diner, he headed for the freight office, reached his father's company two minutes later, and met an anxious Simon outside the office.

"I thought you forgot about me, Max," he said when Max drew close.

"Nope. Just needed to check out the shop and give you some time to get the papers drawn up."

"No, sir. Jim already dropped 'em off, so do you want to head over to the land office and get this taken care of?"

Max smiled at Simon's anxiety and replied, "Let's go and make you the new owner of the freight company, Simon."

Simon grinned back, and they headed to the land office to complete the sale, which didn't take long. After Max and Simon signed the contract, Simon gave him the draft for a thousand dollars and Max signed over the deed to the company. The clerk notarized everything, and Simon was now the owner of the freight company.

"What's the new name going to be?" Max asked as they left the land office, then stood outside on the boardwalk.

"I was going to go with Whitley Freight, but it doesn't have a ring to it."

"How about Whitley Shipping?" Max suggested.

Simon's face lit up as he said, "That sounds great, Max. I was just messing around with the name part."

"Glad to help."

They shook hands and Simon returned to his warehouse while Max turned in the opposite direction and headed for the bank.

After making the deposit, he decided it was time to get the transportation issue resolved and get a horse to take its rightful spot in the small barn behind his shop.

As he headed for the livery, he wondered if Bob Johnson was still there because he had been talking about getting out of the business before Max had gone off to prison.

When he arrived, he found that Bob hadn't gone anywhere.

"Bob, how are you?" he asked loudly as he walked through the wide livery doors.

Bob Johnson dropped his hammer, removed two shoeing nails from his between his lips, and, just as loudly replied, "Max! I heard you were back in town. Good to see you!"

"Good to see you, too, Bob," Max said as he approached the liveryman and shook his hand.

Bob had always been shorter than Max, but thicker in the chest and shoulders. Now, he practically dwarfed Bob, and thankfully, Bob didn't comment about how different he looked. It was getting old.

"What can I do for you, Max?"

"I need a whole new rig, Bob. Horse, tack, scabbard."

"I've got six in back right now. I think there are two you'd like," he said.

"Let's go and check them out."

Bob turned and headed for the back door of the livery with Max following before they entered the attached corral. They had barely entered the fenced area when Max identified the two horses Bob had expected would attract his interest.

"Those two are handsome animals, Bob."

"Just got them in last week. Which one do you like better?"

Max walked up to both horses. Both were tall, which he felt was necessary. One was a mare the other was a gelding. The mare was a tan, almost gold color with a mahogany brown mane and tail, and no markings at all. He was leaning toward the gelding, though. He had a bigger chest and fire in his eyes. He usually didn't see that in geldings. The gelding was such a deep red that he almost appeared to be black, had a black mane and tail, and his only marking was a star on his forehead.

"What's the story on the gelding?" Max asked.

"I thought he'd catch your eye. He's a young lad, only six. He takes after his sire. He's saddle-broke, but still a bit feisty. I shod him right after I got him."

"How much?"

"Fifty dollars."

"Got any saddles?"

"Nope. Sorry. You're gonna have to buy a new one."

"Alright, you've got me, Bob. I'll take the gelding and won't even dicker on the price, but can I get you to deliver a bale of hay and a sack of oats to the barn behind my shop?"

"It's a deal," Bob said with a grin.

They shook hands and Max gave him the fifty dollars, knowing the horse was worth it.

76

"I'll be back when I get my tack, Bob," he said before he waved to Bob and headed for Harrison's leather shop.

Charlie Harrison was an artist in his leather work, so Max wasn't that upset to have to buy new.

He entered the shop and was greeted by Charlie Harrison a few seconds later as he emerged from his workroom in back.

"Howdy, Max. Heard you were back. Hard to recognize you, though."

Max smiled and said, "So everyone keeps telling me. I need a whole new rig, Charlie. Can you help me out?"

"That's what I'm here for. Let's see what you like."

It only took a few minutes to find exactly what he liked and paid more than double for the tack as he did for the horse, but again, he felt it was worth it. He carried the saddle back to the livery while Charlie carried the rest of the tack.

After Charlie returned to his shop, Max said, "I'll leave him and the tack here until you get a chance to drop off the hay and oats, Bob."

"Tomorrow morning be alright?"

"Perfect. Now, I need to go and find some new guns."

"Enjoy it. Paul got a new shipment of firearms a couple of weeks back, so he has a good stock."

"Great. See you tomorrow, Bob."

He left the livery, then turned down the main street and headed for Schneider's General Store to rearm himself.

When he entered the store, he spotted Paul behind the counter, talking to a woman he didn't know, so he just walked down the first aisle, looking at the shelves and recalling how rare it would have been to have most of the items just last week.

The woman left the store, so Max approached the counter, smiled, and said, "Good afternoon, Paul."

"Howdy, Max. What can I do for you?"

"Two things. I need to restock my pantry, so could I get it delivered to the house?"

"Not a problem. I figured you'd need a bit."

"Bob tells me that you got a new shipment of weapons a couple of weeks ago. Anything interesting?"

"Come on over and I'll show you," he replied then left his spot behind the counter and walked to the far end.

Max walked over to the far end of the counter where Paul kept the firearms and spotted something new right away.

"I see a Winchester '76 over there."

"That's one. Do you want to see it?"

"Of course, I do. I can tell you right now, I'll buy it and some of those .45 centerfire cartridges as well. Let me have three boxes."

"I have two of the rifles, did you want to check them out?"

"Sure. I'm going to tweak them anyway, but I may as well have a good starting point."

Paul handed him one of the new Winchesters.

MAX

Max felt the weight and balance. He liked some of the new pieces. The block was made of a better grade of steel and the stock's butt had a brass plate. He cycled the lever and it felt a little stiff. He could fix it, but he tried the second one before he made his choice and found that it was much smoother.

"I'll take this one, Paul. What else can I waste my money on?"

"I have three Colt 1873s and two of the Russians."

"You have two of the Smith & Wessons?"

"Yes, sir."

"Let me see one."

Max's eyes were gleaming as he took the proffered pistol. He liked the feel of the gun more than the much more popular Colt and preferred the innovative design for changing cartridges. He cracked it open and made sure it was empty before dry firing the pistol.

"Let me see the other Russian."

Paul handed him the second Smith & Wesson Model 3 and Max did the same to the second pistol. He was impressed with both pistols and decided to add both of them to his new arsenal.

"I'll take both of them and give me six boxes of the .44 cartridges. I need to get some practice with the Russians."

Paul laid the two new pistols next to the Winchester and then added six more boxes of cartridges.

Max nodded in satisfaction, then said, "I'll need to get a rig for those pistols. I'll be right back."

Max walked down to the leather section. Most of the items were made by Charlie Harrison, so he knew the quality was the best. He found a dark brown two-gun rig that he liked, then carried it up front and added it to the pile. Then he headed for the clothing section. Finding some pants wasn't hard but searching for shirts that would fit proved difficult. He finally found two at the bottom of a stack and walked them up front as well.

"Paul, if you give me a piece of paper and a pencil, I'll write out the food order."

The proprietor slid a pad of paper and a pencil onto the counter and asked, "When do you want it delivered?"

"Can you do it sometime later today? I'll be heading back to the house straightaway after leaving here."

"I'll have it there in two hours."

"Perfect."

Max began writing down his food order which took him a while.

When he finished his list and handed it to Paul, he asked, "Did you think of anything I might have forgotten?"

Paul ran his index finger down the list and asked, "Eggs? Butter? Milk?"

Max rolled his eyes and said, "Add them to the list. It's been a while."

Paul added them and then began adding the prices to the right of each item. It was a lot of food.

He finally looked up and said, "Total, including the guns, is $87.45."

Max wrote out a draft for the large order because the horse and tack had taken a big chunk out of his cash. He handed the draft to Paul, put the holsters on, and slipped the Russians into their new homes, then picked up the Winchester. Paul slid all nine boxes of ammunition into a bag with his clothes and handed it to him.

"Thanks, Max."

"Have a good day, Paul," Max said as he accepted the heavy bag.

"I already have, Max," he replied before he laughed.

Max laughed as well before he waved, headed out the door and back to his house, stepping lively so he could get home and do a closer examination of his new firearms.

He arrived and walked in the front door, hoping that Amanda hadn't returned for some reason. He had to make sure he wasn't in the house when she was there. She was still a very good-looking woman, despite her new subservient attitude, and would rather not be tempted.

He walked to the kitchen, set the guns on the table, stacked the boxes of cartridges next to them then just dropped the box of clothes on the floor. He'd go and empty his drawers of the clothing for the charity donation later. Right now, he only wanted to explore his new weapons.

He spent almost an hour checking out the Winchester and Russians before he finally loaded the Smith & Wessons and returned them to the holsters, hooked the cartridge loops in place, and put the rig over his hips. Next, he loaded the

Winchester with its more powerful .45-70 cartridges, then picked up the Winchester and the bag with his new shirts and pants and walked to the main bedroom. He would have stayed in his room except he appreciated the extra size of the bed in the main bedroom. He removed his gunbelt and hung it over the bedpost and hadn't put any of the clothes away when there was a knock on the back door.

Max left the pistols where they were, returned to the kitchen, and opened the door finding an older boy standing on the back porch looking up at him.

Max smiled and asked, "Howdy. What's your name?"

"I'm Jack Schneider," he replied as he stared, apparently in awe of the big man.

"You've grown a lot, Jack. I see you're working with your father now. Let's get all that stuff inside."

Jack paused for a couple of seconds before saying, "Okay," then turned to go back to the food-laden wagon with Max following.

They had the wagon unloaded and all in the kitchen in five minutes, with Max handling all of the heavy items.

When the last bag was in the kitchen, Max pulled a quarter out of his pocket and handed it to Jack, who stared at the coin in his palm. No one ever tipped him before, much less this much money. He wasn't even sure if it was legal.

He looked back up at Max, and asked, "Are you sure, Mister Wagner?"

"Absolutely. You helped a lot, Jack."

The boy broke into a big grin, said "Thanks, Mr. Wagner!" then bounced across the porch and climbed into the wagon before waving and driving away.

Max smiled as he watched Jack leave and noted that the entire town had all remarked how much he had changed, but young Jack Schneider had changed a lot more. It was just that they had all witnessed the gradual change over the years while his change had been so abrupt. For him, seeing Jack put an exclamation point on how much things had changed in Burden since he'd gone.

Pondering the past, Max set about unloading his order from the bags. It was mostly food, but there was soap and all the other toiletry and cleaning items he'd need as well.

He began to place the food items into their assigned locations, as determined by his mother. He smiled as he recalled her admonishment once for putting a can of beans in the wrong spot, so he didn't make the same mistake today.

After five years of bland prison fare, he had ordered some spices to add flavor to his meals, including ground pepper, cinnamon, nutmeg, and chili powder. He even added some brown sugar and molasses in addition to the white sugar, meaning he was all set if he wanted to do some serious baking, but snickered at the thought based on his ineptitude in the kitchen. He could do a decent breakfast of eggs and bacon, but baking? It was one of the unknown arts to him.

He had it all put away by early evening, but it was too late to cook anything, so he thought he'd head for Sunny's for dinner. He walked to the bedroom, removed his gunbelt from the bedpost, strapped it on, and left the house.

Max reached the diner five minutes later and found a table. It was about half full of diners again, and he noticed that there was a new waitress. She looked familiar, but then again, everyone looked familiar. It was just the folks that were over twenty when he left that he'd been able to recognize. The ability to put a name to a face diminished with the age of the person when he went to prison, like Jack Schneider.

He still hadn't put a name to the face of the pretty young waitress as she approached his table.

"Good evening, what can I get you?" she asked with a normal smile.

"What's on the menu tonight?" he asked as he smiled back at her.

"I'd recommend the fried chicken. It's very good."

"Then I'll have that and some coffee."

"I'll be right back," she said before heading back to the kitchen.

Max watched with admiration. She was also the first attractive woman not to make eyes at him, putting her at the top of the list of young women he'd like to know better. He just had a hard time placing her, and it was so close, but not able to make the mental leap. She certainly was pretty and with an impressive figure, too. But it was her auburn hair and green eyes that marked her as exceptional.

She returned with the coffee, set down the cup, and began pouring.

Max said, "Excuse me, I'm not trying to be forward or anything, but I've been gone a while and I don't recall your name."

84

She laughed and said, "I'm sorry. I would have been fourteen when you left, Max. My name is Colleen Emerson."

Max almost died inside. *She was Walt's sister!* This was awkward, to say the least.

"I'm sorry, Colleen. If you'd rather not serve me, I'll understand."

She looked at him curiously and said, "Why would I not serve you, Max? I'm not a child. I know what happened five years ago, but I also know the whole story, well, most of it. One of these days, you'll have to tell me all of it."

"I'd like to do that, Colleen."

"Well, you can tell me whenever you'd like."

"Are you still living on the farm?" he asked.

"No, I moved out over a year ago. I'm staying at Mrs. Kirkland's rooming house now."

"I just got into town last night, so I'm still trying to get settled. I'll be spending most of my time cleaning up my workshop and getting it ready to be useful again. So, if you'd like to stop by sometime, that's where you'll find me."

"I may do that," she said before smiling and adding, "I'll go and get your dinner."

As she left, he began sipping his coffee and thinking about not only Colleen but the rest of the Emersons as well, and wasn't sure how this could ever work out even if she did stop by his workshop. He'd killed her brother, and Max was sure that Walt's father still hated him for it. *How could anything serious develop with that kind of background?* But that young lady was already beginning to work his way into his mind. *Why did she have to be an Emerson?*

Yet she had already shown her willingness to confront the difficult issues by her acceptance of Walt's death as accidental, or at least not blaming him. He continued to drink his coffee and thought that it might be wiser not to think about Colleen Emerson as anything more than a waitress. That thought lasted for about another ninety seconds when he spotted Colleen returning with a tray. *Damn, that woman was special!*

She arrived with his dinner and set it down, met his eyes, smiled briefly, and then turned to go to a different table.

There was a lot behind those deep green eyes. This was no empty-headed schoolgirl. This was a serious young woman, but there was something else and he couldn't put a finger on it. Granted, he could read Chinese better than he could read women, but still, there was something in those eyes.

He returned to his dinner and began eating. The chicken, as Colleen had said, was very good, as were the mashed potatoes and gravy. He took his time eating as he watched Colleen wait on other customers. Throughout the dinner, she only looked his way twice, probably to check to see if he'd finished eating, unlike the other waitress who practically stared at him, smiling at him for the entire time he was in the diner. Maybe she wasn't interested after all. It would make things easier, but still disappointing.

When he finished, he stood, left a silver dollar for the fifty-cent meal, then walked out of the diner, waving to Colleen as he left, as another woman just to Colleen's left broke into one of those broad smiles. Colleen had a small, but pleasant smile on her face as Max left.

MAX

As Max walked down the street in the fading light, he began to wonder if Colleen secretly harbored a desire for revenge for what had happened in the stagecoach office that morning five years earlier. *What if she was trying to get close to him so she could pay him back for what he had done?* It all came back to trust. *Could he trust her? Could he trust any woman?*

Finally, he just shook his head. It seemed that as long as he was out of sight of Colleen Emerson, it was a lot easier to think, but knew that even that would probably change if he saw her again. She was a hard person to forget.

He reached his house, popped onto the front porch, entered, and closed the door behind him. It was going to be a long night with a lot of thinking to do.

———

In the Peters household, Amanda was trying to get Johann interested after his liaison with Alice. She had undressed, put on just a shirt, and even left the top three buttons undone to let him know her intentions to make him happy.

Johann was getting ready for bed, but for the sole purpose of sleeping. He had told Amanda that he was tired, but from what, he didn't say. He'd just slipped under the comforters when Amanda entered and smiled at him.

"What do you think, Johann?" she asked as she turned, showing her long legs.

Johann had noticed but wasn't impressed. He'd grown tired of Amanda years ago. Now, here she was trying to tempt him to show some form of interest after he was drained from the afternoon with Alice. Alice was the fourth woman he'd taken to his bed since he'd been married to Amanda. She did keep the house clean and was a good cook, though. She even worked which allowed him time to bring his women into his house. Alice was the second unmarried one, but she, unlike the first one, wanted more, and that put him at a risk. She had already hinted that she wanted him to get rid of Amanda, but that wasn't going to happen, not that he'd told that to Alice. Amanda was the perfect shield for his affairs, and he'd counted on her fidelity. He still found it hard to believe that even after all this time, she not only still trusted him but didn't seem to care that he didn't work. Now, here she was trying to impress him, and he had to deal with it again.

He smiled at her and said, "Amanda, it looks very nice, but I'm not in the mood. I'm just too tired."

Amanda wanted to cry or confront him yet again but instead, she turned and took her nightdress out of the drawer, went into the bathroom, and changed before returning to crawl into bed.

"That's better. Good night, Amanda," Johann said before rolling over without even so much as a goodnight kiss.

"Good night, Johann," a frustrated Amanda replied as she lay on her back in her flannel nightdress staring at the ceiling.

It was getting harder and harder to please Johann, and she finally began to wonder if he loved her at all.

CHAPTER 4

The next morning, Amanda was making Johann's breakfast. It was already eight, but Johann liked to sleep late.

He came walking into the kitchen, passed by without saying a word, and left the house to use the privy, giving Amanda the time to set the table for him.

When he returned and sat down at the kitchen table, Amanda obligingly put a plate of bacon and eggs in front of him and filled his cup with coffee, and he began to eat, scooping up a large forkful of eggs and shoving them into his mouth.

Amanda set her coffee on the table next to him, sat down, smiled, and said, "I have some good news, Johann."

He swallowed and asked, "What's that?"

"My pay for cleaning just doubled. I'm going to get ten dollars a month now. Isn't that nice?"

"Why did that smarmy lawyer give you more money? Is he trying to get you into his bed?" Johann asked before ripping off a big bite of bacon.

"No, no. It's not like that at all. In fact, it wasn't even Mister Garson. Max Wagner returned and he's living there now. He said he didn't want to do the cleaning, so he raised my pay because he said five dollars a month wasn't enough."

Johann dropped the other half of his strip of bacon and snapped, "*That bastard is out of prison already?* Well, you tell him to keep his damned money. You ain't taking any dirty money from some ex-con."

A startled Amanda said, "But Johann, we need the money."

"We don't need his money. You just tell him you ain't gonna do no cleaning. He'll probably just try and trap you in that house and rape you. You don't know how these men are, Amanda. Just tell him you ain't gonna work there anymore. You tell him today."

"Alright, I'll tell him," she replied quietly.

Amanda was sick knowing that she'd lose ten dollars a month. Even the five dollars that she'd been getting before was barely enough to make ends meet.

Johann suddenly realized that had also thrown away his private time now that Amanda wouldn't be leaving once a week to do the cleaning. He'd have to find someplace else to meet with Alice. If it hadn't been from that damned Max Wagner, he would have agreed with Amanda that it was good news.

———

Max had finally returned to his shop that morning and was really working on getting it back into some semblance of order. His tools were all still in good shape because he kept them wrapped in a canvas tarp when they weren't in use. He just had to coat them with some machine oil and let them sit under the tarp while he cleaned the dust out of the place.

He started with good old-fashioned sweeping, working from the inside out. It took over two hours to get most of the dust out of the shop. He then filled a bucket with water and began to mop the floor. It took almost an hour of steady mopping and wringing filthy water out of the mop before the shop finally began to resemble a shop and not an abandoned dust factory. He then emptied the bucket of muddy water out back, refilled it, soaked a towel, and began wiping down the other surfaces. By the time he finally had the shop reasonably dust-free, it was noon.

He realized that he hadn't found the one thing in his shop that was valuable, a least to him. He went into his living area and opened the drawer in the small cabinet near his bed. He smiled as he pulled out the pocket watch his parents had given him on his sixteenth birthday. He wound it and was gratified that it still worked. It should work because he had taken it apart and made it perfect two days after he had received it. He changed the time to close to what he thought it was and slipped it into his pocket. He'd go down to the train depot and match it to the station clock later.

He washed his hands and headed down the street to Sunny's for lunch, leaving the door to the shop open.

When he arrived, he found the ever-smiling waitress on duty, so Max ate his lunch quickly and returned to his shop to restore it to working order and began by working on the small barn in back to prepare it for his new horse.

When he swung the door open, he found that it wasn't in poor condition at all. It was a barn, after all, and a certain amount of dirt and dust is not only tolerated but expected. He had just finished the barn when Bob Johnson arrived with his oats and hay, so he unloaded the hay as Bob took care of the oats.

When they finished, Max said, "I'll be down in a little while for the horse and tack, Bob. Say, Bob, what can you tell me about that mare?"

Bob stopped and replied, "Well, I can tell you that your gelding ain't gonna keep her in foal."

Max laughed, and replied, "Really? He's not a stud gelding?"

Bob laughed and said, "She's just had her first foal, so she's just past bein' a filly. She's five years old and really gentle. Pretty, too."

"How much for her?"

"Seein' as how you're a repeat customer, I'd let her go for forty dollars."

Matt smiled and said, "You're a tough salesman, Bob, but I know when I'm licked. It's a deal."

He pulled out the money and handed it to Bob who asked, "Did you want me to bring her down with the gelding?"

"Sure. But I've got to see Charlie and get another rig, too."

Bob asked, "Why do you need two saddles? You gonna ride 'em both at the same time?"

Max wasn't sure himself, but somehow meeting Colleen Emerson had triggered the idea, so he answered, "Beats me, Bob."

Bob shrugged and said, "After you visit Charlie, bring it all over, we'll saddle 'em both up and you can just bring them back yourself."

"Sounds fair. I'll hitch a ride with you back that way."

"Gonna start gettin' fat if you start ridin' instead of walkin'," Bob said with a snicker.

"I'll worry about it when that problem arrives," he replied as he hopped onto the wagon and sat on the driver's seat next to Bob who flicked the reins to get the team moving.

He jumped off the moving wagon at Charlie's shop and was soon lugging another saddle and the rest of the setup over to the livery. Charlie had another customer and had draped it all around his neck and shoulders as he carried the saddle. Bob already had the mare brushed down, and Matt had to agree that was a very pretty horse.

They saddled both animals and Max stepped up on the gelding and led the mare down the street to his shop. The gelding had a smooth gait, and he noticed that the mare was even smoother. It was such an exhilarating, free sensation to be on horseback again.

He pulled in behind his shop and put both horses into the small corral beside the barn. He had built it large enough to handle four horses, so two was no problem. He stripped off the tack, and put it all in the barn, then checked his watch. It was only 1:20, so he went into his shop and walked to the front, and opened the doors wide to let some air into the place.

As the doors arced into the street, the right door almost smacked into Colleen Emerson, startling them both.

"Oh! Sorry, Colleen. I should have given you some warning before opening the doors," Max said as he grabbed the door to stop its swing.

She laughed and replied, "Or maybe I should have stood back a bit."

"Come on in. It's reasonably clean now."

She walked through the wide doors and began looking about the shop.

"This is an interesting place. You seem to have a wide assortment of tools."

"I'll fix anything from a pocket watch to a steam engine, so I need them all."

She followed him into the living area and said, "I heard that. Are you going to continue doing that now that you've returned?"

"I hope so. It's what I do. Have a seat. I'd offer you some coffee, but all of my food is back at the house."

"That's all right. I'm a tea drinker anyway."

She sat at the small table and asked, "Do you live back here?"

"Not anymore. I used to before the stagecoach office incident," he replied and almost grimaced for bringing it up so soon.

But Amanda seemed nonplussed and said, "You told me that you'd tell me the whole story. Will you tell me now?"

Max sat down across the table from Colleen and wondered how much of the truth he could tell her. *Did he keep the omission of what he'd discovered Walt and Mary doing, or did he reveal Mary's part in the drama?*

"I will, but before I start, I'd like to thank you."

She tilted her head and asked, "Thank me for what?"

"For being the only female that I've met since I've been released that hasn't given me that 'come hither' look."

She laughed, and answered, "I had an advantage. Maddie told me that you were in town. She didn't know who you were, but I figured it out."

"Who's Maddie?" he asked.

"Madeline Wheeler, she's the other waitress at Sunny's."

"That's Madeline Wheeler? She was just a skinny little girl when I left."

"Maddie has filled out some. She's been talking about you almost non-stop since you've been back."

Max scratched the back of his neck and said, "Well, even though you were forewarned, thank you for acting normally. It was sincerely appreciated."

Then, as he looked into those inquisitive green eyes, he decided which tale to tell her.

"Anyway, onto the story. That wall to the east is a common wall with the old stagecoach office. I was working on Amanda Peters' clock when I heard a banging against the wall. I ignored it for a little while, but it was getting annoying, so I left the shop and went around back. I found the door ajar to the abandoned office and pulled it open. I saw a girl pressed against the wall with her blouse open, her skirts hiked up and Walt was pushing against her. They both turned when I entered, and as soon as she saw me, she slapped Walt hard and shouted that he was trying to rape her.

"So, I grabbed him by the collar and threw him down. He popped back up and swung at me, so it came down to exchanging blows. Finally, I caught him with an uppercut and sent him flying. He hit his head on an oak table and he died. The girl had fixed her clothing issues, put her hand on my shoulder, and asked if he was dead. Then she asked me not to bring her into the story because it would ruin her reputation. She kissed me on the cheek and promised me that she'd always be there for me. She left, and the marshal arrived. The rest is pretty well-known. It wasn't until I was in prison for a while that I realized what a naïve fool I had been, and she'd taken

95

advantage of that. Walt wasn't assaulting her. He was there at her invitation. I was an idiot and paid for it."

Max then sighed, and said, "So, that's the whole story, Colleen."

Colleen kept her eyes on Max as she said, "All of it except for her name."

"I'll tell you her name because I owe you that. It was Mary Preston."

Colleen sat back as Max watched for her reaction.

After a few seconds, she said, "Well, that explains a lot of things."

"It does? Explains what? I don't understand."

"Mary Preston married a man named Charles Jones from Wichita a year after that. She lives there now. He's some important bigwig in the bank, and she moves around in society circles now."

"What does that have to do with the whole fake rape scene? I thought she was just trying to protect her reputation."

"In a way, you're right. If you are a woman who has ambitions to rub elbows with society types, the hint of a scandal involving being caught in the act and then witness to, or actually the cause of, a death would be to toss any of those dreams into the great abyss."

"Colleen, she was only nineteen. Why would she think such things?"

"You didn't know her as well as the girls did. Mary was always looking to get out of the life she was living. She didn't have it as bad as many other children, but she wanted a lot more, and had the tools to get them, too."

"You mean she was going to, well, prostitute herself to get ahead?"

"That's exactly what I mean. Now, most women do that to some degree or another, meaning they look for husbands who can provide for them and their children, but Mary was much more exact. She wanted to find a wealthy man and seduce him. I think Walt was nothing more than practice."

Max was stunned by the revelation and wished he'd had a sister when he was younger so he could have known such things.

"Do you know when I figured out that it was just routine rutting and not rape? A fellow cellmate pointed out that she hadn't screamed when he first laid hands on her and then he asked if her blouse was ripped or unbuttoned. When he asked that, I suddenly realized that in that brief instant before she slapped him that her head was back, and her eyes were closed. She had her hands on his neck as his head was buried in her chest. That's when I knew. I felt like a bigger fool than I had thought I was in the first place."

"Max, the one thing that had everyone puzzled was why you just pled guilty and let them throw you in prison when you easily could have avoided prison time completely."

"Because after my initial confusion, I was sitting in the jail cell and I realized that regardless of the circumstances, I had taken a life. I had to be punished for what I did, Colleen. I couldn't live with myself. That's why I did all the hard labor, too. It wasn't for the twenty-five cents a day. It was to pay penance for violating the commandments."

Colleen looked down at the table and said quietly, "Max, you didn't need to pay penance for what you did. You became my savior."

That stunned Max. *She was happy that he had killed her brother?*

She took in a deep breath and said softly, "This is between us. Okay?"

"Of course," he answered.

"Walt was four years older than my sister Patty, who was one year older than me. He was always the big brother. When we reached our teen years, we noticed that Walt was always hanging around. We'd catch him looking at us when we were in bed, then we found knot holes that had been pushed out of the wood, so he could watch us from his bedroom.

"We told my father about it, but he didn't do anything. Then, almost as if he'd been given the go-ahead, Walt became more than just a peeping Tom. He'd grab at us or grope us as we walked past, then he started pulling us onto his lap and enjoying himself. It was hard to get away from him. We didn't know what to do or how far he was going to go. Patty was more physically mature than I was, so she got the brunt of the attention, but I got my share as well. Then, suddenly, he was gone. Just like that," she said as she snapped her fingers.

"My father hates you with a passion for killing Walt, by the way. As soon as she turned eighteen and didn't need my father's permission, Patty married and was out of the house like a bullet. She took the first proposal she received and married Joe Endicott and lives southwest of town at his ranch. I go and visit sometimes. Then, for a year, I was alone in the house with my father. When I finally reached eighteen, I moved out that day into the rooming house and took the job as a waitress."

Max wondered why she didn't take the first marriage proposal she received as she must have had them by the bushel but didn't ask.

"I'm so sorry, Colleen. Didn't you have anyone to turn to?"

"Not a soul. My father was the head of the household. Do you know what that means to any woman that lives in that house? He can beat her, abuse her, and it's all okay because he'll claim it was just a method of discipline and he's entitled."

"I really am sorry, Colleen. I've been so naïve to so many things in my sheltered life. I had wonderful parents that loved me."

"I apologize for venting like this, Max. It was just bottled up for so long. No one except Patty knows."

"No one else will ever know, Colleen. Not from me."

"Thank you."

"Colleen, you said that your father really hated me for what happened to Walt. How far would you think he'd go?"

"Do you mean would he murder you? I think if he thought he could get away with it, he would."

"Colleen, my father died in what they said was an accident when he was crushed by a freight wagon. Those of us who knew him understood that he was diligent in his concern for safety when working on the wagons. Is it possible that your father could have murdered my father in revenge?"

"I never thought about it, but I suppose it's possible."

"I'll think about it. Colleen, on a less gloomy topic, what do you do for entertainment?"

"Not much. Why?"

"Do you just go out riding?"

"If I had a horse, I'd love to. But the best I can manage is a good walk now and then."

"Come with me for a second," he said as he stood.

He turned, opened the back door, and walked outside as Colleen followed him out the door, then saw the two horses in the corral.

"Max, those are beautiful horses!" she exclaimed.

"I bought the gelding but felt bad leaving that beautiful mare. So, I bought her this morning, too. It's kind of silly, really, but she was too pretty to leave behind."

Colleen approached the mare and rubbed the side of her neck.

"What's her name?"

"I haven't named either one yet. Any suggestions?"

The mare looked at Colleen as she stroked the horse's neck, and she said, "She's so beautiful, I'd call her Venus."

"Then I'd better call the gelding Mars just to offset her. Of course, he is red, so it would fit."

She turned to Max. "Max, would you allow me to take her for a ride?"

"That's what she's there for. Do you have any riding clothes?"

Colleen hesitated before replying, "No. It never occurred to me. I could modify one of my dresses, though."

"Nonsense. Why ruin a perfectly good dress? Let's head over to Schneider's and you get a nice riding skirt and blouse. You can go back to your room and get changed and I'll saddle up Venus for you. How's that?"

Colleen hesitated again. She was on a tight budget, but she didn't want anything from any man.

Max could see her dilemma but misread it. He assumed it was just pride and not wanting to accept charity.

"Colleen, don't misread this at all, please. But let me buy you the clothes so I can enjoy your company for a nice ride. Would you allow me to do that?"

Colleen was really conflicted. She wanted to ride the horse, but she didn't want to be in anyone's debt, especially not a man's. She continued to absent-mindedly rub Venus' neck as she thought about her answer.

Max suddenly came up with another solution.

"Colleen, if that makes you uncomfortable, as I imagine it does, how about this? When I returned home, I went through the house and found drawers full of women's clothing. I'm sure I saw some riding clothes in there. I was going to donate them to charity anyway. Do you want to just go to the house and find some that fit? I'll stay here."

Colleen bit her lower lip, then finally said, "If you were going to donate them anyway, I suppose that it would be all right."

"Colleen, if you find anything else that you'd like, set it aside and you can take it with you when you get back. There were some very nice dresses in there, too."

She was still uncomfortable, but nodded and said, "Alright. I'll be back in about twenty minutes."

"I'll get the horses saddled."

She smiled weakly, then turned and stepped off quickly.

Max watched her leave and realized what a delicate situation he was in. Colleen probably trusted men a lot less than he trusted women, and he couldn't blame her, either. Living with a brother who watched and groped her and a father who, instead of taking Walter to task, let him get away with it must have been horrible. Patty was probably just as hurt and wondered how her marriage was working out.

He turned and walked into the barn and removed the saddle blankets first.

Colleen arrived at the Wagner house, found it unlocked, and walked inside. She had never been in the house before and was impressed with how big and well-constructed it was. It was nothing like the ramshackle house she had grown up in on the farm. She found the main bedroom and saw one of Max's shirts folded on the dresser. She picked it up and let it unfold, its sheer size giving her a rush. She sighed and quickly folded it again before going through the drawers.

Max had been right. There were several very nice dresses in the drawers that were much nicer than the three she owned. There were undergarments as well.

She wanted everything, but it would look bad, so she found a riding skirt and blouse and took them out of the drawer. But after she pulled them out, she found a box at the bottom of the drawer, and curiosity compelled her to take it out and open it.

When she lifted the blue felt cover, she found a stunning necklace that probably belonged to his mother. It was a beautiful piece of jewelry, not overly ornate, just a single emerald with a small diamond on each side. She replaced the necklace and the box into their original location, closed the drawer, then the bedroom door, and looked around the room, finding no peepholes. She almost laughed at herself but didn't think it was humorous at all.

She changed quickly and left her old dress over a chair before she opened the door and as she was getting ready to leave, decided to go out the back door and peek at the kitchen just out of curiosity.

The kitchen was much larger than the one at the farmhouse, which didn't surprise her. Max had obviously just restocked the food supply, and it was the one aspect of her life that she missed. She loved to cook, and here was everything she needed to make anything. He had even bought cinnamon and nutmeg. She sighed, then left through the back door and walked quickly back to Max's shop using the back alley.

When she was still a few hundred feet away, she saw him smiling at her and holding the reins of the two horses and couldn't help but smile back.

"Ready for the ride, Miss Emerson?" he asked as she drew near.

"More than you could imagine, Mr. Wagner."

He gave her the reins to Venus before he climbed up on Mars.

"Where to?" he asked.

"Can we go and visit my sister?"

"Sure, you lead the way."

She grinned and turned out to the roadway with Max following. He was pleased to see her so happy on the horse, even if that undercurrent of discomfort was still there.

She turned west leaving town and Max caught up with her and soon trotted next to Colleen.

He asked loudly, "How does she ride? She seemed very smooth when I trailed her down to the corral."

"She's perfect. It's like I'm floating," she replied, unable to contain her smile.

Max nodded as they kept the horses at a medium trot.

The road branched off to the southwest and Colleen angled Venus to the turnoff. Colleen hadn't stopped smiling since she first stepped up on Venus.

"How much further, Colleen?"

"About three miles."

"Let's let them run!" he shouted as he let Mars take his head.

He shot past Venus and Colleen let the mare go. Soon, they were both charging down the road, leaving a huge plume of dust behind.

Max swiveled his head to see Colleen wearing a giant grin as her auburn hair flew out behind her. He was still pulling away, but barely. After a mile or so, he slowed Mars down to a fast trot and Colleen caught up, then slowed down, and soon both horses had reduced their speed to a walk.

"That was the most fun I've had in years!" exclaimed Colleen.

"Same here. They both can really get down the road, can't they?"

"Yes, they can."

"Colleen, Venus will be in the corral. Whenever you want to take her for a ride, the tack will be in the barn. Just saddle her up and go."

"You won't mind?"

"Not a bit."

They rode for another couple of minutes when they arrived at a ranch access road. There wasn't any sign over the road to identify the ranch.

"This is Patty's place," Colleen announced as she turned Venus down the entrance road.

Max didn't comment as they continued walking the horses toward a ranch house that seemed a bit run down. They reached the house and Colleen slid down from the saddle rather than step down. Max stayed put until he was invited.

Colleen turned to Max. "Come on, Max, you don't have to stay up there."

He was invited, so he dismounted.

Colleen shouted, "Patty!" and was rewarded with a rush of footsteps from the house, the door opened, and her sister's smiling countenance emerged before she crossed the porch and hurried down the steps.

Patty Endicott embraced her younger sister, and as she did, her eyes wandered to Max, then after a few more seconds, she stepped back.

"Colleen, are you going to introduce me to your friend?" she asked.

"You already know him, Patty. This is Max Wagner."

Patty's jaw dropped, and she walked toward Max, closing her mouth as she drew closer.

"Max? Really?"

Max smiled and replied, "Yes, ma'am. How are you, Patty?"

She suddenly hugged Max like a long-lost relative, except her arms never made it close to his back. Then she stepped back, smiling.

"I'm sorry for that. I was just happy to see you," she said with a blush.

"That was my impression."

"Well, come on in," she said before turning, taking Colleen's hand, and walking onto the porch.

Patty led them into the main room and sat down. The furniture was clean but worn.

"Where's Joe?" Colleen asked as she took a seat while Max remained standing.

"He went into town for some supplies. I'm surprised you didn't see him."

Max wondered about that. His shop was almost directly across from Schneider's and he hadn't seen a wagon pull up while he was there. Maybe he just rode in.

"Where did you get that beautiful mare, Colleen?" Patty asked.

"She's Max's horse. He said I could borrow her whenever I want, so I can visit you more often now."

"That's wonderful," she said, then turned to Max and asked, "So, when did you get back, Max?"

"Three days ago."

"I'm sure you've heard this before, but you've changed a lot."

He smiled and said, "That's an understatement, it seems to be the number one topic of conversation. Colleen is the only one who hasn't commented, but she said she had been forewarned by Maddie."

"Max, we all were curious about why you pled guilty."

"Colleen has all the details, but the simple reason was that I was guilty. I killed Walt, and the circumstances really didn't matter. I served my sentence and now I'm back."

Patty didn't know what to make of the answer, but asked, "Did Colleen tell you about Walt?"

"She did."

"Then you understand my reaction when I saw you."

"I did. It didn't alter what I did, but I'm glad you both got out of that situation. How are you doing now, Patty?"

"I'm fine. Joe and I get along okay."

Max thought that didn't exactly sound like a ringing endorsement of her marriage. He didn't remember Joe Endicott that well because he left school in his sixth year and mostly stayed at the ranch.

"How many head are you running?"

"About two hundred or so. We need to get some of the young heifers castrated and we're behind on branding, though."

"Do you have any hired hands?"

"John Perkins from the Slash P next door used to help, but he just got married and moved in with his wife's family on the other side of the county."

"I'd offer to help, but I've never gotten within twenty feet of a cow."

She laughed and said, "Sometimes, I wish I hadn't."

There was the sound of hooves outside, making them all turn to the doorway, but the horse passed by the front of the house.

"Sounds like Joe's home," Patty said, then asked, "How bad was it in prison, Max?"

"Not too bad for someone like me. The small guys were just like mice to the big cats. I worked every day, so I got outside a lot. Just being outside, you can close your eyes for a few seconds and imagine you're not a prisoner. Then, when they found out I could fix anything, they kept me busy. You'd be surprised with what some of the prisoners owned. One even had a thermometer and barometer setup. I even worked on things like steam engines outside of prison."

"Can you really fix anything?" she asked.

"Pretty much. I probably know a lot more now than when I went in. I was able to read a lot of technical manuals and engineering books when I wasn't working."

"Really? Where…"

Patty's question was interrupted by the arrival of her husband.

"Whose horses are outside?" he asked loudly from the kitchen.

"Colleen and Max Wagner are visiting," Patty answered just as loudly.

Joe walked down the hallway into the main room and Max could smell the alcohol on him when he got within ten feet.

"Hello, Colleen. Is that you, Max?" he asked, surprisingly without a hint of drunkenness.

Max smiled and replied, "It is. How are you, Joe? I haven't seen you for a while, five years for some reason."

Joe laughed, but not pleasantly as he said, "I imagine so. I hear the state had you under their protection for a while. So, what are you doing here with Colleen?"

"Just riding, but she wanted to visit Patty."

He looked at Colleen and then back at Max.

"You're taking her riding already? Moving in kinda fast, aren't you?"

Max looked at Joe and saw something that surprised him. He was jealous, of what, he wasn't certain. *Was he jealous that he was with Colleen? Or was he jealous because he was talking to Patty?*

Before Colleen could answer, Max replied, "I'm not moving anywhere, Joe. Colleen saw my new mare and I offered to let her take her for a ride. She wanted to come and visit her sister, and as I hadn't ridden the gelding yet, I came along."

"Well, just remember that Colleen's family to me. Don't go getting any ideas."

Max had no response to that comment, so he just let it go. Obviously, neither of the sisters had any intention of replying either.

"Are you going to stay for dinner?" asked Patty.

"I need to get back, but if Colleen wants to stay, that's all right. She can leave the mare in the corral whenever she does get back."

"I'll stay, if that's alright with you, Max," Colleen said.

Max nodded and replied, "That's fine. I'll be getting along. Nice to see you both again."

Max was still standing, so he just gave a small wave before heading out the door, crossed the porch, then unhitched Mars and climbed aboard. He wheeled him around and headed back down the access road wondering just how much of an alcoholic Joe was. For him to put away that much whiskey and not feel the effects was an indicator. He knew that if he had even two drinks, he'd be out cold, despite his bulk. And then, there was the jealousy. *What was that all about?* The liquor probably made him a bit looser with his tongue, but that just meant he had the feelings in the first place. So, he was jealous that he was with Colleen, yet she chose to stay. Max was so confused by the whole thing, so he just wanted to go home and get some sleep.

He arrived at his shop just forty minutes later and brought Mars around back and unsaddled him. After he had put the saddle away, he brushed him down and let him drink as he poured some oats into his feed bin, all the while thinking of Colleen and how happy she had been on the ride to the ranch, and then the decision to stay rather than to ride back with him. It bothered him more than he dared to admit.

He locked up his shop and headed back to the house, reminding himself to move some of the food, especially the coffee, from the house to his living quarters behind the shop. He stopped more than halfway to the house and returned to Schneider's.

"What can I get for you, Max?" asked Paul when he entered.

"I forgot something from my food order."

Max went down to where the coffee was and bought a two-pound box of tea and a tea strainer. He also added a teapot and kettle. As he carried them to the counter, he smiled to himself thinking that these were something he never thought he'd be buying when he was sitting on his cot in the Kansas State Prison.

"Fancy some tea, Max?" Paul Schneider asked as he smiled.

"Just a hankerin', Paul."

He paid for the order and carried the bag with him back to the house. When he went to put the tea away in the kitchen, he noticed for the first time that his mother had a box labeled 'TEA'. It was empty, but he soon remedied the situation by pouring the contents of the container of tea into the box. When he opened the drawer to put the tea strainer, he found another already there. He smiled and shook his head. May as well bring the new one and some tea to the shop in case Colleen ever stops by again but wasn't sure she would. He wondered if he had gone too far in the first place as he set aside the tea strainer and teapot and began to cook his dinner.

―――――

Back at the ranch, Colleen and Patty were cooking dinner as well while Joe lay snoring on the couch.

Patty looked at her sister and said, "That was embarrassing, Colleen. I'm sorry."

"You didn't do anything wrong. Are things all right for you these days, Patty?"

"It's all right. It's not like when Walt was around."

"At least if your husband was pulling you onto his lap and fondling you, it would be appreciated."

She sighed, then said, "Yes, it most assuredly would be appreciated. Not that it happens. So, is Max interested, Colleen?"

"I'm not ready, Patty. I like Max, but I'm just not ready. I can't. I really wish I could."

"I know. It took me a little while to get used to it, too, almost six months. But then, by the time I did, Joe lost all interest. I knew he had a drinking problem when we got married, and I thought he'd change, but he didn't. If anything, he drinks more now. The work's not getting done, and he sleeps a lot, too. I don't know what I can do."

"Does he hit you, Patty?"

"Not too often, and only when he's drunk."

"He's drunk a lot of the time, Patty," Colleen said.

"This isn't too bad, but I believe it's going to get worse because of the money. Our savings are almost gone, and we can't hire anyone to help with the cattle. I know you don't have much money either, but at least you're on your own."

"It makes a difference. I have some money saved up from tips. I could let you have thirty dollars. Would that help?"

"No. He'd probably just find it and buy some more whiskey," then Patty looked at her clothes and said, "That's a nice outfit, though. Did you just buy that?"

"No. Max was going to buy me something new, but when I balked, he mentioned that he found a lot of women's clothing in the house that was his mother's. He said he was going to donate it to charity anyway, so I went through the drawers and found this."

"Was there anything else nice?" asked an interested Patty.

"Oh, yes. There were at least a half dozen really nice dresses as well as undergarments, nightdresses, and stockings. There were even some shoes. I saw two nice coats in the closet, too. Everything looked almost new."

"Do you think he's going to give them away?"

"He said he was. He even said I could take what I wanted. Maybe I could ask for a couple of the dresses. That wouldn't be too bad, would it?"

"Could you do that? I'd like a nice dress. This is the best one I have now, and it's getting a bit worn in spots."

"I'll see what I can do. I don't want to owe him anything, though. At least these won't be a gift."

"I don't think it matters, but I'd appreciate anything you could get."

————

Max had finished his dinner and cleaned up the dishes before he walked into his bedroom and saw Colleen's dress hanging over the chair. He picked it up and looked at the thin fabric. It was all right now with the weather warming toward summer, but it would never do in the autumn and winter chill.

He returned to the kitchen and took out the four large canvas bags that he had used to bring the food into the house then brought the bags into his bedroom and began to empty the drawers. He started with the four pairs of shoes. He didn't know if they fit, but they seemed about the right size. Then he began to fold the dresses and other feminine attire as tightly as he could to get as much as possible into each bag but didn't quite make it. He reached the last drawer and pulled out the remaining clothes and saw the blue velvet box underneath.

He took the box in his thick fingers and smiled, knowing what was inside before he slowly opened the cover and gazed at the emerald and diamond necklace.

His father had bought the necklace for his mother for their twentieth anniversary, just weeks before he had been sent to prison. He had watched as his father had put it around her delicate neck. She was crying as he fastened the clasp and kissed her.

Tears began to slide from his eyes as he continued to stare at the necklace. He would never see his mama's smile again or feel his papa's rough handshake. He finally managed to bring himself under control and began to wonder about his father's death again. He decided that he would exhume the body and have an autopsy performed. It would cost him more than just money, but it would be worth it if he found his father had been murdered, and he already had a suspect.

He placed the necklace back into the now empty drawer. He needed at least one more container of sorts, so he went into his old bedroom, the one he slept in for eighteen years, and opened the closet. There were still some of his old clothes there, which would become more donations but in the back of the closet was a large travel bag. He pulled it out and brought it into what was now his new bedroom, then put the last of the clothes inside, as well as Colleen's old dress, and still had enough room for the two coats.

He tied the bags together, then picked up all four bags and the travel bag and left the house. He waddled his way into the sunset to Mrs. Kirkland's rooming house and once on the front porch, put his right-hand load down and opened the door. He walked inside and almost ran down Mrs. Kirkland.

"Good evening, Mrs. Kirkland. Miss Emerson asked that I drop these off."

"Well, just leave them in the hallway by her room. It's the third room on the right," Beatrice Kirkland said.

"I'll be right back."

Max waddled his way up the stairway and down the hallway to the third door. He just left the bags against her door. If she never talked to him again because of what she perceived as a gift, then so be it. At least she'd have something to wear.

He returned down the stairs, saw Mrs. Kirkland waiting for him to come back, then tipped his hat and said, "Thank you, ma'am."

"Do I know you, young man?" she asked.

"Yes, ma'am. I'm Max Wagner."

She stared at him for a few seconds and said, "By golly, you're right! I'm glad to see that you're back, Max. I'm sorry that I didn't recognize you."

"That seems to be a common occurrence, Mrs. Kirkland. You have a nice evening."

He waved and jogged down the porch steps and back up the street to the house, almost dreading Colleen's return.

————

Twenty minutes later, a very upset Colleen Emerson returned Venus to her corral. She really didn't want to ask Max for the dresses, despite the assurances she gave Patty. What made it worse was that she knew both she and her sister could really use the clothes. The riding outfit she was wearing was easily the nicest thing she owned. Then she remembered that she had left her dress in Max's bedroom. *How awkward would it be to get it back?* She only had one other dress.

She brushed down the golden mare and sighed. She'd decide what to do in the morning.

She walked half a block to the rooming house and climbed the steps to the short porch. After entering, she stepped up the stairway to the second floor, reached the top landing, and saw the bags stacked in front of her door, she stopped in her tracks for a few seconds, then slowly walked down the hallway. At first, she didn't recognize what they were. Then she saw a petticoat bulging out of one of the bags and hurriedly opened the door to her room and began bringing the cloth bags and travel bag inside.

After closing the door, she began pulling the clothing out of the bags in a confusing mix of suspicion, relief, gratitude, and ingratitude.

It must be the entire wardrobe of women's clothing! All of it, even the coats and her dress that she had been so worried about retrieving were in the bags. She didn't need to ask for anything at all, but now she had another problem. *What would Max expect from her?* She didn't know if she could ever face him again, but she needed to use Venus at least once more to deliver the clothes to Patty. It saddened her to think that she wouldn't be riding the mare more often. It was the most enjoyment she'd had from life in years.

But right now, all she did was go through the dresses and pick out three for herself and three for Patty. She divided the shoes, which did fit perfectly, so she knew Patty could wear them as well. Finally, she split up the coats. She began putting one stack back into the canvas bags. The rest she put in her drawers and closet. She knew she'd have to borrow Venus again to deliver the clothes but smiled when she thought of Patty's reaction tomorrow. She knew how unhappy her sister was and this would brighten her life, if only for a short time.

CHAPTER 5

The next morning, after he had made himself a real breakfast, Max walked over to Jim Garson's office.

He walked in and found the attorney at his desk reading some law review before he looked up.

"Morning, Max. What can I do for you today?"

Max sat down and asked, "Jim, how do I go about getting my father's body exhumed and having an official autopsy performed?"

Jim sat back, and his eyebrows rose slightly as he replied, "Seriously? You can request it on your own because you're the only surviving relative. An official autopsy would mean you'd have to have a forensic pathologist brought in to do the job and write the report. The nearest one is probably in Topeka or Kansas City. I'd have to check. Why do you want to do it?"

"I think he was murdered, Jim."

The attorney leaned forward quickly and asked, "Murdered? Are you sure?"

"Jim, nothing about this accident makes sense to me. Simon thought the same thing. Those of us that worked with him or understood him knew he'd never only use two jacks to do work under a freight wagon."

"He only had two jacks under there?"

"That's what Simon told me."

"Alright. I'll draw up the paperwork for the exhumation and find the nearest forensic pathologist. It'll take me a few days."

"Thanks, Jim," Max said as he stood and shook his hand.

After leaving Jim Garson's office, he walked to his shop and opened the barn doors wide. It was cloudy and threatening, but he could close the doors quickly if it became necessary. He had remembered to bring the coffee for his back room, as well as some of the tea, sugar, and the second strainer, just in case.

He put the coffee and tea away then went outside to the horses and noticed that Venus was back, so he brushed her down as he wondered how Colleen was taking the clothing delivery. She'd probably be angry with him, judging by her reaction to his initial offer to offer to buy the riding clothes.

He returned to his shop and continued to get everything in shape. He was still mulling over the whole Emerson situation when Amanda walked into the shop.

"Good morning, Amanda," he said as he smiled at her.

She didn't seem happy, and Max was confused. She had seemed practically ecstatic when she'd left the house.

"I can't clean for you, Max. I'm sorry," she blurted out before she rapidly turned around and almost ran away, hurriedly walking back down the street.

He had heard the obvious strain in her voice and had no idea why she had turned down the job. He really didn't need a cleaning lady anyway, but that wasn't the point. He knew she was stretched for money with Johann not working and guessed that Johann had put his foot down. He shook his head. *Aren't there any normal, well-balanced women in this town?*

Down the road, Johann was out of the house and walking to the Western Union office. He stepped inside and sent a short telegram that cost him a precious forty cents, then left and returned to the house before Amanda returned.

No one would ever know how close he and Mary Preston had been in the years after the Max episode. She had been the first of the four women he had bedded while married to Amanda and she had been the best, too. Then she had gone off to Wichita and married that banker, and he'd always hoped to rekindle the liaison. With the news of Max's return, he saw the value to Mary in the news which would increase the probability of that happening.

Max was busy with his old Winchester Yellowboy. He had it disassembled and was cleaning and oiling each piece when he heard noise from behind the shop. He was going to go and check but figured it was probably Colleen taking some clothes to Patty, so he continued working. When he heard hooves departing a short time later, he finally stood and walked outside just to make sure no one had stolen his gelding. He saw that Venus was gone, so he went back inside.

He finished the Winchester and was pleased to have it feel the way it should and loaded it with fresh .44 cartridges. Now he needed to fix his old Colt '73.

———

Colleen arrived at Patty's ranch a little while later. She had two bags of clothes for her older sister and happily walked up the stairs.

"Patty! I'm back," she shouted, but there was no answer.

She walked up the steps, crossed the porch, and called her sister's name again, but still received no response. She slowly opened the door, stepped inside, and found her sister lying on the floor. Colleen dropped the bags and ran to her sister, took a knee, and rolled Patty onto her back. She was on the verge of panic when Patty moaned.

"Patty! Are you all right? This is Colleen," she asked quickly.

"Colleen?" Patty whispered through narrow eye slits.

"What happened, Patty?"

"It was bad, Colleen. I shouldn't have said anything. But I think I'll be okay in a while. Can you help me up?"

"Of course," Colleen said.

Colleen stood and then bent over at the waist to help Patty stand.

Her sister wobbled as Colleen fought to keep her upright before Colleen swung Patty around and managed to get her into a chair.

She crouched down before her sister and asked, "Patty, where does it hurt?"

"Just on the side of my chest and my head. I'll be okay. Don't worry, please."

"Patty, how can I not worry? You could barely stand."

"Joe was mad at me. I made a mistake. I told him that Max was going to give you some dresses for me. He got really mad and hit me hard. I fell to the floor and he kicked me in the side of my chest. That's why it hurt. Then I passed out, but I'll be okay now."

Colleen rose to her feet as rage filled her, asking, "Where is Joe now?"

"He went to town, probably to get something to drink."

Colleen looked at her older sister who was now going to be her baby sister and said, "You're coming with me, Patty."

"Where can I go? I have no place to go, Colleen."

"I know someplace. Come with me and we'll take all these dresses along."

"You did bring a dress for me, Colleen? Is it nice?" Patty asked, almost as if she were in another place.

"It's very nice. All three of them. Now, I need you to stand."

Patty was in rough shape, but she managed to stand, then after Colleen grabbed the two bags, Patty used her as support by putting her hand on Colleen's shoulder as they walked out to the porch and down the steps.

Colleen hung the two bags over the saddle horn, helped Patty into the saddle, then climbed up behind her and turned Venus back toward Burden.

———

Max had the Colt in pieces on his workbench. There were a few pieces that needed serious sanding to remove some rust spots, but at least there was no pitting of the metal. He was bent over the trigger assembly when he heard Venus return.

He wasn't going to say anything until he heard Colleen shout, "Max!", which startled him.

He dropped the hammer assembly and jogged out the back door and was stunned to see Colleen on Venus with Patty in front of her in obvious pain.

"Max, Patty's hurt. Can we bring her to your house?"

"Sure. You know where it is. I'll go and get Doctor McKenna, okay?"

"Alright. I'll put her in one of the spare bedrooms."

"Go ahead. I'll have the doc there shortly."

Colleen turned the horse back toward the east and stayed in the alley, so Joe couldn't see them.

Max trotted out of his shop, crossed the street, and then over three doors to Doctor Patrick McKenna's office. After entering, he found the doc napping at his desk, which meant he'd probably delivered a baby sometime in the wee hours of the morning.

Max stepped over to the desk, shook the doctor's shoulder, and said, "Doc! Wake up. We need you."

Doctor McKenna sputtered awake, looked at Max, and asked, "What's wrong?"

"Patty Endicott is injured. Her sister took her to my house, but I don't know what happened."

"Okay. Let's go," he replied, instantly awake as he grabbed his black bag.

Max led the doctor out of the house, then they walked quickly across the main road and down the side street to his house. Max saw Venus tied up outside the house, and they soon passed the horse as they walked through the open front gate, down the walk, and onto the porch. He opened the door and let Doctor McKenna into the house and was met by Colleen.

Colleen said to the doctor, "She's in the second bedroom on the left. Her husband hit her, she fell and then he kicked her in the chest."

"Alright. Colleen, I'll need you to stay with me while I examine her," the doctor said.

"Okay."

Max headed for the kitchen while Colleen and the doctor entered what was now Patty's bedroom, and Colleen closed the door after they entered.

Max started the cookstove fire, closed the firebox door, and filled a coffee pot with water as well as his mother's tea kettle, then put them both on the stove's hotplates. He was already running through different solutions for this new problem as he took a seat at the kitchen table. He couldn't let Patty return to the ranch, not after what Colleen had said. She could stay here, which meant that Colleen had to stay as well to take care of her. That meant he'd move back to his shop living area. He'd lived there for a couple of years, so he was used to it. He'd have to get some more food for his shop. But the wild card in all this was Joe Endicott. The law wouldn't prosecute a husband for just beating his wife, nor would they offer any protection for her. If Colleen was in the house, then maybe she should be armed.

He leaned back in the chair and put his hands behind his neck. *How did he get involved with this?* And then there was the Amanda situation. *What was that all about?* He felt like pulling his hair out and began yearning for the simpler days of prison life, which was something he never thought possible, much less just four days after walking out of those gates.

It seemed like just seconds later when the water began boiling in both containers, so he pulled them off the cooking area and put coffee in one, and poured the boiling water from the tea kettle into the teapot with its strainer full of tea He put out a few cups and checked to make sure the sugar bowl was full, then went into the cold room and poured some milk into a small pitcher. He closed the cold room and put the pitcher on the table.

This was getting so bizarre. Here he was making tea and putting milk and sugar on the table. If his cellmates could see him now, there'd be no end to it.

A few minutes later, Dr. McKenna and Colleen exited the door and walked to the smell of coffee.

"Coffee, Doc?" he asked.

"Absolutely. I'm in desperate need of the caffeine."

Max poured him a cup and asked, "Tea, Colleen?"

"You have tea? I don't suppose you have milk and sugar?"

"On the table."

He poured a cup of tea for Colleen and then a cup of black coffee for himself and took a seat.

Doctor McKenna turned to Max and said, "Max, this is an awkward situation. I've recommended to Colleen that Patty stay in bed for at least three days. Colleen will have to stay here with her. What can you do?"

Colleen looked at Max, hoping he wouldn't say he'd be living in the same house. If he did, she'd have to move Patty, and she had no idea where she could.

"I've already figured out that would have to be the case, Doc. I'll move back to my shop. I've lived there for two years, and it's still better than my accommodations for the past five years. I can leave with you."

"That's good. Let me finish my coffee."

Colleen breathed a sigh of relief knowing that she and Patty would be left alone.

Max then looked at Colleen and said, "Colleen, I want you to lock the doors after we're gone. I'll leave you the key then I'll go and bring in the two bags of dresses. That will cover your needs until this is over."

Colleen just nodded.

"Doc, I'll be right back," Max said as he stood.

Max trotted out the front door and grabbed the two bags from Venus and went back inside, brought them to the kitchen, and set them down near the table.

"There's enough food here for a while, Colleen, so I don't think you'll need anything. Do you need to tell them down at Dolly's that you won't be available for five days?"

"If you could tell them, I would appreciate it. Better make it a week."

"Alright. Doc, you ready to go?"

"Sure."

The two men left the house as they walked down the street, Max asked, "How bad was it, Doc?"

"She had a lot of old bruises, Max. He must have stayed away from her face, though. I don't know why women put up with it. I see it more often than I'd care to admit. We all knew Joe was a drunk. He's been hard drinking for at least five years, and some of that stuff would kill a horse."

"What other options do they have, Doc? They can't get a job. The law protects the husbands, so they have to stick with it, especially if there are children involved."

"I know. It doesn't make it any better."

"Nope. Not at all."

Doctor McKenna turned to head for his office then Max returned to the house and retrieved Venus. He walked her down the street and to his small corral where he stripped her of her gear and rubbed her down. When he finished, he cut through his shop and went to Schneider's to get some food for his shop. He also picked up two sheets, a new blanket, a pillow, and a pillowcase. Then after leaving the purchases in his shop's living area, he walked to the café to tell Maddie that Colleen wouldn't be available for a week. As it turned out she was glad for the chance to make more money.

He returned to his shop and spent an hour getting the room ready for habitation, then he walked outside just in time to see Joe Endicott leaving the saloon and climbing on his mule. He headed west, probably expecting dinner to be on the table.

———

At 242 Station Street in Wichita, a messenger had just delivered a telegram. Mary Jones read it and made a face. Max

Wagner was back. She'd been dreading this day and had hoped that he might be killed in prison as it was a common enough occurrence. If that hadn't happened, she had assumed the last place he'd go after his sentence was completed was Burden, but he'd done exactly that, and now she was worried that he'd be so vindictive for going to prison that he'd tell everyone what he'd found in that abandoned stagecoach office. No one could know about what had happened five years ago. It would ruin her social standing and her husband might even divorce her, and that couldn't happen. She had to act and act quickly.

She called the carriage driver. He had friends of dubious reputation and was only too happy to do favors for the lady of the house.

After he arrived, she explained to Carl, without going into details, that Max might present a problem for her, but she left it to him to figure out how to solve it. She wasn't concerned about how he would handle it, either. She simply wanted Max gone.

———

An hour later, Max had the Colt in working order. He really wanted to test the guns but knew it wasn't a good time. He was going to make some lunch but decided to head over to Sunny's instead.

He cleaned up from the gun oil, put his Stetson on his head, and strapped on his pistols. He wasn't going to stay unarmed any longer. Things were getting too tense.

He stepped into Sunny's and had barely made it past the threshold when Maddie spied his entry and hurried over.

"Good afternoon, Maddie. What's the special?" he asked.

Maddie was beside herself. Max had called her by her name.

"Roast beef and mashed potatoes. Is that okay?"

"Perfect," he replied as he smiled at her.

Maddie thought she would melt as she turned to get his coffee.

Max figured that Maddie wasn't complex, at least not that he could see, but he was beginning to believe that once he got to know her, she'd probably have some dark, hidden secret that would make Colleen's problems appear to be minor difficulties.

She brought him his coffee quickly and presented it with the expected broad smile, then left. As he took a sip he continued to think about any possible solutions to the Colleen and Patty issues but couldn't come up with anything. He didn't think it would blow over after Patty was doing better either. He suspected that Joe Endicott would be more than simply irate when he discovered Patty missing.

Maddie brought him his lunch quickly, which was the advantage of ordering the special. Max knew it was a lot better than anything he could make, then quickly finished his lunch leaving Maddie a large tip and waving to her as he left.

After leaving the diner, he headed back to Schneider's, and after entering, found Paul helping Mrs. Whitley.

Max sauntered to the gun case, looked inside, found what he wanted, and waited for Paul to finish.

Mrs. Whitley smiled at Max and he returned her smile as she left the store.

"Paul, let me have three of the Remington derringers, would you?"

"Three, Max?"

"Sure. I'm going to mess around with them. I think I can make them better."

"Oh. Now I get it," he said as he pulled three of the small pistols from the case, then asked, "Ammunition?"

"Let me have two boxes if you have them."

"I do. Anything else?"

"Nope. That should do it."

Max paid the $38.50 bill and left the store with the small, but weighty bag. He walked to his shop and sat down at his bench. He wasn't passing that big of a fib when he said he was going to disassemble them and smooth out their action. They were very simple guns, but ingenious as well.

He took the first apart and smoothed out all the factory burrs, then oiled and polished each piece before putting it back together. It was a quick job, and the trigger and hammer mechanisms were much smoother. He repeated it with the other two derringers, and when all three were done, he loaded one and slipped it into his pants pocket.

He loaded the other two and dropped four spare cartridges into his vest pocket, left the back of the shop, and headed for the house using the back alley rather than the road.

After he arrived, he walked to the back door and tapped loudly on the adjacent window.

Colleen's head appeared in the window, then a few seconds later, she unlocked the door.

"Max, what's the matter?" she asked.

"Nothing. I just felt a little nervous letting you two stay here by yourselves without protection, so I picked these up."

He handed her the two derringers and asked, "Do you know how to use them?"

"No."

"It's really simple. Just pull back the hammer, point it, and pull the trigger. If you need a second shot, do the same thing again. Alright?"

"Okay."

He handed her the pistols, then said, "I talked to Maddie and she was happy about the extra money, and about an hour ago, I watched Joe Endicott leave the saloon and ride home. I'll keep an eye out if he comes riding back."

Without another word, Max turned on his heels and headed back. He was in no mood for any more protests or admonishments and could already see some discomfort in her eyes, probably because she thought he might enter his own house.

He would do what was necessary to keep them safe, but after things had settled down, he began to seriously consider selling the house and the shop and just leaving town.

Colleen was relieved that he hadn't tried to come inside and locked the door after he had gone.

———

In Wichita, the carriage driver, Carl Arnold, was talking to an old acquaintance, 'Stud' Smith. The man was only three inches above five feet in height and weighed all of a hundred and twenty-five pounds, but he wore the moniker proudly, not realizing that he was given the nickname as a joke by friends who had seen him naked. What he lacked in physical size, he made up for in sheer meanness.

"So, what do I need to do?" Stud asked.

"Simple. You head down to Burden and just pop this guy. The faster the better. He just got outta prison, so they'll suspect some ex-con he pissed off inside caught up with him. He should be living in a house just off the main street. Here's where it is, according to someone who knows these things," he said as he drew a crude map on a sheet of paper on the table.

"How much?"

"One hundred now and another two hundred when the job is done. We'll pay for the train ticket, too."

"Alright, but I've got to take my horse with me. That way, I can sneak outta there and ride back. It's only fifty miles or so, so I'll get to do the job just at dusk. It'll give me enough light to take the shot and then make my getaway."

"Smart thinking."

Carl handed him the hundred dollars and another thirty for the ticket before he left Stud's apartment and returned to the big house. The mistress needed the carriage tonight. She and that sissy husband of hers were going to some gala or whatever and the thought made him snicker.

———

MAX

Max was back in his shop, and after cleaning the workbench from the derringer modifications, he checked his watch. It was only 3:40, so he picked up the Winchester '76, a box of .44 cartridges for his pistols, and walked out behind his shop.

After he walked for more than a half mile, he found his old shooting range where he set up a target and stepped back to his pistol shooting distance, sixty feet. He set down the Winchester, then released his hammer loops from his Russians, and took his first shot with the right-hand pistol. He felt a little slower than he had been before his stint in the prison, but not too bad. It was the same with the left. The accuracy hadn't suffered, though. He reloaded and tried with both Russians and felt better. It was really close to where he'd been before his incarceration, which really surprised him. He expected to have seen a serious deterioration in his level of skills but had no explanation for why he hadn't. A few more days of serious practice and he'd be at least as good as before, and he knew he was better than most.

He reloaded the pistols and holstered them. After slipping the hammer loops in place, he picked up the new Winchester. This ought to be fun. He walked out to his one-hundred-yard marker. His target was a small log that had already borne the brunt of twenty .44 caliber rounds from his '66, and now it was time to use the more powerful Winchester '76.

He was curious if the power of the new cartridge was noticeable as he levered in a fresh round and caught the ejected round in his hand, putting it in his pocket. He aimed, fired, and saw the log jump, which was very impressive. He rapidly fired six more rounds, almost cutting the log in half and leaving an enormous cloud of gunsmoke, which is why he had to stop after six shots. He was pleased with the new rifle, as he waited for the smoke to clear and decided he may as well empty it. When he could see the target clearly, he fired nine more rounds in succession, leaving the log in chunks on the ground. As he waited for the barrel to cool, he picked up all of his spent brass and dropped them into his pockets, then turned and walked back to his shop to clean the weapons, satisfied with his and his new weapons' performance.

———

Colleen had checked in on Patty and found that she was doing much better already. Then Colleen sat with Patty and they just chatted about things that didn't involve men, but only peripherally as they talked about Max's house, Max's dropping off the clothing, and even Max's tea.

It was a small thing, tea, but it showed thoughtfulness that neither woman had experienced in their lives. They knew that Max didn't drink tea, so the only ones who would drink the beverage were Patty and Colleen. Patty correctly suspected that it was bought for Colleen's consumption but didn't mention it. She was still very sensitive when it came to men, probably excessively so, but she was the only one who understood why.

Colleen was preparing dinner for her and Patty when the whistle sounded from the evening train from the east, but it meant nothing to either of them.

———

Max had just finished cleaning his guns and was wondering what to make for dinner. He was debating about whether to have breakfast or to forego cooking his dinner entirely and head to Sunny's.

The train pulled into the station at 5:25. It was a little early, and Stud Smith was the first one off the train. He walked to the corral and watched them unload his mare. The map he had in his pocket was poorly drawn but seemed to be accurate. He could see where he wanted to go from here and was already mapping out his escape route when he took his horse and started to walk across the street.

Max had decided to take the lazy route and let someone else cook. He walked out into the street and saw the small stranger leading his horse across the street. It was an odd thing to do and piqued his curiosity. *He wasn't heading to the livery, so why was he leading his horse in that direction? Why is he leading his horse at all?*

He turned from his first path heading to the diner to a new one heading for the other end of town and his house. He picked up the pace, his long legs eating up the distance.

Stud Smith glanced down the road and saw Max rapidly approaching and wondered if he was the target. Carl said he was tall but hadn't said anything about the bulk. He stopped and watched Max get closer, suspecting that he might be the law.

Max noticed that he had stopped and was watching him, so he slowed down slightly and removed the hammer loops from both Smith & Wessons.

Stud noticed the move and did the same. He was carrying a single Colt but prided himself on his ability to use it and smiled as Max drew closer.

There was no one else in the street as the two men more or less faced off at sixty feet.

"You Max Wagner?" Stud asked.

"Who's asking?"

"Name's Stud Smith."

Despite the situation, Max laughed lightly and said, "You've got to be joking. Really?"

Stud wasn't pleased with the response and snarled, "Well are you or ain't you?"

"Why do you care?" Max asked more soberly.

"Somebody in Wichita doesn't like you, Wagner."

Max was surprised by the answer and asked, "Who the hell knows me in Wichita?"

Stud didn't verbally respond, his question about Max's identity answered, but instead, dropped his right hand to his Colt, slapped his small hand around the grip, and pulled it from its holster, cocking the hammer as he brought it level.

Max saw his hand go to his gun and without a conscious thought reached for both Smith & Wessons as he watched the small man's sights align on his chest. He was a fraction of a second behind as Smith fired but squeezed both triggers in that fraction of a second later. In the calm night, the sounds of three .44 caliber pistols exploding at the same time echoed like thunder through the streets of Burden while in the waning light, the flames from the pistols erupted almost two feet from their muzzles.

Stud's shot hit Max in the back of his left armpit, catching only the fleshy part of the muscle. Both of Max's shots took Stud in the chest, about six inches apart. The bullets crashed through ribs and lungs and one clipped the top of his heart. His eyes were still working and reported to his brain that the dusty ground of Burden, Kansas was rushing to meet them. He bounced off the ground but didn't move as that dust billowed around him.

Incredibly, it was Max's choice to use both guns that saved him from a more serious injury. If he had only used his right gun, Stud's bullet would have caught the left side of his chest. But as he had raised the left pistol straight, it elevated and rotated him slightly to the right, so the left-hand pistol could point at the target, making Stud Smith's lone shot hit him more to the left.

The noise awakened the town and heads began appearing from doors and windows. Marshal Emil Becker had just sat down to his dinner in his home when the clear sound of gunfire shattered his quiet night. He raced from his house and ran toward the train depot where the sound had originated and soon saw Max Wagner bending over a small human form on the ground. Stud's horse hadn't wandered.

In Max's house, Colleen heard the gunfire and wondered if it had something to do with Joe Endicott, so she pulled the derringer from her purse and walked into Patty's room, and waited.

Marshal Becker reached Max and asked, "Max, what happened?"

"You know, Marshal, I almost have no idea. I saw this little guy come from the station leading his horse across the street. It just looked odd to me. Where was he going leading his horse? So, I thought I'd check it out. I walked down the street and he stopped and looked at me. We both released our hammer loops and I kept walking. Then he yells out and asks me if I'm Max Wagner, so I asked him who he was, and he said he was Stud Smith."

"That's Stud Smith? Are you sure he said that?"

"Positive. Then he said that someone in Wichita didn't like me very much and pulled his pistol. I pulled both of mine, but I was slower than he was. His shot just caught me below the left armpit. I got him with both of mine. What I don't get is why would someone from Wichita want me dead?"

"You got me. But if that's Stud Smith, you got a hefty reward coming. He is one nasty son of a bitch. Usually, he works from behind, though. You're finding him out in the open was a real stroke of luck, Max."

"If you consider this good luck," he said as he looked at the blood still oozing into his shirt, "I suppose I need to go and see the doc for this thing."

"I'd think so. I'll go through his things. You're entitled to all his gear, too. If he has any cash on him, we'll pay for this burial and you can have what's left if there is any."

"Thanks, Emil. I'll go and see Doc McKenna."

Max stood and walked across the street and entered the doctor's office. He lived upstairs, so all he had to do was make a modicum of noise before the good doctor made an appearance.

"Back again so soon, Max? Were you the cause of all that ruckus in the street?" he asked as he took a quick look at the wound.

"Not the cause, Doc, but I did finish it. Strange thing, too. The man was sent to kill me by somebody in Wichita and I don't even know anybody in Wichita."

"Well, let it be a mystery for a while. Come on back and I'll clean you up and sew that closed."

Max walked to the examining room and took a seat on the table while Doc McKenna cut away his new shirt and began cleaning. It only took a half hour to suture the wound closed.

"What do I owe you, Doc? I think I have two bills due. You didn't collect for Patty Endicott."

"Don't worry about it. You're entertainment value."

"Nonsense, Doc. The last time I knew, you didn't receive any papal dispensation from eating," he said, then tossed a ten-dollar gold piece to the doctor, who snatched it out of the air like the athlete he had been in college.

"Papal dispensation, Max? I didn't know you were Catholic."

"I'm not. The papal dispensation was used as a joke in prison. Probably from some Irish sinner."

"There were probably a lot more of you heathen Germans in there than sons of Ireland."

"I'll grant you that," he said as he laughed, "Thanks, Doc. I'll try to avoid creating any more entertainment in the future."

He left the doctor's office and headed down the street to Marshal Becker's office.

The marshal was at his desk, looking through wanted posters as he walked through the door.

He looked up and said excitedly, "Max, come over here! Look at this!"

Max walked to the other side of the desk and glanced over the shoulder of the marshal.

"I've never seen one this high before. No wonder, either. Look what that little bastard is wanted for."

Max looked and was amazed by what he read, four counts of murder, six assaults, three robberies, and an arson.

"Arson?" Max asked.

"I guess he wanted to diversify. Look at the reward. Twelve hundred dollars! I've never seen one bigger than five hundred before. I don't know how I missed this poster. Must've come in with a stack of 'em. He also had over a hundred and forty dollars in his pocket, so I think someone paid him to assassinate you. You'll get over a hundred dollars after we pay for his burial, and his horse and tack look pretty good."

"Say, Emil, do you have any idea why anyone would want me dead? I mean, I paid my penalty and I've been out of circulation for five years."

"I haven't got a clue."

"Well, I'm going to head back to my shop and get rid of this shirt. It's even too far gone to go into the rag pile, which really makes me mad because it was a new shirt, too."

"Come back in the morning. I'll send out a telegram to the ones offering the reward and certify his death."

"I appreciate it, Emil."

Max left the marshal's office and was suddenly tired. It must be because of the narrow brush with death. He was only too aware of how close that bullet was to killing him, maybe an inch to his right and it would have ripped the left side of his chest to pieces. At least Stud would have gone with him.

He reached his shop and closed the door behind him, then carefully took off the shirt and tossed it into the rag pile anyway. He walked back to his bunk, sat down, pulled off his boots, tossed his hat onto the table, and pulled off his pistols. He'd clean them in the morning.

MAX

Max laid there thinking how odd it was that he felt so guilty for what was really an accidental killing of Walt Emerson, yet he felt no guilt whatsoever for intentionally killing Stud Smith.

———

Colleen had decided that whatever the gunfire was, it didn't involve her, so she changed into one of the nightdresses and went to sleep in the big bed.

———

Johann had heard the gunfire and assumed that Max was dead. He smiled as he curled up with his back facing Amanda, who had heard the gunfire as well and was, as most people were, totally mystified.

———

Joe Endicott heard nothing. Aside from the distance, he had passed out on the living room floor, not even noticing the absence of his wife.

———

Max slept on his right side but still managed to get a decent night's sleep, despite waking twice when he rolled onto the freshly sutured wound.

CHAPTER 6

Max woke the next morning to the sound of his stomach grumbling and his side aching. He started to stretch and quickly squelched the idea. Instead, he rolled out of bed and walked to the back of the shop but didn't bother walking to the privy. He just made sure he was far enough away from his back door.

He washed as best he could before he put on another new shirt, which left him with just one spare, and needed to do a wash soon, too. He put on his Stetson and his gunbelt, deciding to clean the pistols after breakfast, then pulled on his boots, left the shop, walked to Sunny's, and headed for an empty table.

Maddie almost sprinted to his location before his bottom contacted wood.

"Are you all right, Max? I heard you were in that gunfight last night."

"I'm fine, Maddie."

"Where did you get hit? I heard you were shot, and I almost cried myself to sleep."

"He hit me right in the back fold of my left armpit. The doc sewed me up and I'll be as good as new in a week or so," he replied as he smiled at her, touched to see the genuine concern in her eyes.

"That's good. I heard that he was a murderer, too."

"He was, so it was good riddance. The world doesn't need trash like that."

"No, we don't. I'm glad you're all right, Max."

He grinned at her and said, "Me, too, Maddie."

She smiled and asked, "Bacon, four eggs over easy, biscuits and coffee?"

"That'll work, Maddie."

She smiled once more and zipped off to the kitchen as Max watched her leave.

Maddie may still be a teenager in her age and behavior, but she sure was a woman in other things. But even as he watched her, he knew he would only ever admire Maddie. She'd never survive even a casual relationship, and he knew that wouldn't work because he would never hurt anyone as sweet as Maddie.

She brought his breakfast just three minutes later.

———

At the other end of town, Colleen was fixing breakfast for her and Patty. Patty was doing a lot better this morning and had even offered to help, which her sister declined. Colleen was still in awe of the kitchen and the amount of food that she could choose from, so she made a big breakfast for each of them.

"What was that shooting last night, Colleen?" Patty asked as she ate.

"I don't know. It doesn't involve us, so we probably won't find out for a few days."

"Still, I am curious."

"Me, too."

———

Amanda left the house with one dollar in her skirt pocket, needing to buy some flour, salt, and coffee. When she reached Schneider's, she saw a crowd around the counter and surmised that they were talking about the shooting last night. So, she headed down the aisle and picked up the flour, a poke of salt, and two pounds of coffee.

When she approached the counter, she heard one of the men finishing up his sentence, saying, "…Max sure was lucky. That Stud Smith done murdered four people that they know about."

That got her attention, then she listened as another man talked about how close Max was to cashing in his chips, but his shooting was incredibly accurate with both shots just six inches apart. Another mentioned the huge reward coming his way.

Amanda was shaken by all of the revelations, but finally made it to the front and paid for her purchase, leaving her with thirty-seven cents in change.

She left the store and hurried back to the house to tell Johann what she heard. Maybe he'd be in a better mood today.

———

Joe Endicott finally crawled along the floor to a chair and pulled himself into a sitting position. His head hurt, he felt lousy and was also turning a light shade of yellowish-brown.

"Must be the sun," he thought.

"Patty? Where are you, woman?" he shouted but heard no reply.

MAX

He was getting angry, needed something to calm his stomach and that bitch wasn't anywhere to be found. He stood and let his head and stomach settle before he stomped around the house looking for his wife but didn't find her anywhere.

The first thing he thought was that she had run off with Max, and his anger exploded. But after the initial surge of hostility, he stopped and gave it some thought, befuddled as his mind may have been. He then realized that he was free of her, so maybe it wasn't so bad after all. Let the big galoot put up with her.

Joe suddenly believed that he was single again, so he went to the kitchen sink, pumped some water, splashed some on his face and head, and felt better. He walked over to the kitchen shelf and took the last three silver dollars out of the household cash in the jar. He could buy two bottles with three dollars, and that was a lot better than buying them by the glass at the saloon. He'd buy the bottles and then come home and drink as much as he wanted with no nagging wife to tell him to stop.

It was a cheerful Joe Endicott who went outside and saddled his mule. He was feeling darned good about the world right now and would feel a lot better when he got those bottles.

"You're all right, Max," Joe said aloud, then giggled as he mounted before adding, "You're a good feller for takin' that nag off of my hands."

———

That good Max feller was leaving the marshal's office. After paying for the burial, Max was handed an envelope with $117.50 in it, and Stud's gunbelt with the Colt that had failed him when he needed it the most. The horse was tied to the hitchrail in front of the jail.

Max checked the horse and was pleased with his newest equine acquisition. She was a nice mare, chocolate brown with four white stockings and a star. She wasn't that tall which would make sense considering her owner and seemed pleasant. The rig looked good as well.

He led the horse back to his corral and introduced her to Venus and Mars, wondering what he'd call her. She didn't look fast enough for Mercury, besides Mercury was a guy. He went through the planets and the best one he could use was Saturn, but she didn't look that big. So, he skipped planets and settled on Luna, which seemed to fit her perfectly.

He carefully unsaddled Luna to avoid another visit to the doctor to repair his stitches and put her gear into the barn. After brushing her down, she looked almost as pretty as Venus. She was shorter but had a way about her. He felt bad that she had to put up with such a despicable rider.

He let the horses become familiar with each other and have some water and oats as he returned to his shop to examine Stud's Colt.

———

Amanda was excitedly telling Johann about what she had heard at the store, and even as she spoke, was stunned by his reaction. He was angry, and the more she said, the angrier he got. She finally stopped before saying how big the reward was, believing it would push him over the edge.

After she'd stopped talking, he said, "I've got to send a telegram. How much money do you have?"

She reached into her purse and pulled out the thirty-seven cents and handed it to him.

"Is this all? Where did you spend all the money?"

"I spent sixty-three cents on flour, salt, and coffee. You said you wanted coffee."

He grabbed her tightly by the arm and shouted, "You, stupid cow! How the hell am I going to send a telegram when all we have is thirty-seven cents?"

Amanda was beside herself. Johann was hurting her, and she didn't know what she had done. What was even worse, he had called her a stupid cow.

Then, without realizing it, she chose to say the worst possible thing she could have when she said, "I can get some more money, Johann. I can ask Max if I can clean for a day and he'd pay me enough to let you send your telegram."

Johann's grip tightened as he snarled, "So, that's it, is it? You wanna go see your precious Max. What, so you can spread your legs for him, just like every other damned woman in this town wants to do? That son of a bitch is supposed to be dead, and here you are wanting to go and beg him for some money. You have to be the stupidest woman God ever put on the earth. I'll go and get some money. You get your ass out of my sight!"

With that, Johann grabbed Amanda by the back of her collar with his left hand and threw her across the room. She hit the floor hard and rolled into a chair knocking it back three feet, shocked that he would do such a thing.

He stomped out of the house, slamming the door behind him, as Amanda lay hurt on the floor. She hurt more in her heart than her body. Amanda had suddenly come to see Johann for what he had been for years, but she had been too blind to see. Everything finally coalesced in her mind: Alice Roth, the laziness, and now calling her names and throwing her to the floor.

Suddenly, she despised the man she had been married to for six years now. *How could she have failed to see all of it for so long?* She realized that if she had just stepped away, she could have seen him for who he really was, but she still saw him as the cute boy from school…until now.

————

Max had Stud's Colt disassembled after having just cleaned his Model 3 Smith & Wessons and returning them fully loaded to his holsters. He had even taken to wearing the guns while working unless the job required him to take them off.

He was sanding and polishing the pieces before oiling them and wasn't paying any attention to what was going on outside.

————

Johann was stalking down the street as he headed for the saloon. He had friends there, and he only needed a dollar, for God's sake. After passing through the batwing doors, he scanned the place and spotted four men he knew chatting and laughing at the bar. He walked up to them and put on his good ol' boy face.

"Howdy, boys. What's goin' on?" he asked loudly.

One turned and replied, "Oh, howdy, Johann. We're all talking about that shootin' last night. You shoulda seen those two holes in Stud Smith! Looked like giant nipples!"

They all rolled in guffaws and howls as one slapped the bar. Johann tried to laugh, but the subject matter was beyond his ability to find humorous.

He then asked, "Say, I just found out that the wife took the last of the household cash. Any of you fellers got a buck? I need to send a telegram."

Another of them replied, "Maybe you outta go and see Max. He's loaded now. Gonna get a twelve-hundred-dollar reward for shootin' that Stud Smith. I don't know why, either. That was the least studly Stud I've ever seen!"

They all broke out in howls of laughter again, slapping each other on the backs.

Johann was getting more anxious as he asked, "How about fifty cents? Come on, boys. Somebody's gotta help me out."

The first jokester then answered, "Go and ask Stud Smith. He must be a charitable sort. He sure looks holy to me!"

Johann seethed as they erupted in a new round of raucous laughter, then turned on his heels and stormed from the bar.

Once outside, he stopped on the boardwalk, then looked down the street, and his anger grew when he saw the open doors of Max's shop. He didn't have a gun, but maybe he didn't need one. Maybe the idiot would give him the money to send the telegram to let Mary know that he wasn't dead...yet.

He snickered, and with his eyes focused on Max's shop, stepped down into the street, and was almost run over by a mule. *A mule?*

"Hey! Watch where you're going!" Joe yelled at Johann who just turned and glared at him.

Johann stared at Joe and screamed, "Me? Why don't you watch where you're riding that damned animal, you, stupid son of a bitch?"

Joe glared back and shouted, "Listen, you lily-livered bastard, I ain't puttin' up with your smart mouth! Come over here and let's see what you got!"

Joe Endicott then slipped down from his mule and immediately took a wild swing at Johann and missed badly. While Joe was off-balance, Johann slammed his fist hard into Joe's belly, dropping him to the ground. When Joe crashed to the dirt, one of his precious silver dollars rolled from his pocket stopping just inches from Johann's right boot.

Johann didn't waste any time. It was too providential to pass up, so he snatched the coin as Johann writhed in pain before Johann trotted up the street toward the Western Union office.

Mrs. Kirkpatrick was sweeping her portion of the boardwalk and had watched the entire incident, and as Johann jogged back up the street clutching his money, she dropped her broom, stepped down, and walked quickly over to the still moaning Joe Endicott.

"Are you all right, Joe?" she asked as she bent over him.

She could smell the booze that permeated his system, even as he appeared sober, and it was strong enough to make her eyes water.

Joe finally groaned and rasped, "Get the doctor. I ain't feelin' so good."

She turned and fast-walked down the street to see Doctor McKenna.

———

MAX

Max was finishing the assembly of the Colt, totally unaware of the drama that has just played out just yards from him, and even less aware of its consequences.

Five minutes later, Doctor McKenna trotted down the dusty street with his black bag, followed by Mrs. Kirkpatrick, and soon reached the still moaning Joe Endicott.

"Where does it hurt, Joe?" he asked, taking a knee and trying to keep his stomach from rioting with the smell.

"In my gut, Doc. You gotta help me," Joe replied weakly.

"What happened?"

"Got into an argument with Johann Peters and he hit me in the belly. It hurts real bad, Doc."

"Can you stand up?"

"No. It hurts too bad."

"Hold on."

The doctor trotted over to Max's workshop before he reached the open doors and shouted, "Max! You in there? I need your help!"

Max was just testing the Colt, so he put it down quickly, stood, walked out of his shop, and saw Doctor McKenna heading his way.

"What's up, Doc?" he asked.

"I need you to carry someone to my office. He can't walk."

"Right behind you," Max said as the doctor turned and headed back for Joe and Max finally spotted who the patient was.

When Max saw Joe Endicott squirming on the ground, he had a real dilemma. Of all people to have to carry, Joe Endicott was right there at the bottom of the list. He knew why the doc had to treat him, but he sure wasn't bound by any oath, Hippocratic or otherwise. Maybe he could accidentally drop him on his head on the way to the doc's office.

He walked up to Joe and bent at the knees, slipped his arms under Joe, and lifted his two-hundred-plus pounds to his chest. The doctor started walking back, and Max carried the reeking patient as quickly as he could, taking big gulps of air through his mouth periodically to avoid breathing through his nose.

It seemed like forever as he carried Joe Endicott to Doctor McKenna's office, and began mentally counting the steps to throw his mind off the horrible odors. He reached the office, carried him inside, and laid Joe on the examining table.

"Want me to open the windows, Doc?" Max asked with watery eyes.

"If you would, I'd appreciate it."

Max opened both windows as wide as he could as Doctor McKenna began examining his patient.

The doctor finished his preliminary exam quickly and waved Max over as he left the examination room.

"Max, he was suffering from cirrhosis of the liver for a while. See how jaundiced his skin is? Johann's punch seems to have pretty much damaged the liver beyond repair. He'll die within a few days and there's nothing I can do about it. I'm going to be here with him for a while. Can you tell his wife?"

"Sure, Doc. I'll take care of it. Was it Johann Peters that hit him?"

"It was. Thanks for doing this, Max, and I'm really grateful for carrying him to my office. I couldn't think of any other way and be sure to check your stitches when you get a chance."

"I'll do that," Max said before adding, "You're a good man, Doc. I'll head over to my house and tell Patty."

As he was leaving, Marshal Becker intercepted him.

"Max, what happened?"

"Doc told me that Joe Endicott was hit by Johann Peters. Joe had a liver disease and the punch pretty much finished him off and he'll die in a few days."

"Where did Peters go?"

"I have no idea. I was in my shop when the doc called me outside to carry him to his office."

"Okay. I'm going to his house and find out what's going on."

"You need any help, Emil?"

"Not yet. But check with me later."

"I will."

The two men left the doctor's office going in different directions. The marshal went east towards the end of town where Johann Peters' house was, and Max went north toward his house.

Max didn't know how Patty would react. Joe had just beaten her and left her damned near penniless, but you never knew.

He arrived at the house and knocked on the front door. He had to look through the window to make eye contact with Colleen before she opened the door and stood there.

"What do you need, Max?"

"I need to talk to Patty."

"About what?"

"Colleen, I don't have time now. Please. You can follow along, but I need to talk to Patty."

"I'm sorry. Come in."

Max walked inside, then quickly stepped through the parlor and walked to the bedroom where he found Patty sitting up in bed. She smiled at him as he entered, then saw his somber face.

Colleen sat down in a chair as Max sat down on the edge of the bed.

"Patty, I just had to carry Joe to Doc McKenna's office."

She interrupted him, asking, "What happened? Did you shoot him?"

Max was getting irritated as he replied, "No, Patty. I didn't shoot him. Johann Peters and Joe got into some kind of fight outside the saloon. Johann punched Joe in the stomach, and I carried him down to the doc's office. The doc told me to tell you that he had an advanced liver disease and that the punch damaged the liver so badly that Joe wasn't going to make it. He said he'd only last a few days."

"Joe's going to die?"

"That's what the doc said."

Max awaited the reaction as he watched her face.

Patty was in serious emotional and moral conflict. Deep down, she was elated. There would be no more beatings, no more having to scrimp and save to buy flour. But she felt guilty for feeling that way. She was married to Joe and she should feel some sorrow for his situation.

"I'm a horrible person," she finally said, "I should be upset about what happened, but I'm not. I'm relieved. I feel free, just like when Walt died. But what am I going to do?"

Max replied, "First, don't feel guilty one second. Joe wasn't acting like a man. He didn't take care of you like he should have. He did just the opposite. That's not a real man in my book. So, feel better and get well. Don't worry about Joe. He's not going to bother you. You and Colleen stay in the house as long as you want. Okay?"

"But where will you live?"

"I'll stay in the shop," he replied, then stood, turned, and left the room.

He walked down the hallway just as quickly as he'd entered, crossed the parlor, and closed the door behind him without saying another word. He had just faced off a killer yesterday but wasn't about to face Colleen's questioning today.

155

He decided to head toward the Peters house and see what the marshal found. He had taken two steps when out of his unconscious mind flew a line uttered by Colleen just a few days earlier.

"Mary Preston married Charles Jones from Wichita. She lives there now."

Why would Mary Preston want him dead? Surely it can't be because he knew she was trying to get it on with Walt Emerson. That was five years ago, and Walt was dead.

Colleen had mentioned that she moved in high social circles now because her husband worked in a bank. Charles Jones works in a bank in Wichita, Colleen had said. If she's so wrapped up in her own importance, then maybe she really is that frightened of his being around to spread the rumors.

Now, he was torn. *Did he just confront her and tell her to back off and that her secret was safe, or did he try and get her arrested?* Proving that she had something to do with the assassination attempt would be difficult. Maybe he could just take her down a peg or two. Maybe he should just leave town altogether as he thought of doing earlier. He had the money, and with the reward, it would be over ten thousand dollars. The question was where could he go? Maybe he should contact Mr. Trask in Lansing after all.

In all his mental wandering, he almost walked past the Peters residence, but caught himself in time, turned down the walkway, and saw the marshal inside talking to Amanda through the open door.

He knocked on the door jamb and the marshal waved him in.

"Come on in, Max. This may concern you."

"Is it about Wichita?" he asked.

"I'm not sure. Amanda, tell Max what you told me."

Amanda looked up at Max with red eyes, and Max felt an enormous amount of pity for her. *Where was the sweet, innocent, yet lively Amanda from just a few years ago?*

"I was telling Johann about the gunfight last night and when he found out you were still alive, he got really mad. He said he needed to send a telegram, but I only had thirty-seven cents change after buying some flour, salt, and coffee. He got even angrier and started calling me a cow and even threw me to the floor. He said that you should be dead, and he'd go and get money to send another telegram."

"Amanda, do you feel safe here?" Max asked.

"No. I'm afraid he'll come back and hurt me now."

"Emil, I think if you check, you'll find that the telegram was sent to Wichita to let them know that their assassination attempt failed. I bet that I even know who is behind it, too."

"Who do you think?"

"Mary Preston. She married some rich banker named Charles Jones and she lives in Wichita now."

"Why would she risk all that to have you killed?"

"Because I jeopardize her position by being alive. Now that this is out, I don't feel obligated to keep a promise I made to her five years ago," he said and then told Emil the unabridged story of that afternoon.

He finished the story by saying, "She wanted Walt to have her, Emil. Now, if she's so high in society that this story could ruin her standing, it may be important enough for her to have me killed."

"Jesus, Max! Now you really make yourself out to be an idiot. Why the hell didn't you tell me in the first place?"

"Because I had promised her I wouldn't, and I still killed Walt and the circumstances didn't matter. I deserved to go to prison, Emil."

There was no answer possible as Amanda just stared at Max.

He turned to Amanda again and said, "Amanda, get your things. You're coming with me."

"Where?"

"To someplace safe. I'll take you to my house."

"Alright. I don't have much anyway," before she left to retrieve her clothes.

"Emil, I'm going to drop her off at my house. She can stay with Colleen and Patty, and it'll give each of them some flexibility to leave the house if they need to. If I'm gone, keep an eye on them for me, will you?"

"Where are you going?"

"Wichita."

"I guessed as much. What are you going to do?

"I have no idea yet."

The marshal nodded and said, "I've got to find out where Johann went off to. He can't be far."

Amanda came out of the back rooms carrying a canvas bag with a surprisingly small amount of clothing, then said, "I'm ready."

"Okay, Amanda come along."

He waved to the marshal, then Max and Amanda walked out the front door, turned onto the street, and began stepping toward his house as Max scanned the surroundings for signs of Johann but didn't see any signs of him. There weren't a lot of hiding spots in this section of town. Like the marshal, he wondered where he had gone.

As he walked with Amanda, he asked, "Amanda, do you have everything you need?"

"I don't have some things."

"When you get to the house, I'll wait for you in the main room. Check and see if there's anything you still need after looking around. If you do, come and see me and we'll head down to see Paul and you can buy whatever you need. I'll pay for it, so you don't have to worry."

Unlike Colleen, Amanda didn't argue, but simply said, "Thank you, Max."

"Someone needs to look after you, Amanda. You were always such a good person. You deserve better treatment."

"I'm glad someone noticed."

They arrived at the house and Max had to knock on the door again and wait to let Colleen see his face before she opened the door.

"Colleen, Amanda is going to be staying with you. Johann is a threat to her now. I'm going to hang around for a little bit until she can find what she needs. If you want to take the time to go to your room at Mrs. Kirkpatrick's and bring the remaining clothing back, this would be a good time. I'll probably be making a trip to Schneider's to pick up some things for Amanda, so if there's anything you need, let me know. Okay?"

Colleen thought for a few seconds before saying, "I'll go and get those bags. I'll be right back."

"Don't forget to say hello to Venus. Oh, and introduce yourself to Luna, too."

"Luna?"

"You'll see."

Colleen looked confused as she left the house but still hurried down the street.

Max then entered the house with Amanda and said, "Amanda, you'll probably be in the last bedroom on the left, just before the kitchen. Unless you want to use one of the bedrooms on the second floor."

"No, this one will be fine," she replied as she headed down the hallway, still a bit numb from the sudden change in her life.

Max sat on a chair in the parlor, facing the door to keep the two injured women safe. He heard Amanda unpacking if it reached that level of dignity. She had just dumped the bag's contents onto the bed, and then began searching, until she figured out what she still needed, then walked back out to the parlor.

"Whenever you're ready, Max."

"We're just waiting on Colleen. Let me take a second to go and ask Patty something."

He trotted back to Patty's room, stuck his head in the door, and asked, "Patty, do you need anything from Schneider's?"

"No. I have everything I need, Max."

"Do you have riding clothes?"

"No. Do I need them?"

"Eventually," he replied before he returned to the parlor.

"Amanda, I'll ask you the same question I just asked Patty. Do you have any riding clothes?"

"No. I haven't needed any. Why?"

"I'll show you on the way to Schneider's, or maybe you can find out when Colleen comes back. But you can buy yourself a set and pick out some for Patty as well."

"Alright, if you think it's necessary."

"It is."

Colleen returned carrying the two bags and the travel bag with a smile on her face before she said, "So, that's Luna."

"That's Luna. I couldn't find another planet to match her personality, but Luna worked."

"It does. She's beautiful. Did you buy her, too?"

"No, she was a gift from the man who shot me."

She and Amanda both looked shocked as Amanda exclaimed, "I didn't know you'd been shot!"

"It wasn't much. Just took a chunk out of the back of my left armpit. Doc sewed it up in just a few minutes. You ready to go, Amanda?"

She smiled at Max, then replied, "Ready."

"We'll be back in a few minutes. At least now, Patty doesn't have to worry. Joe isn't going anywhere."

"I hadn't thought of that. That's the reason we're here."

"No, you're here to get Patty better. That includes financially as well. We'll be back in a bit."

Max offered Amanda his arm, which she took gladly, and they left the house. Colleen watched as they stepped down from the porch and told herself that she wasn't jealous, not at all.

"So, Amanda what do you need?" Max asked as they walked along.

"Some toiletry items. I don't have my toothbrush."

"You know. I just thought of something. I don't have anything in the house for ladies to use. You know, hairbrushes and things like that. You three may be there for a while, so why don't you find anything that might be useful to women that big lummoxes like me wouldn't have around the house. Okay?"

"Alright. Are you going to show me the mysterious Luna?"

"I'll show you Luna and Mars and Venus. How is that?"

"That sounds even more mysterious," she said as she clutched his arm and felt amazingly content and safe.

He steered Amanda behind his shop and she soon spotted the three horses in the corral.

Amanda finally released his arm and exclaimed, "Max! They're beautiful! Let me guess which one is which. The big gelding is Mars. I'm guessing he's your primary ride. The tall mare is Venus and the small one is Luna. How'd I do?"

"Perfectly. Now you know why you need riding clothes. If you have riding clothes, any of you can come down here and ride a horse any time you want and can go anywhere."

"What if all three of us want to ride?"

"Then you all ride. I don't know how much longer I'm going to be here."

"I heard you say you were going to Wichita."

Before he could answer, Max heard a thumping noise from his shop, followed by what sounded like a Winchester being cycled. *Damn!* He had left the shop unlocked and there were two loaded Winchesters in there. He looked at Amanda, put his finger to his lips and she nodded. He pulled his right-hand pistol and he gently pushed Amanda to the right. She stepped aside with fear in her eyes, as Max cocked his hammer.

Johann had heard the voices from behind the shop. It sounded like his cow of a wife and a man's voice, probably Max Wagner. He pushed himself further into the corner as he swung the cocked Winchester's muzzle to the door leading to the living area.

Max pulled open the back door slowly, grateful that he had oiled it just yesterday.

He let his eyes adjust to the loss of light, then took a step into his living area, then another step, and finally a third. He was well inside the living area of his shop when he stopped and listened. He could hear some faint rustling to his left, just inside the shop. He suspected that Johann was sitting there with his Winchester cocked, and must be sitting deep in the corner. He was hoping that Johann didn't take the new Winchester, not wanting to have the rifle sullied by his use.

Now, he was in a quandary. If Johann had just gotten into a fight with Joe Endicott, it wasn't even involuntary manslaughter, the same crime he'd done five years in prison for committing. Then, he really wanted Johann to tell him what he knew about Mary Preston, so killing him should be avoided, if possible, although he knew it was unlikely if he had to fire.

He had to take a chance that Johann would give up, so he said in a normal voice, "Johann, drop the rifle. So far, you haven't done anything that can even get you arrested. Come on out of there and we can talk. I need to know about Mary Preston."

Johann listened to what he had said, and it made sense because he'd just gotten into a fight and everyone knew that Max shouldn't have gone to prison for killing Walt Emerson. Joe Endicott was still alive, too.

But then, Max had mentioned Mary Preston and he knew he couldn't give up. They'd find out that he had been the reason for Stud Smith's arrival in Burden and then, they'd hang him. So, Johann stayed silent.

After almost a minute of silence, Max knew that Johann wasn't going to surrender and had to get him out of there.

MAX

He knew that Johann was probably tense and had an itchy trigger finger as he sat in the dark workshop. If he fired the Winchester, there would be a three-second window for Max to get into his shop and take a snap pistol shot at Johann.

So, he slowly reached over, picked up a tin cup with his left hand, then quietly walked closer to the door separating the living quarters from the shop. He stopped, then whipped the cup across the workshop, hitting one of the front doors.

Johann saw the glint of metal and the clang to his left, swiveled the Winchester in that direction, and pulled the trigger. He was momentarily blinded by the flash but still began to lever a new round into the breech.

Max didn't hesitate after seeing the muzzle flash and immediately took one long stride into his shop, turned to his left, and fired at point-blank range.

The .44 blew through Johann's upper chest from the right upper lung through the left lung and left his body before drilling into the wall and finally burying itself in the floor of the abandoned stagecoach office.

Johann's wide eyes still showed the look of shock as the Winchester slowly dropped from his hands, the lever halfway through its cycle. It was the Yellowboy.

Max waited for a few seconds to make sure he was dead, then quickly left the shop and went back out the back door, hoping to prevent Amanda from entering.

Amanda saw him come out the door and asked, "Are you hurt?"

"No. I'm fine. Amanda, I'm not going to sugarcoat this. Johann is dead. He was waiting inside with the Winchester. He was going to shoot whoever came through that door. I tried to get him to surrender, but he wouldn't, so I tossed a cup against the wall and he fired. I entered my shop and returned fire."

"He's dead?" she asked numbly.

"Yes. I'm sorry, Amanda. I didn't have a choice."

She took a deep breath, feeling an incredible sense of relief, which was astonishing as even she knew that if Max had shot him two days ago, she'd probably be weeping or ready to claw Max's eyes out.

"I understand, Max. I'm all right. Do I have to go back to my house now?"

"No, Amanda. I'd rather you stay with Colleen and Patty. You all need support from each other now."

"Thank you, Max. I am so very grateful. I never want to set foot in that house again."

"Amanda, I need to wait for the marshal. I don't want you to have to see this. Are you still okay with going to Schneider's, or would you rather just head back to the house?"

"I'm all right, Max. I can go to the store and wait for you."

"I'll join you shortly to pay for anything you buy. And Amanda, don't skimp. You've done without for far too long now. Buy anything you want."

Amanda was overwhelmed. Max had said that like he meant it, but no one really means it. *Do they?*

Max escorted Amanda around the front of the building and not surprisingly, Marshal Emil Becker arrived at the same time.

"Max, now what happened?"

"I was showing Amanda the horses and heard a noise from inside my shop, followed by a Winchester levering in a new round. I knew the only one it could be was Johann, so I went inside with my pistol drawn and didn't see him. So, I suspected he might be out of sight in a corner somewhere with one of my Winchesters.

"I tried to talk him into surrendering, Emil. I mean, all he did was get into a fight with Joe, and I really wanted to know what he could tell me about Mary. But he didn't answer, so I tossed a tin cup into the far wall and he fired, giving his position away. As he was levering in a new round, I jumped around the corner and shot him. He's dead. I haven't been in there since. I'm going to let Amanda go to the store while we check out Johann. Is that okay?"

"Sure. She shouldn't see this."

Amanda nodded and turned to cross the street to Schneider's.

Max opened the door, noticed the large hole on the left side of the doors, right near the spot the tin cup hit, and pointed out the hole to the marshal.

Marshal Becker stuck his finger through the hole and said, "Guess you're gonna have to plug this one of these days."

"Likely."

They entered the room and found Johann, sitting in the corner, the Winchester still on his lap with the lever pulled open and the look of surprise still on his face.

"Glad you were here instead of me, Max."

"That was my biggest concern, Emil. What if someone opened that door to the shop? Johann would have shot without even knowing who was coming inside. I couldn't risk letting him stay there. I just couldn't come up with another solution."

"So, what's gonna happen to Amanda?"

"I told her that she should stay in my house with Patty and Colleen. She doesn't want to go back to her own house and I'm guessing Patty doesn't want to return to the ranch, either. They both can stay at my house as long as they want to. I'll stay here in my shop. If Colleen wants to stay with her sister, she can stay there, too. Do you want to handle getting Johann out of there, or do you want me to do it?"

"Can you drag him out back? Then you can lock your shop up."

"Good idea. I really should bring those weapons back to the house, but it's never been a problem before. Times are changing, Emil."

"They are. I'm not sure it's for the better, either. I'll go tell the undertaker to pick him up. Does he have enough money to pay for his funeral?"

"Remember, Emil, Amanda said they didn't have enough to pay for a telegram. I'll pay for his burial."

"I appreciate it, Max."

Max entered his shop, pulled the Winchester out of Johann's hands, then dragged him out of the shop and left him in the back alley. He thought about covering him with a tarp but figured the undertaker would be by soon, so he locked the shop and headed over to Schneider's.

He found Amanda putting more items on the counter. She turned when he entered and smiled sheepishly.

"I think I got everything."

"Riding clothes for you and Patty?"

"Yes."

"Western boots for all of you?"

"No."

"Go."

She returned with three pairs of boots.

"Did you remember the toothbrushes, tooth powder, and some scented soaps? Not to mention the hairbrushes."

"Oh."

She returned with all the items and put them on the pile.

"That's all. Really."

"Give me a total, Paul, and give me ten cents worth of penny candy, too."

Paul totaled the order and said, "$47.45, Max."

Max counted out the money and handed it to him. Paul gave him his change, smiling all the time. He and Max then packed the order into large bags.

Max left the store carrying all but one of the bags, which he left for Amanda. It wasn't heavy, as it contained only clothing, but it was bulky.

They made their way to the house and stepped up to the door. Amanda had to knock because Max's arms were full, and Colleen opened the door a few seconds later.

As they entered, Colleen asked, "Did I hear shooting again?"

Max set the bags down on the parlor floor and replied, "Yes, ma'am. Amanda can tell you what happened. I need to leave now and take care of things. You ladies go through the bags, and if you need anything else, I'll be in my shop."

Without waiting for a reply, he quickly turned, crossed the parlor, and left the house, closing the door behind him.

Amanda and Colleen watched him leave and both wondered why he was so abrupt.

After a short delay, Colleen asked, "What on earth did you buy, Amanda?"

"A lot of things. Max told me to buy whatever I wanted, and then he came and added some more things for all of us. Let's take these to Patty's room and I'll show you."

She and Colleen had to make two trips to get everything into Patty's bedroom and then began taking things out of the bags.

———

Max headed back to his shop, using the alley, and found the undertaker loading Johann into his hearse.

"Hello, Max. Emil tells me you're paying for this one."

"I am. What's the bill, John?"

"Twenty-seven dollars."

Max dug through his pockets again, found the exact amount, and handed the money to the undertaker.

"You're keeping me busy, Max."

"Not intentionally, John."

"I know. Humor is hard in this business."

Max nodded and walked into his shop as the hearse drove away.

He closed the door, feeling exhausted again. All of this was beginning to wear him down, even more than a week in the work gang.

He sat at the table and just stared at the empty wall before him, still trying to get his mind over everything that had happened since he'd left prison. He had expected to return to find his father happy to see him again, his shop waiting for him to start business again, and maybe even settling down. But this was all so overwhelming.

Now, he had three young women living in his house, one now a new widow because he'd just shot and killed her husband, the other soon to be a widow, and the one he had believed might be the one he wanted to settle down with acting as if he had measles or worse. Add the assassination attempt and possible future problems because of Mary Preston and he felt like running down the main street of Burden screaming like a wild man.

But he knew he'd do no such thing. He had to handle each of the problems as they arose and that would mean a trip to Wichita to deal with Mary Preston. Once that problem was solved, leaving Burden might be the best solution for the others.

He finally stood, removed his pistols, hoping to remember to clean the one he'd just used and the Winchester in the morning, tossed his hat on the table, pulled off his boots, and just flopped onto the nearby bed. He was asleep in minutes, even though it was only early evening.

———

The women went through Amanda's purchases. They each had a new hairbrush, toothbrush, boots, and even scented soap for the bath. But it was the penny candy that really surprised them. It was such a minor thing compared to all the other items, but it meant so much more. They each took a single piece and as they put it onto their tongues, for some inexplicable reason, the candy brought them back to the everyday world from the almost surreal world that they'd each found themselves.

CHAPTER 7

Max struggled to wake up after having slept for more than twelve hours. He finally sat up in the bed and swung his feet to the floor, feeling as if he should have slept for another twelve.

Once he decided that it wasn't a very productive thing to do, he stood, took care of his morning necessities, and decided he'd let someone else cook. A habit he'd have to get away from, he promised himself.

He left the shop, locked the door, walked down to Sunny's, and found a seat. Maddie, as usual, hustled to his table.

"The usual, Max?" she asked.

"Thanks, Maddie. That's what I need, and lots of coffee."

She was getting accustomed to his use of her first name, but she still enjoyed it.

Forty minutes later, Max left the diner and checked his watch. It was only a little after seven o'clock, so he returned to his shop and spent another forty minutes cleaning his Yellowboy and his right-hand pistol before reloading each weapon.

With his guns done, he had to clean the blood from the corner where Johann had died, another death that didn't bother him. He was going to try to kill him just like Stud Smith had, which reminded him that he needed to get Mary to stop her campaign.

He strapped on his newly cleaned and reloaded guns and left the shop, locking it behind him. Suddenly, it dawned on him that he forgot to go and see Jim about the exhumation and decided he might as well take care of that before he left for Wichita, so he reversed course and headed for the attorney's office.

He entered just five minutes later, saw Jim at his desk, and said, "Morning, Jim."

He stood quickly and practically shouted, "Max! *What the hell has been going on?* I hear you were involved in two gunfights."

Max spent ten minutes describing the details, before a calmer Jim Garson asked, "So, you think Mary is behind the shootings?"

"She's the only one I know in Wichita, and she has a motive."

"How are you going to deal with it?"

"I'm going to write you a letter describing the incident in the stagecoach office five years ago, the shootout with Stud Smith with his statement, and what Johann said about my being dead. I'll seal it and then you can write me a letter saying I left you the letter with that information that will be opened on my death. It might make Mary think twice before trying again."

"Good idea. I'm guessing you remembered the request you made concerning your father?"

"That's it."

"I contacted Doctor Phillip Francis in Wichita. He's used by the U.S. Marshal's service, so his word is gospel. Do you want to proceed, even if you're in Wichita?"

"Yes. How much will the cost of the exhumation and autopsy be?"

"The exhumation will be thirty dollars, and the fee for Dr. Francis will be a hundred and ten."

"Fine, I'll leave the cash with you. I need to get some more money anyway."

"I hear you've installed three young women in your house."

"Amanda is now a widow with no money. Patty is almost in the same situation, but she's recovering from injuries from her husband's beatings, too. But at least they both have property now. Colleen is looking after her sister. It's the least I can do, Jim."

"I know. I'm just ribbing you a bit."

"I know. Anyway, I'll be back with the money in a little while. I'm going to go and check on the women first. Then I need to clear my head before I go to Wichita. Jim, one more thing about those ladies. I want to make a quick will before I go. I want them each to get a third of my money and joint ownership of the house and the contents."

"Are you sure, Max?"

"Jim, who else can I leave it to? At least they wouldn't have to worry so much."

"I'll draw it up. You can stop by around three o'clock and I'll have it ready."

"Thanks, Jim."

"Take care, Max."

Max waved and walked out the door, then once on the boardwalk, headed for the house. He didn't even think of it as his house anymore. It's just *the* house.

Five minutes later, he stepped up to the front door and knocked.

He was pleasantly surprised when Patty opened the door as he didn't want to be grilled by Colleen again.

"Well, this is a pleasant surprise, Patty. I'm glad to see you up and about."

"It's about time. Come in, Max."

He stepped inside and after Patty sat down, all three young women were sitting in the parlor looking at him.

"Good morning, ladies. I'm just checking in and see how everyone is doing and if you needed anything."

Patty replied, "We're fine. Are you all right, Max? You've been in two shootouts in two days."

"I'm fine, Patty."

"When are you going to Wichita?" asked Amanda.

"Tomorrow morning. I should be back in two or three days. And while I'm on the subject of the trip, before I go, I'm having Jim Garson draw up a will for me. I'm leaving each of you a third of my money and you'll all have joint ownership of the house and its contents. You can jointly decide to sell it or continue to live here. I'm just making sure that in the event something bad happens, the state doesn't take it all."

All of them were stunned by the news and sat there staring at him for a good thirty seconds.

Patty finally asked, "Was that gunshot wound that close, Max?"

"I'll be honest with you. If I hadn't been shooting with both hands, that bullet probably would have hit the left side of my chest. I don't know if it would have been fatal, but it does give one a hard dose of reality."

None of the women could reply and continued to sit quietly so Max figured it was time to go.

"Well, I'm going to head back to the shop. If you think of anything, I'll be there for a little while," he said, then turned and took one step before Colleen spoke, stopping him.

She asked, "Max, when I was putting clothes in the drawers, I found a necklace in a box. It's very beautiful. Was that your mother's?"

Max nodded and replied, "It was. It was a gift from my father on their twentieth anniversary. She was sitting right there, where you are, Amanda. My father stood in front of her and opened the box. She put her hand over her mouth and started crying as he placed it around her neck."

"I'm sorry, Max. It must be a very sad memory."

"It was never a sad memory, Colleen. It's just the opposite. It's how I remember them both. If you could have been here and felt the love between them, it was almost palpable. My father looked at my mother just as he probably did when she stood next to him at the altar. She looked up at him the same way. It's one of the most beautiful things I can recall. I'll never forget it. It's something that I've hoped for my entire life."

He blew out his breath, then quickly said, "Well. I need to get back and take care of things. I need to get ready to head to Wichita."

Max again turned and hurriedly left the room and the house, closing the door behind him. The answer he had given to Colleen about the necklace was so very true that the memories had begun to flash in his mind, and he knew he couldn't stay composed much longer.

He needed a distraction, and that would be Wichita. He went straight to the bank and withdrew another five hundred dollars, then walked down to Schneider's. He found a travel bag that was a bit too much like a carpetbagger's, but it was the best he could do. He wondered if he could find a decent jacket in his size. He doubted it but checked anyway.

He found one that was a bit tight around the shoulders, but not too bad, and thought he would probably find one better in Wichita. He found a pair of pants that were very close in color and cloth to the jacket, then added a vest and two new shirts. His Stetson was a bit sweat-stained, so he found a nice light gray one that worked well with the medium gray jacket and pants and bought a new belt which completed his purchases.

He paid Paul for the items and returned to his shop. He'd buy one item he knew he could get in Wichita that he couldn't get here. He'd only travel with the Remington derringer, but he needed more stopping power, so he'd buy a Webley Bulldog when he arrived in the city. It used the same .44 caliber cartridge as the Winchester '66 and his Smith & Wessons, but it had a shorter barrel and was smaller overall but felt like a normal-sized pistol. It only carried five rounds, but he didn't expect to get into any drawn-out gun battles. He just didn't want to get caught with only the derringer between him and the morgue. He'd get a shoulder harness for it and could carry it anywhere without notice. The other advantage of the pistol was that it was double action and didn't have to have the hammer pulled back. He wondered if he'd do it reflexively anyway if he found one.

He pulled out his pocket watch, knew he needed some lunch, and didn't want the food in his shop to go bad, so he decided to eat in, meaning he'd have to cook.

An hour later, he finished his lunch, admitting that it wasn't the tastiest of meals, but it was filling. By the time he finished cleaning up, it was time to return to Jim Garson's.

Five minutes later, he was sitting at Jim's desk and handed Jim the money for the exhumation. Jim gave him some paper and a pen for his Wichita letter, which didn't take him long to write and only needed a single sheet. He let it dry and addressed an envelope while Jim wrote the letter explaining Max's letter and that it would be held in a secure location known only to three unnamed people.

Max finished the envelope, folded his letter, and slid it inside. He handed the letter to Jim and he sealed it with wax. Max took the letter Jim had written and folded it before slipping it into his inside vest pocket.

Then Jim slipped more paper across the desktop saying, "Here's your will, Max. Like you said, it's very simple. I'll just need you to sign it and I'll witness it."

Max signed two copies, as did Jim, and after it had dried, Max took his copy.

"Is that all we need for today, Jim?" Max asked.

"You're all set, Max. Good luck in Wichita."

"I'll need it," Max replied as he stood and shook Jim's hand.

Max returned to the shop to give it a cleaning before he headed to Wichita. He decided to empty both Winchesters of cartridges after last night's incident. He also moved the rifles and his two-gun rig to a long crate under his bed, hiding them from plain sight.

Then, he went outside and checked on the horses.

When he reached the corral, all three animals walked over to him. He hoped there wasn't some equine sixth sense that warned of imminent death, but figured they really just wanted some more oats.

He rubbed their necks and wished he had a treat for them, but instead, he filled the oat bin with the remaining grain from the bag. The more he looked at Luna, the more he appreciated the small mare. She was too small for him, but ideal for a woman. He'd probably need a fourth horse for either Amanda or Patty, assuming that Colleen eventually figures out that Venus is hers.

It probably didn't matter anyway. Colleen had surprised him. He thought she was the least abused of the three, yet she had become more distant than either Amanda or Patty. Maybe she was hiding something that had happened. She had lived a year alone in the house with her father and maybe he hadn't just defended his son. Maybe he was more aggressive to his daughter, the only woman in his house. She had been so pleasant to talk to until Max started getting too close, and it hadn't even been that close at all. Then she became almost cold and distant and he suspected that he'd never know the reason why.

He had enough hay for the horses for a few days, so they could go without oats for a day or two. He wondered if the women would go riding while he was gone. It still might be tough on Patty, though. Speaking of Patty, he hadn't heard a word about Joe Endicott's condition from Doctor McKenna.

Then, as he was going down the list of problems he was leaving behind when he went to Wichita, he arrived at Jerome Emerson, Patty and Colleen's father, and his prime suspect in his father's murder. He was already convinced that he had been murdered, but the problem would be if the murderer really did just drop the wagon on him, then there would be no evidence found in the exhumation.

But what would he do if he found evidence of a murder? He didn't have anything like motive or eyewitness accounts. He was literally clueless.

He returned to his shop. The train departed tomorrow morning at 9:20 and arrived in Wichita at 10:50. He had planned on staying in Wichita for two days. Maybe he could get it done in one day if things worked out right, but somehow, he didn't think they would.

———

Four miles east of Burden, Jerome Emerson sat drinking a cup of coffee. One of his neighbors, Bill Ferguson, had stopped by to borrow one of his mules and had mentioned in passing about the big shootouts in town and that his son-in-law had been killed by Max Wagner. Not only that, his two girls were living with Max Wagner in his house.

Jerome turned down his request to borrow the mule. He might want to go into town in the next day or two.

He was getting mighty lonely since Colleen had gone and didn't understand completely why she had left him. He had seen how Walt enjoyed being around his sisters and he had been without a woman since his wife had died, so he let Walt have the daytime and he had the nights.

He'd just crawl into their beds when they were sleeping and feel them evolving into more mature women.

Patty had fought him tooth and nail, so he had backed off after the first few times, but Colleen just curled up into a ball, so he spent his nights with her. Even though she was wrapped up, it didn't mean he couldn't enjoy himself with her.

There was nothing wrong with it in his mind. He didn't take her or anything. He just fondled his daughter at first as she was tightly curled up in her nightdress, then he began pulling her nightdress up and slide up close against her skin. He still dreamed about that skin-to-skin contact and wished she hadn't gone. She never complained, either, except for some mild whimpering.

He sure did miss that girl and now she was sleeping with that murderer, the same man who had killed his son, and that wasn't right. She should be home, sleeping with her father. Maybe this time he'd treat her like his wife, believing that she would be thrilled with the idea.

———

Max was ready to go. It wasn't quite dinner time, so maybe he'd go and pay the women another visit, then he thought better of it. He'd already stopped by earlier that day and didn't want to be a nuisance, so he tried to think of anything he may have missed.

———

MAX

After Max had gone that afternoon, the first thing that Amanda and Patty did was to have Colleen show them the necklace.

Now, all three women were in the kitchen cooking dinner. Amanda was still adjusting to a life of plenty. Like Patty and Colleen, she had been stunned by the quantity and variety of food. She also was very aware, as they both were, that Max had never eaten one bite of it.

"Colleen, why did you ask Max about the necklace?" asked Patty.

"Curiosity more than anything. I assumed it belonged to his mother."

"It meant a lot to him," commented Amanda.

"I was wondering about that. Max's father died less than a year after his wife died. After the way Max described how much they loved each other when he gave her the necklace, I'm beginning to think that Max's father wasn't murdered. I think he might have committed suicide," suggested Amanda.

"Suicide? Really? Why didn't he just shoot himself?" asked Patty.

"Because it attaches a social stigma to the family. If he died in an accident, no one would say anything. But to have an accident that seemed out of place just a few months after his wife died just seems too much of a coincidence."

"But he didn't leave a note or anything," said Colleen.

"He wouldn't leave one out where anyone could find it because it would defeat the purpose of doing it the way he did. He'd leave it in a secret place that only Max knew about."

"I hope you're wrong, Amanda," said Patty.

"So, do I," Amanda replied.

―――――

Max left his shop and walked to Sunny's for dinner. As expected, the only waitress was Maddie. She looked tired but still smiled at Max as she walked to his table at normal walking speed.

"Hello, Max. What can I get for you?"

"Maddie, you look exhausted. Can you have a seat for a few minutes?"

"I wish I could, but it's still busy."

"You just bring me whatever is easy, alright?"

"Okay. I'll be back in a minute."

He watched Maddie walk away and felt bad for her. He'd ask Colleen if she could pull a few shifts to give her a break.

Maddie brought him his coffee and said she'd be back shortly.

He sipped his coffee and thought about Wichita again with its many different possible scenarios and even more potential results.

Maddie brought him a roast pork dinner with roasted potatoes.

"This looks really good, Maddie. Thank you for your choice," he said as he smiled at her.

Maddie smiled back, but the energy was gone as she returned to the kitchen.

He finished his meal leaving two dollars for the fifty-cent meal, returned to his shop, and prepared for the trip to Wichita. The doors were wide open to allow the evening light to bathe the shop.

He'd just bring his new travel bag with the minimal necessities. He wasn't going to be gone that long, so it didn't take long to pack and when he finished, he just stretched out on the bed with his boots on so he could think.

Since he'd returned, he'd been embroiled in two family messes that weren't his own, been shot, and killed two men. Yet he hadn't repaired a single thing, whether it was mechanical or human.

He wondered why no one had brought him a single thing to fix. He knew all sorts of mechanical things were still breaking, but nothing had entered his shop.

He had the money to do what he wanted to do, maybe it was time to move on. Maybe he should sell everything except the house and then go and see Mr. Trask. But he'd never worked for anyone before, except for those five years he worked for the state and wasn't sure he'd like it. Maybe he should just open up his own shop in a big city like Kansas City. He had the capital to start his business.

He knew one thing; he couldn't keep going the way things have been going these past few days.

CHAPTER 8

The first one up the next day was Jerome Emerson after having decided that Colleen would be coming home today. If Wagner had ruined her, he would kill the son of a bitch. She probably missed him already. He'd bring his rifle, but he had to load it before he left. He hadn't used it in a while and thought that maybe he should test it first. He walked to the powder keg that he kept in the kitchen pantry, still thinking about how he'd shoot that Wagner bastard.

He took his powder cup from the shelf and scooped it full of powder, not paying much attention as he thought about what he needed to do. He poured in the powder, noticing the greenish tinge to the gunpowder but paying it no mind, shoved in a wad and rammed the Minie ball home. The rifle had served him well in the War Between the States, and many a Johnny Reb had fallen victim to his marksmanship.

He had his breakfast and went outside and saddled the mule. He didn't bother testing the rifle, he just put a fresh percussion cap on the nipple, so all he'd have to do is cock it and fire if Wagner showed his face. He hoped he did because that would be justice as far as Jerome was concerned.

As he rode along, he smiled at the thought of getting justice for Walt and then getting Colleen back into his bed tonight.

―――――

Max was dressed and having breakfast at Sunny's and Maddie seemed in better spirits. She was almost back to her usual bouncing self and was very happy with the concern shown to her by Max, including that enormous tip he had left for her. When she brought his breakfast, she added some raspberry preserves for his biscuits.

Max expressed his thanks as he smiled up at her.

He finished his breakfast and left a dollar for the twenty-five-cent bill. He was in a good mood and had made up his mind to leave Burden after he cleared up this Mary problem and found his answer about his father's death.

He returned to his shop an hour later. He was ready to go. He was dressed in his new clothes and looked like a well-heeled rancher, which was his purpose. His only weapon was the derringer in his jacket pocket.

His travel bag was ready, and he had $267 in his pocket. He thought about visiting the women but thought it would be better if he just left. He didn't have anything to tell them anyway.

He exited his shop, locked it, and stepped out into the street and another beautiful late spring morning. Enjoy it now before the summer heat arrived, he thought.

As he walked eastward, Jerome Emerson was riding his mule westward. He was about a half mile out of town, his rifle in his left hand.

Max was on the boardwalk, passing the marshal's office when he saw a rider approaching from the east, stopped and stared, then chastised himself for being on edge so much these days. It was probably just a rancher or farmer coming in for supplies, he thought until he saw the rider holding a rifle and watched more closely.

After another two minutes he thought that the rider looked like Jerome Emerson, so he began to walk slowly to the train station, getting a better look with each step, until he was sure it was Jerome, and he was bringing a rifle with him, which was unusual. He looked around and thought about heading back to Emil's office, but then he saw Jerome turn his mule toward his house. *Damn it!*

Max dropped his travel bag and broke into a jog, quickly reaching the opposite side of the street and heading for the cross street and his house. He pulled out his Remington derringer and picked up the pace until he was moving at a loping run.

Jerome had seen the motion out of the corner of his eye and turned as Max closed to within a hundred yards. *It was him! That son-killing, daughter-spoiling bastard was running right at him!* This was perfect, he thought as he climbed down from the mule and cocked the hammer of his rifle.

Max saw him and realized he was in trouble. Jerome had an old Springfield, and that beast fired a .58 caliber Minie ball that would devastate anyone it hit, so he began to zig-zag as he got closer.

Jerome had seen soldiers try that stunt a lot of times during the war. Those Rebs would try to escape from his aim, but he anticipated their moves. He waited until Wagner had just finished a turn as he closed within fifty yards and pulled the trigger. The hammer was released and rammed into the percussion cap, igniting the powder. The trusty old rifle spewed the Minie ball and a huge cloud of gunsmoke as the loud crack of sound followed the lead out of the muzzle.

Max was stunned when he felt the hammer of the Minie ball as it hit him in the left upper chest knocking him off stride, but not killing him which was all that mattered as he maintained his stride but stopped zigzagging.

Jerome was stunned, knowing that he hadn't missed. He had seen the round strike the big man right on the left side of his chest. He didn't know why Wagner wasn't dying in the street but grabbed the barrel of his rifle, held it over his head, and prepared to use the rifle as a weapon, wishing he had his bayonet. He couldn't see the derringer in Max's right hand.

In the house nearby, all three women ran to the windows to see the cause of the gunfire, and Colleen was the first to recognize her father standing there with his rifle over his head. Patty recognized him an instant later and then saw Max boring down on him.

Max saw him start to swing the rifle as he reached him, and automatically brought his right arm up to deflect the blow. It wasn't a direct hit but glanced off his forearm. It still hurt, but it didn't slow him down as he plowed into Jerome and crushed him to the ground. Max didn't give him a chance to defend himself as he could feel his blood wetting his new jacket and didn't know how much time he had to make this right. He pounded Jerome with a hard right knocking out some teeth and then grabbed him by his shirt.

Max shouted, "You bastard! You let that worthless son of yours abuse your daughters!"

Jerome started laughing, blood spitting out of his mouth as he said loudly, "Colleen loves me and you ain't ever gonna have her. She's mine. She liked it when I was in her bed and you're never gonna get her in yours."

Despite his shocking claim, Max quickly screamed, "*Why did you kill my father, you, worthless son of a bitch?*"

Jerome looked genuinely confused and yelled back, "Why the hell would I care about your old man? I wanted you dead. Not him."

Max had enough of Jerome. He wanted to crush him but knew that it would be murder, so he picked him up and started dragging him to the marshal's office, but never made it. Emil Becker was running as fast as he could and saw Max manhandling Jerome as he walked his way and could see Max's jacket with a big hole in the front surrounded by a growing stain of blood.

He reached Max and asked, "Max, now what?"

"I have no idea. This bastard was riding toward the house with an old Springfield. I ran that way and he shot me. I've got to go and bother Doctor McKenna again. Can you take him?"

"I've got him. Get over there."

Max didn't know why he wasn't dead. He should be. That Minie ball hit him in the left side of the chest. *Why was he still breathing normally?*

He made it to the doctor's office and walked inside, finding Doctor McKenna with a patient. He didn't want to bother him yet but wanted to see why he was still alive, so he opened his jacket gently, then his new, ruined vest. He began unbuttoning his new, ruined shirt, peeled it away, and couldn't believe what he saw. He could see the back end of the Minie ball. It was buried into his muscle and wondered if Jerome was using bad powder from the Civil War. It could last a lifetime if he kept it dry, but if he let it get contaminated, it was a different story.

Doctor McKenna exited his exam room with Mrs. Kirkpatrick. She glanced at Max, then without comment, hurriedly left the office.

"Max, get in here!" Doctor McKenna said after seeing the unusual sight of a patient examining a bullet wound in his waiting room.

Max stood and followed the doctor into his office and sat on the examining table.

"Were you going to sit out there all day?" asked the frustrated physician.

"I had to see why I didn't die. Jerome shot me with a .58 caliber Minie ball at sixty yards right in the chest. I should be dead, Doc."

"Jerome Emerson?"

"Yes, sir."

"Lie down. I'll take a look."

Max did as he asked. Because Max had already pulled back all the cloth, Dr. McKenna simply peeled all of the layers back a little more before his eyes went wide as he saw what Max had just seen.

"I don't believe it! Hold on, Max. I'll get it out of there."

He took a pair of forceps and pulled the Minie ball out, making a sucking noise as he did. He dropped the round on a side table and cleaned the wound, pulling out fragments of cloth from the hole. Max lay there grimacing as the doctor probed the open wound, wondering what Jerome had said. He had slept with Colleen. *Was that why she was so distant?* He also said that he hadn't murdered his father, and for some reason, he believed him. Jerome was so angry, yet he had admitted to molesting his daughter and said he wanted to kill Max, so if he had killed his father, he would probably have bragged about it.

Regardless of anything else Jerome had done, Max knew that he'd be in prison for the rest of his life for attempted murder.

As the doctor finished suturing the hole, Max suddenly realized that his trip to Wichita had been delayed, and he'd have to buy some new clothes…again.

"Okay, Max. Now you have more sutures that need to be removed."

"Can I have the bullet, doc?"

"Here," he replied, handing him the Minie ball.

"Thanks, Doc. What's the bill?"

"You overpaid last time, Max. We're even."

"Alright. I need to go back to the shop and clean up."

"Good idea."

Max stood up and left the office, suddenly wondering where the derringer was, so he walked over to where Jerome's rifle lay on the ground near his house. He got there and after a minute of searching found the small gun in the grass. He had worried that Jerome might have found it and slipped it into his pocket. He slid the derringer into his pocket, picked up the heavy Springfield rifle, and headed back to the marshal's office, believing that at least the women didn't see this mess. They must have been in the kitchen.

He opened the door to the marshal's office and found Emil sitting behind his desk. Jerome was sitting on the same cot that he had used five years ago, scowling as Max handed the rifle to the marshal.

"Emil, do you want me to write a statement?" Max asked.

"Can you do that? How the hell are you still standing?"

Max reached into his pocket and placed the Minie ball on his desk.

"He must have used contaminated powder from the War Between the States. It just made a hole and sat there in my chest. I could see the back end of it."

"It's still attempted murder."

"I assumed as much."

"Go ahead and write your statement if you can."

He slipped a sheet of paper and a pencil to Max, who wrote the statement quickly, feeling the need to get back to his shop so he could get cleaned and changed. After five minutes, he slid the paper back to the marshal.

"Good enough, Max. I'll notify the county to come and get him. I'll notify you when the trial will be held. It'll probably be in a couple of days."

"Alright," Max replied as he stood and then left the office.

Two more days, he thought as he walked down the street. He hoped it didn't matter and thought he should stop at Jim Garson's office and call off the exhumation but decided to do it after he was clean.

He reached his shop, unlocked the door, walked back to his living area, and took off his jacket and then his vest. He finally peeled off his shirt. He was still covered in blood, so he left the clothes on the floor and began pumping water into the sink. He took a towel, soaked it in the cold water, and began to wipe the blood from his chest and stomach. At least his pants weren't bloody. There was a little on the waistband, but not enough to notice, but they'd need a good laundering. He wished there was a laundry in town, so he could avoid the task. He may not be much of a cook, but he hated doing his laundry.

He put on a clean shirt and pulled out his pocket watch. It was only 9:20. He could still catch the train if he hurried and actually thought about it. Maybe he could get there, talk to Mary and get back before the trial. But then he realized that if he didn't get back in time, Jerome might walk away without any punishment, and he deserved a lot more than what he was going to get, even if it was life in prison. Max wished he had really pummeled him. He had only delivered one hard shot before screaming at him.

He laid down on the bed, wondering if everything was conspiring against him. *How much more could happen?* He'd been shot twice in just a few days. Granted, neither was little more than a minor inconvenience, but with just a minor difference, both could have been fatal. He didn't want to tempt fate again and it also reinforced his decision to leave Burden after returning from Wichita.

He stood again and picked up the bloody jacket, shirt, and vest. They were all beyond repair, and the materials didn't make for good rags, except maybe the shirt, but it was so soaked with blood, he decided not to bother. He started a fire in the heat stove and tossed in the shirt first, then the vest, and finally the jacket. He closed the stove door and decided to go pay a visit to the horses. He pulled on his Stetson and his gun rig before going outside, half expecting to find another gunman. He looked at the horses and they all stared back as he smiled.

"Which of us is the dumber animal?" he asked aloud.

He locked up the shop and saddled Mars, led him from the corral, closed the gate then trotted out into the street and turned east. He set Mars to a fast trot and rode out of town, knowing where he was going.

After four miles, he turned into the Emerson farm. He didn't know what he'd find, but he wanted to make sure nothing was there that could cause either Colleen or Patty to be humiliated and even contemplated burning the house down.

He stopped in front of the farmhouse and stepped down, looping the reins around the hitching rail. He walked inside, got his bearings, and looked for Jerome's bedroom first. He walked inside the only bedroom that had evidence of recent occupation and began searching. He found women's underclothing in the drawers with Jerome's clothing and held onto them so he could put them in another bedroom's drawer.

He also noticed that one of the knots in the wall had been removed, which wasn't incriminating, just creepy. He was about to leave when he stopped and looked at the bed again, then stepped over and ripped the blanket from the bed and found a nightdress on the sheet. He picked it up and added it to the collection of underwear. He noticed it had a 'C' embroidered on the front, then walked back into the hallway and into another bedroom. The drawers were all empty, as were the drawers in the last bedroom.

After leaving the last bedroom, he looked at the collection of cloth in his hand and thought it would be best if he just burned it all.

Max started a fire in the cook stove and once it was going, he tossed the clothes into the fire. They blazed quickly and soon were reduced to ash, and with them, all evidence of what Jerome had done to Colleen and Patty. He opened the pantry door and found the keg of gunpowder, crouched down, and looked at it. He scooped some up in his hand and saw that it was full of a mold of some kind. It smelled different, too. He dumped it back into the keg and shut the door. Now he understood why he was still alive.

He was still fuming inside about what Jerome had done to his daughters when he left the house. There was no place in hell hot enough for Jerome Emerson.

He left the house and mounted Mars, set him to a slow trot, and headed back to Burden. He needed to think about this. He knew he had to tell Colleen and Patty about their father, *but should he tell Colleen about what he had said and what he had found?* He fully understood now why she wouldn't allow him to get close.

Her father had destroyed her ability to be intimate with any man. She must have gotten the worst of it because Patty was gone, *but if he told her that he knew, would that push her away even further?* His heart was aching for both women, especially Colleen. To have to put up with that for years was almost unimaginable. No wonder she didn't want him, or probably any other man to touch her. It was such a terrible waste, he thought. Colleen was so perfect. It was just his luck to find her and not be able to do anything about it.

Max reached the edge of town and turned to the side street toward the house.

"Here he comes!" shouted Amanda, who had been looking out the window. Ever since the shooting, the women had wondered when Max was going to come and tell them what had happened. Amanda had wanted to go to the doctor's office and see how he was, but because he had walked off, they thought he was all right, despite the blood on his jacket. Now, they'd get their answers. Patty and Colleen were particularly keen to find out what happened to that bastard who called himself their father.

Max stepped down and tied off Mars, then walked slowly to the door, still unsure of what he was going to do. He never got a chance to knock as the door swung open as he neared.

MAX

Patty exclaimed, "Max! Come in! How are you doing? We saw what happened and were waiting for you."

Max walked inside, now more nervous after having believed the women hadn't witnessed what had happened.

As he walked into the parlor, he replied, "I'm fine, Patty. Come on in and I'll fill you all in on the details."

Less than a minute later, everyone was sitting in the parlor as Max began his story.

"I was heading toward the depot to take the train to Wichita and I saw Jerome riding his mule into town. I noticed he was carrying his rifle and knew he was up to no good, but when he turned toward the house, I thought he was going to try to hurt you or Colleen.

"So, I dropped my travel bag and pulled out my derringer. It was all I had. He saw me running toward him, took out his rifle, and fired. He must have been using messed-up powder he had from the war because the Minie ball hit me square in the chest but didn't penetrate enough to do any serious damage. Then I crashed into him and let him have a few shots before dragging him off to the marshal."

"What's going to happen to him, Max?" asked Colleen quietly.

Max could see the fear in her eyes just talking about him.

"He'll go to trial in a couple of days for attempted murder. I'll testify, and he'll probably go to prison for the rest of his life."

"Do you think there's a chance he could get off?" asked Patty.

The same fear was in her eyes, Max noticed, but not as intense.

"There's always a chance with juries, but I'm going to do what I can to make sure that doesn't happen."

"What happens to the farm, Max?" Patty asked.

"That's a good question. I'll ask Jim Garson about it. Your father won't be able to pay the property taxes on it, so if you don't, it'll be forfeited, and the county will auction it off. There should be a way, after he's convicted, for you to sell the farm, maybe as part of a plea agreement, he would get a reduced sentence if he deeded the farm to you both."

"I'd rather him keep the damned farm rather than let him get a lesser sentence," spat Colleen.

"Me, too," agreed Patty.

"I'll ask Jim about the law on this. I may go and have a chat with the bastard in a bit, too."

"What about Wichita, Max?" asked Amanda.

"I'll delay it by at least two days. I hope Mary doesn't try anything and I don't think the assassination route was the way to go anyway. I thought she'd do something a lot subtler, like a bribe or something."

"Does the 'or something' include using her feminine charms?" asked Patty.

"It does."

"Max, if you only had a derringer, why did you charge at him like that? Why didn't you go and get one of your Winchesters?" asked Colleen.

He glanced into those green eyes but couldn't bear to look much longer.

"Because I thought he might be trying to hurt you or Patty. I didn't have the time to go back to the shop. He would have been at the house in less than a minute. If I left to get my other guns, I would be too late. I had to take the risk."

"If he had better gunpowder, what would have happened?" Colleen asked softly.

"I don't know. Maybe the shot would have been too high," he lied.

At the distance he was firing, that Minie ball would have killed him. He hoped they'd buy the lie. They didn't, but they let it go.

"Where did you go, Max? We saw you ride Mars east," asked Amanda.

"I just needed to clear my head," he lied again and hoped this wasn't becoming a habit.

Then he said, "I need to have Jim Garson cancel the exhumation, too. When I grabbed Jerome, I asked him why he had murdered my father. He denied it, and for some reason, I believed him. So, I'm going to let that go."

"Max," Amanda began hesitantly, "was there any secret place in the house that you or your parents used to store things? Most people do."

Max wondered why she would ask but simply answered the question.

"Sure. Want me to show you where it is?"

"No, but have you looked inside since you've been back?"

"No. I haven't, but I suppose that I should have."

"That's what we thought," Amanda said.

"I'll go look. Do you want to come along?"

"No, we'll stay here until you get back."

None of the women wanted to be there if he found a suicide note, so they sat nervously after he left.

Max walked back to the kitchen and opened the pantry door. There was a small knot hole in what looked like a full-height board. Max put his finger in the hole and pulled. The board had been cut with the seam covered by the shelf edge. He removed the board and took out a small metal box. He walked the box to the kitchen table and opened it. There were two sealed envelopes inside along with about two hundred dollars in cash. Both envelopes were addressed to him. He sat down and stared at the envelopes. One was in his mother's handwriting and the second was in his father's.

He was both dreading and excited about what was inside, took a deep breath and opened the one from his mother. There was a single page. Her handwriting was shaky, so she must have written it while she was sick.

He took a deep breath and read:

My Beloved Son,

I am so sorry for leaving you. You were such a light in my life. Doctor McKenna, good man that he is, told me the truth and I can't fight off the pneumonia much longer.

I'm still saddened by your decision to go to prison, but I am also proud of you for making that decision. You have become the man I always expected you to be.

I have asked your father not to bury me with my necklace. He knows how much it means to me, but it doesn't deserve to sit in the ground. Give it to the woman who will complete you. You'll know her when you meet her. She will be as happy with you as I am with my Hermann.

I am worried for your papa. I know how lonely he will be. He has told me that he could not live without me. Please care for him when you return.

I am tired now. Just remember that I loved you more than you'll ever know. When you have your own children, you will understand. If you have a daughter, I wouldn't be upset if you named her Elsa.

With all the love in my heart,

Mama

He was so upset by reading his mother's words, that he wasn't sure he could read his father's letter. He decided that he owed it to his father to read it, so took another deep breath, then blew it out before he opened the second letter:

My Dearest Son,

I wish I could be here when you return, but I can no longer bear the loneliness. I miss my Elsa so much every day. I thought after a few months, it would fade, but it grows worse instead. I see her face everywhere. I don't know how much longer I can live without my Elsa. I know it is a selfish thing that I am planning to do. I am going through this life now as though I am already dead, I don't care about anything but her.

Last week, I finally decided to join my Elsa. I want to see her again so badly it hurts. My last thoughts though, are for you. I know why you went to prison, and I know you seem to blame all women for what Mary did. Remember that your mother, my beloved Elsa, was a woman, and the very best of women.

As your mother wished, I leave Elsa's necklace for you to place around her neck as I did for my Elsa. Love her as much as I loved my bride. Let her fill your life as Elsa filled mine.

I will see her soon. Do not think less of me for what I do. It will appear to be an accident, so no stigma will be left to hurt you.

I love you, my son, and wish you all the happiness you can find. But you will only have that happiness if you find your Elsa.

Your Loving Father

He slowly lowered the letter to the table, letting his tears silently drip onto the wood surface. Now he knew. There was no murder. He felt so empty but didn't think any less of his father at all and understood. He had loved his mother deeply, but children all understand that they will, sooner or later, be living without their parents. His father thought he'd grow old with his wife and it must have torn his soul apart when she died.

MAX

How could he find his Elsa when the only woman that he thought could be that woman was so damaged by her own father that she probably wouldn't let him touch her?

He stayed sitting at the table with the letters in his left hand, then wiped his face dry, and took another deep breath before he finally stood and walked back to the parlor where the women sat waiting.

When he arrived in the room, he simply handed the letters to Colleen, said he needed to go talk to Jim Garson right away and he'd be back when he finished, then continued out the door.

Colleen quickly read the first note from his mother and handed it to Patty, who read it and passed it to Amanda. Colleen read his father's letter and mechanically handed it to Patty.

———

Max walked quickly to Jim Garson's office, opened the door, and found Jim reading a file.

"Max! I heard you were shot again. How are you doing?"

"I'm fine, Jim. I need you to stop the exhumation and autopsy. I found out what happened."

"Okay. I'll send a telegram to Dr. Francis shortly. What did you find out?"

"Is this private, Jim? I mean, I know you don't gossip, but this is important."

"Of course, it's private, it's attorney-client confidentiality."

"I found a note from my father. He committed suicide, Jim. He missed my mother too much, and it ate at him."

Jim sat back and said, "I know how much he missed her. We were all waiting for him to return from his depressed behavior, but he seemed to be getting worse. Honestly, Max? Some of us suspected that."

"Alright. Go ahead and notify Dr. Francis. And another thing, Jim. Jerome Emerson. He'll be charged with attempted murder. Do you think there's any chance he can get off?"

"Almost none. He'll do twenty-five to thirty in the state prison for it."

"That's what I thought. The problem is the farm. After he's convicted, how can we get the deed transferred to Patty and Colleen? They'll probably want to sell it."

"We petition the county court. Usually, in a case like this, when the deed holder is sent up for a long sentence, the court wants to do that anyway."

"Fine. I'll let them know. Thanks, Jim."

"Oh. And here's your hundred and forty dollars back. I thought you might change your mind," he said as slid an envelope across the desk.

Max took ten dollars out and left it on the desk.

"You've got to charge me sometimes, Jim. See you later."

"Anytime, Max."

Max left the office and was going to stop at the jail and talk to Jerome but decided it wouldn't be necessary or wise, so he headed back to the house. He had also decided to talk to Patty and then to Colleen privately.

The women were a bag of mixed emotions when Max returned and just took his seat. The letters were sitting on the table, so Max picked them up, folded them, and slid them into his pocket.

"Patty, Colleen, I talked to Jim Garson. After the trial, if he's convicted, and Jim thinks his chances of getting off are almost zero, we petition the court to have the deed to the farm transferred to both of you. Then, you'll be free to sell it. Amanda, are you going to sell the house?"

"I'd like to get rid of it."

"Patty, what about the ranch?"

"I definitely want to sell it. Why don't we have the farm put in Colleen's name? I will already get the proceeds from the sale of the ranch."

"Patty, the farm should belong to both of us," protested Colleen.

Before it went any further, Max said to Amanda. "Amanda, could you start making lunch? I need to talk to Patty and Colleen in private."

"Sure. I understand. I'll go and start cooking."

"Thank you, Amanda."

After she had gone, Max looked at the Emerson sisters.

"Now, I understand what you both went through with Walt. What I did this morning was to go out to the farm and destroy any evidence of anything that could cause either of you pain. The farm is nothing more than a farm now. I wanted to let you know that. Now, Colleen, I know that you want to protest about Patty giving up her share of the farm, but what she's saying is just common sense. She'll probably get more than five thousand dollars for the ranch and cattle. The farm will sell for around four thousand.

"It seems to me that it's just common sense for both of you to have around the same amount of money. Amanda will only have about a thousand dollars from the sale of the house, if that. I'd be more comfortable if you each had enough money to give you options, but still, hope that you'll all stay here as long as you wish. It'll give you much more than a roof over your heads because you'll all have each other for support."

Colleen still looked hesitant about the farm, but Patty spoke up.

"Thank you, Max. I agree. Colleen needs the money, too. I won't have it any other way. Colleen, you are getting the farm and I'll hear no more arguments."

Colleen managed a weak smile, then said, "Alright. You were always the bossy one, anyway."

"Max, if we all live here, what will you do?" asked Patty.

"I'm not sure. After I solve the Mary problem, I'll probably leave. I was offered a job by Mr. Trask in Lansing for keeping his equipment operating, but I'm not sure."

"You'd leave us?" asked a stunned Colleen.

"You need each other more than you need me. Once the word gets out about three pretty, unmarried women living in one house, this place will be swarming with eligible bachelors."

Then he shifted his eyes to Colleen and asked, "Colleen, could I talk to you for a minute in your room?"

"Okay."

Patty looked at Max curiously. She didn't know if this was about being an eligible bachelor himself or something else, but she knew that Colleen was still deeply impacted by her father's behavior, much more than she was. She also knew that Colleen had to live alone with that bastard for more than a year after she'd gone. She hoped that Max knew that she was vulnerable, but she also trusted Max. She'd probably find out what he told her from Colleen after he was gone.

Colleen walked into her room and sat down on her bed. Max closed the door and took a chair.

"Colleen, I didn't want to say anything in front of Patty or Amanda. When I grabbed your father and asked him if he had murdered my father, do you know why I believed him?"

She shook her head, obviously uncomfortable with any mention of her father.

"It was because he already had readily admitted to what he did to you. That was why I went to the farm this morning. I had to make sure that there was nothing that anyone could find that would cause you embarrassment or hurt."

"Did you find anything?" she asked softly.

"Yes, I did. I found women's undergarments in his drawers and your nightdress on his sheets."

Colleen felt a cold wave rush down her back as her stomach flipped.

"I burned them all, Colleen. I made sure it was just a farm."

"Okay."

"Colleen, I know this is all painful for you to hear or talk about, but you need to understand that you aren't alone. You have Patty and Amanda. Patty will understand more easily, but each of you has been abused. Talk to them both, Colleen. Let it out.

"I'll be honest with you, Colleen. I was upset with your cold behavior toward me, but I understand now. So, don't worry about me doing anything to make you uncomfortable anymore. I suggest that you ladies get out on the horses often. Go riding and enjoy the freedom. Put it behind you as best you can. More than anything, Colleen, I want you to feel safe and happy. Okay?"

She nodded.

Max stood and opened the door, realizing her hurt was worse than he thought, and that was a lot. He really wanted to go and shoot Jerome for what he did to Colleen.

After he was gone, Colleen continued to sit on the bed just thinking about what he had said. He knew, but he didn't seem to think poorly of her for it, and that surprised her. She would think that any man would take advantage of her knowing what her father had done. She still shuddered when she remembered feeling him against her skin, his arousal obvious. She knew she could never allow another man to get close to her, not even Max, and she really wanted Max to like her.

When she had read his parents' letters, she wondered if she could ever experience the kind of love that they shared. She didn't even know what love was. She'd been proposed to three different times in the past year by young men at the diner and hadn't even told Patty about that. Each of the young men had looked at her with that same look that her father had on his face. A look, she noted, that she never saw in Max. He always looked at her with concern and something else she didn't understand, but it didn't matter.

Max walked out to the kitchen to see Amanda.

"Amanda, you'll be on the short end of the stick financially. You're only going to get around a thousand dollars from the sale of the house. The good news is that you'll have almost no living expenses. I'll leave enough money here so that the house will be stocked with food for at least a year, and there's also that two hundred dollars in the metal box right there. What do you think you'll do?"

"I don't know. But I wouldn't mind getting married again. I'd just have to choose more wisely," she answered as she smiled.

"I think you've learned your lesson."

"What lesson?" Patty asked as she entered the room.

Amanda turned to her and replied, "Max was just asking what I was going to do, and I said I wouldn't mind getting married again, but I'd choose better the next time."

"So, would I," agreed Patty.

Max looked at Patty and gave her a little head tilt toward Colleen's room. Patty nodded, then turned and headed that way.

"Max, why are you thinking of leaving?" Amanda asked.

"I'm not sure, Amanda. I just feel out of place here. I feel like I cause more problems by being here."

"Max, that's just silly. You've helped me and Patty and Colleen."

"I'll still help you as much as I can, Amanda, but I still think it would be best if I wasn't here."

"It's Colleen, isn't it?" she asked quietly.

Max sighed and nodded, then replied, "It doesn't matter, though."

"Of course, it matters."

"I wish it could be otherwise, Amanda. But it can't. Trust me. It'll never happen. That's why I can't stay. It'll just be too uncomfortable and make things worse."

Amanda sighed and returned to cooking.

Behind Colleen's closed door, Patty was getting an inkling of why Max had sent her in. Colleen wasn't even talking to her and Patty didn't know whether to be angry at her sister or to commiserate with her.

Finally, she found the pin to burst her bubble of silence.

"What did Max find at the farm, Colleen?"

Colleen's head jerked up, shocked that Max had told Patty and probably Amanda, too.

"He told you, didn't he?" she snapped.

Patty was surprised by her vehemence and shook her head before replying, "No, he never said a word. He just nodded for me to come and talk to you. What did he tell you to get you so upset? I doubt if he made advances toward you. It's not like him."

"No. He didn't. He did just the opposite. He told me he wouldn't come near me. He said all he wanted was for me to feel safe and happy."

Patty felt like she wasn't getting anywhere and asked, "So, why would that get you upset?"

"It didn't. It's just that…, well, he knows, Patty. He knows because that bastard father of ours told him what he did to me."

Patty rested her hand on Colleen's shoulder, and asked quietly, "Colleen, did he force himself on you? Did he rape you?"

"No. He did everything but that. He would get in bed with me and fondle me and pull up my nightdress and push his naked body against mine. I could feel his arousal, Patty. I was scared. I was so very scared that he would take me. He never did, but every night he would do the same thing.

"I'd curl up into a ball, but it didn't matter. He'd have me almost naked, and all I did was cry and let him feel me and hold me close to him. It was for a whole year, Patty! I thought when I ran away, I'd be all right, but I can't shake it. I can be pleasant enough to men when they're away from me, but when they get close, I feel the fear again. I'm never going to be normal, Patty. Never! And now Max knows. He found my nightdress in our father's bed and burned it, so no one would know, but he knows."

"Yes. He knows, and he still loves you, Colleen," Patty said softly.

"*What?* He doesn't love me! No one can love me, Patty. I'm a mess. Why can't everyone just leave me alone?"

"For the same reason that Max wants to help you, Colleen. We love you, too."

"But you're different. You're my sister. I love you, Patty, but men are different. They don't care about how we feel. They just want to do what our father did, or worse."

"You're very wrong, Colleen. You're selling the entire sex short. I'm sure that many men are just like that, but do you see that look in Max's eyes?"

Colleen admitted, "No. I noticed that he didn't look at me that way."

"Do you know how difficult it is for any man to intentionally keep his hands off a woman that he loves?"

"How would you know? You were married to Joe."

"I know. I've never been in love either. I'll bet if you ask Amanda, she'll tell you that she was all wrong about it as well. But I know that somewhere out there, there's a man for me that will love me for all the right reasons. Just like Max's father loved his Elsa.

"Didn't you see that in those letters? It was a beautiful thing, Colleen. I can't imagine how wonderful it must feel to have someone you love hold you close and kiss you. I'm lost just thinking about it. I just have to have hope. You, on the other hand, have yours just twenty feet away. I'm insanely jealous, too. I imagine Amanda is as well. I've never met a man as considerate and thoughtful as Max. When you add how he's packaged, it makes an incredible, complete man. A man, by the way, who took a risk of death trying to protect you."

"He was trying to protect all of us."

"Believe what you want, Sister. But if you insist on believing that you can never be with Max, it won't be long before he looks elsewhere, and you'll spend the rest of your life wondering."

212

With that, Patty left the room, closing the door behind her.

Max and Amanda had already finished lunch when Patty exited the room, took one of the sandwiches and a glass of water to the table, and sat down.

"Are you all right, Patty?" asked Max.

"I'm fine. I'm not sure I made any headway with Colleen, though. She's still pretty upset."

"I understand. I'm going to head back to the shop. I may stop at the marshal's office on the way," he said, then stood, left through the back door, and walked around to the front of the house.

He unhitched Mars, headed back to the main street, and stopped at the livery instead of the marshal's office.

He looped Mars' reins over the hitching rail and walked inside.

Bob saw him coming and asked, "Back again, Max?"

"Yup."

"How are you doing? For a man that's been shot twice in a week, you're looking pretty good."

"You got that right. I should be dead. Seeing that Minie ball sticking out of my chest was one of the weirdest things I've ever seen."

"I'd imagine. What can I do for you today?"

"Got any new horses?"

Bob laughed, and said, "I can imagine why. You got three fillies over there and only two mares. I think I might have what you want. I went over to Ferguson's ranch yesterday and picked up two new mares. I had a feeling you'd be back."

Max laughed and said, "You're in the wrong business, Bob. You should be in the carnival reading palms."

They walked out in back and Max picked out the new mares instantly. Both were very pretty horses. One particularly caught his attention. She was a light brown Morgan with an even lighter brown mane and tail. She had four white stockings and a streak of white on her forehead.

"I like the light brown mare, Bob. What's her story?"

"Six years old. Docile as they come and has a really nice gait, too."

"How much?"

"I'll give you a quantity discount. How about thirty-five dollars?"

"I suppose I need to see Charlie about another saddle."

"Sorry."

"Alright, I'll take her. As she'll be the last one, I'll be buying, I won't even haggle."

"Well, that ruins my day," he said as he laughed.

"I'll be back in a few minutes with the tack."

"Max, why don't I just lead her over to Charlie's and we can saddle her there?"

MAX

Max said, "I feel like an idiot for carrying those others across the street now, Bob."

Bob laughed and Max crossed the street while Bob put a bridle on the mare to bring to Charlie's leather shop.

Thirty minutes later, Max led both horses back to the corral outside his shop. It was full now, and he thought momentarily about expanding the corral, but then realized he'd be leaving it soon.

He saddled Venus and Luna, before leaving the corral and walking east again toward the house. He needed to get the ladies out of there for their own good.

After reaching the house, he tapped on the back door, then walked in the back entrance and found all of them still at the kitchen table talking.

"Alright, ladies. You've had too much talking and sitting around. Let's go. All of you, into riding clothes right now. We're going for a ride."

"But..." began Patty.

"No buts, Patty. We're going. I'm done talking. Go!"

They all stood and went to their rooms to get changed, having already done the simple arithmetic. One would have to double up, and Patty thought it would be her and Colleen. unless Max thought he could convince Colleen to ride with him, but that was unlikely.

Amanda hoped that she would get to ride with Max. If Colleen was going to reject him, she wouldn't.

Colleen hoped she could ride with Patty and was afraid that Max thought he could get her to ride with him, but Venus was her ride. *Wasn't she?*

They all walked out of their rooms at about the same time and before any could ask, Max said, "Alright, ladies. Let's go," then opened the door.

They trooped out the door and he turned them toward the alley. When they were close enough to the corral, they saw that there were four horses inside the fences. Patty was the only one who hadn't seen them before.

When they reached the corral, Max turned to the women and said, "Okay. Now, Venus is Colleen's horse. Who gets Luna and who gets the new Morgan?"

Patty walked up to Luna and rubbed her neck. Her choice made, Amanda didn't mind a bit as her eye was on the new Morgan.

"Do I get to name her, Max?" she asked.

"She's yours now, Amanda. Name her as you wish."

"Is Luna my horse?" asked Patty.

"She is."

Colleen didn't ask about Venus. Maybe because she always knew that he had bought Venus for her. She loved the horse because the young mare meant so much to her. She meant freedom.

"Let's mount up and head out. Which direction?"

MAX

"Can I stop by the ranch? I need to pick up some things," said Patty.

"Sure. We'll do that."

They all got on their horses and Max opened the gate. He left it open as they took to the road. It was quite a sight.

After they left the town, Max picked up the pace to a fast trot and the ladies followed suit. Soon they were all moving at a good clip.

Max waited for them to catch up, then he let Mars go. The big gelding wanted to run. He had been standing too long.

Colleen had been expecting it and set Venus charging after Max a second later, then Patty and Amanda raced soon afterward. All the women were having the best time they had enjoyed in days.

Max glanced back and saw three smiling faces with hair blowing behind them. It was an amazing sight to behold, and he was glad to see that Patty was free from pain as she rode Luna.

Colleen forgot her depressed state as Venus flew along, her hooves pounding the ground. All she felt was the wind in her face and the scenery flying by. She needed this.

Max slowed down and waited for the women to catch up, but they didn't. They all shot past him, laughing as they did. He smiled, and Mars shot forward, eating up the difference quickly. He moved alongside and passed them all on the left, laughing as they had been. They couldn't catch the long-legged gelding, so they all began slowing down.

When they all were trotting, Amanda was closest to Max.

"Mars sure can fly."

"He's a good horse."

They turned into the ranch access road and a minute later pulled up in front of the house.

"I'll take the horses to water and catch up with you later," Max said as he dismounted, then began gathering the horses' reins.

Patty and Colleen stepped down and went inside, but after Amanda stepped down, she stayed with Max and walked with him as he led the four horses away.

Colleen turned and looked back, keeping her eyes on Amanda until she and Patty entered the house.

Amanda strolled beside Max and asked, "I've been wondering about a name for my horse. I couldn't come up with a good planet name, so what are the names of Mars' moons?"

"You probably don't want to go there, Amanda. They're both gods of grief and unhappiness."

"How do you know so much?" she asked.

"Five years of reading anything I could get my hands on."

"Oh. Any other celestial suggestions?" she asked as she smiled up at him.

"If it was a gelding or a stallion, there are plenty, but females are more difficult. How about Calisto?"

"Who's Calisto?"

"The fourth moon of Jupiter. It's named after a mother goddess that was turned into a bear and then became the constellation Ursa Major, the Big Dipper."

Amanda grinned and replied, "That's perfect. I'll call her Calisto, then."

Max and Amanda led the horses to the trough, and she said, "This was a good idea, Max."

"Everyone needed to get away, including me."

"Are you really going to leave, Max?" she asked quietly.

"I think so. I wasn't joking about the young men. I have a feeling that the rumor is already floating around, and once I'm gone, they'll descend like locusts."

"You are somewhat intimidating."

"I don't try to be."

The horses had watered enough so Max pulled them away before they drank too much, then led them back to the hitching post and tied them off.

Amanda trotted up the stairs and into the house, but Max stayed outside. He decided after talking to Amanda that it was time that he started separating himself from the women as he saw himself more as an obstacle to their healing now.

Five minutes later, they all came out together. Patty had a bag of things that must have been important to her.

"Where to now?" he asked as they stepped down from the porch.

"I think we can go home now," said Patty.

"Okay. Let's head back."

Max climbed up on Mars and turned north after leaving the ranch, almost ignoring the three women as he began running through different approaches to the Mary Jones situation. He finally decided that he'd just go and talk to her if he could.

Once they were on the road, the women were chatting like Max wasn't there, and he thought that was good because, after the trial, he wouldn't be.

They arrived in town, rode the horses to Max's corral, and they all began to dismount.

Max said, "I'll take care of the horses, ladies. You can head back to the house."

Amanda asked, "Max, should you be doing all this work with all those sutures in your chest?"

"I'm fine, Amanda. You can all go back to the house."

"Alright."

The women left, and Max began unsaddling the four horses. It wasn't comfortable but saddling them was worse. He had them all cleaned and brushed down after an hour but needed some more hay and oats, so he wandered back and asked Bob to deliver some to his corral, paid two dollars for the grain, and headed to the marshal's office.

"Howdy, Emil. Any word from the county yet?" he asked as he entered.

"Just heard an hour ago. Trial is set for tomorrow at eleven o'clock. The prosecutor wants to meet with you a couple of hours before that, and your reward came in yesterday. I forgot to mention it in all the excitement. How are you doing?"

"I'm fine," he answered as he took the voucher that the marshal slid across the desk.

"That must have been an odd sensation seeing that Minie ball sticking out of your chest."

"Too bad I couldn't get a photograph taken. It was really bizarre. When I saw that rifle let go, I thought I was gone, Emil. If the idiot hadn't used contaminated powder, I probably wouldn't be here. In fact, if he had kept it dry, it wouldn't have mattered. It still would have punched a hole clear through me. He let it get wet and moldy."

"That's the truth of it. I've gotten some soaking wet, dried it out later, and it still worked fine. I don't know how it'd work if it was all moldy."

"Anyway, I guess I'll be riding to Winfield early tomorrow. See you around, Emil," he said, then waved and left the office.

He had to go and tell Patty and Colleen, so he returned to the house and knocked on the door.

Patty answered it quickly, and said, "Come on in, Max. You really shouldn't knock. It's your house."

"I don't need to come in, Patty. I just wanted to let you and Colleen know that the trial is tomorrow morning at eleven. I'll be riding out of here early to meet with the prosecutor and I should be back by midafternoon."

"We don't have to be there, do we?" she asked, the concern visible in her eyes.

"No. I'd recommend against it anyway. This is between me and him. The reason he had for shooting me shouldn't come up."

"I hope not."

"I'll see you tomorrow afternoon then."

"Max, I don't know if we're ever going to be able to help Colleen."

"I think she'll do better once I'm gone, Patty."

"I don't think so."

Max didn't want to discuss it any longer, so just said, "Anyway, I'll see you tomorrow with the verdict."

"Good luck," Patty said.

Max turned and headed back to his shop, stopping at the bank on the way to deposit the draft. He also stopped at Schneider's to buy another gray vest, finally returning to his shop thirty minutes after leaving the house.

———

Mary had been informed by Carl that his first effort to eliminate the problem with Max Wagner had failed, and she wasn't pleased but told Carl to hold off any further attempts.

Mary had made up her mind to handle this personally and ten minutes after Carl left, she drove the buggy to the bank to see Charles. He had an office on the second floor, as befitting his status. As she walked in, his secretary, a young woman named Clara Crenshaw saw her coming and rose as she entered.

"Good afternoon, Mrs. Jones. Your husband is with a client at the moment but should be done shortly."

"I'll wait," Mary said, then took a seat and studied Miss Crenshaw.

She wondered the same thing that many wives whose husbands had pretty secretaries did. Charles had been working late hours these past few weeks and had even missed dinner a few times.

She watched the door and two minutes later, the client walked out and smiled at her as he passed. She began to stand when Charles came out and didn't see her. He was looking at his secretary, and before Clara could say anything, Charles smiled at Clara, then caught her eye, and turned to see Mary sitting out of sight of his office door.

Mary had seen that smile before, and it wasn't a boss-employee smile.

"Mr. Jones, your wife is here," Clara said quickly, even though Charles had already noticed.

Charles straightened up quickly as his face returned to a strictly business face.

"Why, Mary, this is a pleasant surprise. Come into my office," he said as he smiled at her.

Mary smiled back. She could play this game too, and probably a lot better than he could.

He followed his wife into his office, closed the door behind him, then circled around behind Mary and sat at his desk.

Mary sat in the chair opposite.

"Now, what can I do for you, my dear?" he asked.

"I need to go down to Burden for a couple of days. It's something to do with my parents' ranch. I think there was a problem with the deed."

She wondered how quickly he would jump at the chance to be rid of her for a few days and shouldn't have wasted the time as he answered almost before she finished speaking.

"Of course, I understand. Do you need some cash for the trip?"

"Three hundred should do," she replied, knowing it was more than twice what she'd need.

"Certainly. Let me write you a draft. When will you be leaving?" he asked as he took out a blank draft and began writing.

"Probably the day after tomorrow. Will that leave you in a bind?"

"No, not at all. I'll manage."

"I'll try to get this taken care of as quickly as possible," Mary said.

"If you need to stay longer, send me a wire."

"I will. I'm sure you're a very busy man, so I'll get out of your way. Thank you, Charles."

He handed her the draft and she smiled at him as she left the office, then smiled at Clara as she passed and soon left the bank, pretty sure of what her husband would be busy doing after she left.

MAX

———

Max was out of food in his living quarters, so he went to Sunny's for dinner. Maddie was still there, and there was another waitress as well. Maddie was showing her the ins and outs of being a waitress, and soon both headed for Max.

"Good evening, Max. This is Susan. She'll be taking some of the shifts for me."

Max smiled at her and said, "Hello, Susan. Glad to see someone helping Maddie out. She was working too hard."

Susan was a bit older than Maddie, twenty-one or twenty-two, and seemed in awe of Max.

"Did you really just get shot yesterday?" she asked.

"Sort of. The bullet didn't penetrate very deeply."

"Where did it hit you?" asked Maddie.

"Right here," he said as he pointed to the left side of his chest.

"Does it hurt?" asked Susan.

"Not much."

"You've been shot twice in a week. I hope there isn't a third," Maddie added.

"You're not the only one. I'm not too fond of it, either."

They both giggled, and Maddie finally got around to asking for his order. They both left after he ordered a steak and baked potato and Susan returned with his coffee a minute later.

Max poured his coffee and sipped the hot java as he planned for tomorrow. It was only a twelve-mile ride to the county courthouse, and he'd need to be on the road by seven-thirty, so that wasn't a problem. The problem was with the trial itself. He wondered if the defense attorney would try to twist his purpose for allowing the sisters to stay at his house. If he was any good, he would do just that. He'd try to paint Jerome as a concerned father trying to save his daughters from the clutches of a domineering madman.

Maddie brought him his steak, which he ate mechanically as he thought of ways to avoid the issue of abuse. He was glad that neither attorney had subpoenaed the sisters. That would have been a disaster, at least for Colleen. Patty would probably be all right. She'd probably make Jerome out to be the monster that he was.

He had an idea to deal with any possible problem that might result from that line of questioning, so after dinner, he left the diner and walked quickly back to the house and knocked on the door.

Patty answered shortly, and asked, "Max, is something wrong?"

"I need to talk to Amanda."

"Come on in."

Amanda was sitting in a chair in the parlor and Colleen was sitting across from her.

Max looked at Amanda and said, "Amanda, I need you to come with me tomorrow. Can you do that?"

"Of course, I can. Why do you need me at the trial?" she asked.

226

"As a character witness. I'm concerned that Jerome's defense attorney may try to paint him as an honorable father trying to rescue his poor daughters from some maniac. It might work, too. I want you there to simply testify, if necessary, to your treatment here, that I don't sleep here, and I've never even touched any of you."

"That's ridiculous, Max. Everyone knows that," said Patty.

"Everyone here, but not in Winfield. All it will take is one juror on that panel to believe that Jerome was right, and he's free. If Amanda is there, she can testify that neither Patty nor Colleen want to return to the farm. It may not be necessary, but I don't want to risk the possibility of him being able to walk away from this."

"What time do we leave, Max?" asked Amanda.

"I want to be on the road at 7:30. I'll have Calisto saddled for you, and I'll swing by just before then. Okay?"

"I'll be ready."

"Thank you, Amanda. You may just save the case."

Amanda was smiling broadly as she closed the door and returned to the sitting area. Patty and Colleen both noticed her pleased expression.

"That was pretty smart. Max looked at the case as a stranger would," said Amanda as she returned to her chair.

"Amanda, do you want to know why we would never go back to our father?" asked Patty.

"Heavens, no. That's the last thing I want to know. If the defense attorney asks, I don't want to have to answer the question."

"I hadn't thought of that," she confessed.

"You know, something just occurred to me."

"What's that, Amanda?" asked Colleen.

"When I get to go to Winfield with Max tomorrow, that will be the longest any of us have spent with him since he returned. I don't think he's spent more than ten minutes at a time with any of us. Is that right?"

"You're right. It's like he's afraid of us or something," replied Patty.

"I think it's intentional," Colleen said softly, "I don't think he wants any of us to get too close."

"You should talk, Colleen. You're the only woman I know who's pushed him away. That's ironic, too, because I think you're the only one he's interested in."

"You keep saying that, Patty. But how do you know? I can't let him touch me. Ever."

"How do you know? Have you even held his hand?"

"No."

"Then you're just guessing. You're assuming that you'll feel the same way if Max touched you that you did when our father did. It's not the same, Colleen. Even Joe didn't give me the willies like father did, and I didn't really care for him. If a man like Max loved me, I'd be all over him. I wouldn't even wait for him to ask."

Amanda then said, "I'll second that, Patty. If he even hinted that he was interested, I'd drag him off in a heartbeat."

"It's just not the same," Patty said.

Amanda suddenly realized she was hearing too much about their home lives.

"You both have to stop talking about it. I have to testify tomorrow. Remember?"

Patty said, "Oh. That's right. Sorry. By the way, where did you get Calisto for a name?"

"From Max, of course. I wanted to name her after one of Mars' moons, but he said they were gods of death and destruction, so he suggested Calisto. She was a mother goddess that was turned into a bear and then into the Big Dipper. Isn't that a good story?"

"It is. It's a good name, too."

"Well, I'm going to turn in. Tomorrow is going to be a big day."

After Amanda left, Colleen said nothing, but just sat deep in thought about what both Patty and Amanda had said, especially Amanda when she said she'd be willing to drag Max off to her bed in an instant.

CHAPTER 9

Max was up earlier than he had to be, but dressed quickly, including his gun belt. He wasn't going to take a chance by riding with only a derringer, and he'd take the '76, too.

He was dressed by 6:10 and walked to Sunny's for breakfast. Susan was on her own and took his standard breakfast order.

When he finished eating, he left a tip that matched the cost of the breakfast, thinking he might as well continue the tradition for as little time as he planned on staying in town.

He returned to the shop and picked up the new Winchester, went out to the barn, saddled Mars and Calisto, and smiled at the name for the Morgan. He had to reach for that one.

Once they were both saddled and ready, he pulled out his watch. It was only 7:15, so he walked to the house, leading both horses, and arrived at the kitchen door a few minutes later, hitched the horses, and knocked on the door which was soon opened by Patty.

"Good morning, Max. Come on in."

He took off his hat and entered the kitchen, finding Colleen and Amanda having their morning tea.

"Do you want some coffee?" Patty asked.

"Do you have it made already?"

"Not yet."

"Then don't bother. We'll be leaving in a few minutes."

"Well, come on in and sit down."

Max walked in and took a seat at the table. Colleen was on his right and Max felt decidedly uncomfortable being so close to Colleen. He didn't know if he was making her as nervous as he felt.

"You know, this is the first trial I've ever been to," said Amanda.

"Me, too," replied Max, wondering if they understood the semi-joke.

"That's right. You never had a trial. Do you wish you did now?" she asked.

"No. I don't regret that decision. I regret making the decision to go and investigate the noise, but not the one to take the punishment for what I did."

Colleen knew the story but hearing him say it that way touched something deep inside her. He had spent five years of his life, five years of his young life, in prison because he had killed a man who was so beneath him in every admirable trait, yet he still felt he should be held accountable for that death.

She didn't know why, but she reached out and placed her fingers on his hand. It wasn't much, but when the skin of her fingers touched the back of his hand, she felt an incredible release and didn't feel repulsed at all. She felt a warm rush flow through her like a soothing bath.

Max was aware of the gentle touch of her fingers but didn't react or touch her hand with his free hand. He let her decide what to do next.

Patty noticed and held her breath. but Amanda didn't notice at all.

Max finally turned to Colleen and just smiled, and she smiled back. It was a warm, welcoming smile, a look he hadn't seen on her face in a while.

Patty resumed breathing and thought that maybe, just maybe, Colleen would get better after all.

"I'm ready," announced Amanda, breaking the short, but critical play unfolding beside her.

Colleen quickly removed her fingers but continued to smile at Max.

He returned her smile again and answered, "Okay. We'll be going. We'll be back around two o'clock or so."

"We'll be anxiously awaiting the news," said Colleen.

He gave her one more smile and stood to leave with Amanda, then as he glanced over at Patty, she winked at him.

He smiled at Patty, then he and Amanda left the kitchen. When the door closed, and Patty was sitting alone with her sister, she asked, "How are you doing, Colleen?"

"Better," was all she said, and it was all she needed to say.

―――――

Amanda and Max set their horses to a medium trot, then soon left Burden behind them and were on their way to Winfield.

"There is a chance you won't be called to testify, Amanda. It will all depend on the defense attorney. If he tries to attack me, you're going to be critical to get a conviction. You'll be the prosecutor's secret weapon."

"I'll be glad to help. When Colleen and Patty were talking, I got a hint of what was going on, but I stopped them before they gave me too much detail that I shouldn't know."

"That was very smart. If you don't know, the defense attorney can't ask."

They talked about the trial for most of the trip, arriving in Winfield shortly after eight-thirty, and headed for the county courthouse. They stepped down and let their horses drink before tying them to the hitching rail, then went inside and had to ask for the office of the county prosecutor.

The county prosecutor, Michael Burns, was a middle-aged man with a receding hairline, but sharp, brown eyes, and met with Max earlier than his appointed time.

"Good morning, Mr. Wagner."

"Mr. Burns, this is Amanda Peters. I brought her along for a reason. I'll explain why shortly."

"Fine. Let's go over your testimony."

Max retold the story of the shooting, and the prosecutor was impressed with the detail.

When Max finished, he asked, "Now, why is Miss Peters here?"

"Mrs. Peters is here because I'm concerned that the defense attorney may try to portray Jerome as a loving father who was trying to rescue his misguided daughters from a manipulative man. If you look at the situation from the outside, it may appear strange that I've turned over my house to three attractive young women. A lot could be made of that if the defense attorney is any good."

"He is."

"Mrs. Peters is one of the three women. The other two are his daughters. Neither wanted to see their father again, and Mrs. Peters agreed to come along in case you needed a rebuttal witness."

"Outstanding! Well thought out. That may very well be their only defense. Do you know the reason that the daughters don't want to see their father?"

"I do, but Mrs. Peters does not. She intentionally didn't want to hear their story."

"Another very wise move. Can you tell me why you spent five years in prison?"

"I pled guilty to involuntary manslaughter. I hit a man who fell and struck his head."

"Was it a fair fight?"

"Yes."

"Then why didn't you plead not guilty?"

"Because I did cause his death. It was an accident, but I still felt guilty."

"Was there anything else about the incident?"

"The man I killed was Jerome Emerson's son."

Mr. Burns' eyebrows arched in surprise as he said, "Well, that sheds a whole new light on it. Yes, sir. He wasn't defending his daughters at all. He was trying to kill you."

"That's what he told me when I caught him."

"He did?"

"I thought he had murdered my father in revenge for killing his son. When I asked him why he had done it, he said 'why would I kill your old man. It was you I wanted to kill'."

"Now that's worth keeping in my hat. I see where they have Emerson listed as testifying. If he does, I'll drop that little bomb on him."

He talked to Amanda for a while and was practically giddy with what she told him. Max never entered his own house without knocking, was never there after dark, and had never spent more than two minutes alone with any of them. He was satisfied that the defense attorney wouldn't be able to use his lone argument.

Amanda and Max left his office at 9:45, and Max asked, "Well, Amanda, we have an hour to kill. What do you want to do?"

"Why don't we just sit on that bench under the tree?"

"Perfect."

They chatted for an hour about nothing of consequence, with horses being the biggest topic. At a quarter of ten, they returned to the courthouse and found seats in the courtroom.

Jerome Emerson was walked in by two deputies wearing shackles. He paid no attention to Max as Mr. Burns arrived and took his seat. His defense counterpart, Mr. John Severson, took his chair next to Jerome.

At eleven o'clock, they all rose as Judge Thaddeus Adams strode to his seat at the bench. The trial had begun with his entrance, and after Burns' opening argument, Severson presented his. He did as Max had expected and portrayed him as a convicted felon who preyed on young women, and that Jerome Emerson had heard of his perversions and had tried to rescue his daughters.

Max was the first witness called. After being asked, he told the story of that night, then Severson took his shots.

"Mr. Wagner, you served five years in prison. Which crime were you found guilty of committing?"

"I wasn't found guilty of any crime."

"I beg your pardon? Did you serve five years in the Kansas State Prison?"

"Yes, sir."

"Yet, you insist you weren't found guilty of any crime?"

"That's correct."

"How can that be, Mr. Wagner?"

"I never had a jury trial, Mr. Severson. I pled guilty to the charge of involuntary manslaughter."

"So, you admit that you killed a man."

"Yes."

Mr. Severson had no more questions, so Mr. Burns cross-examined.

"Mr. Wagner, can you give us the circumstances of the incident to which you pled guilty?"

"I was in a fight with the man, hit him and he fell over and struck his head on a table."

"Was it a fair fight?"

"Yes."

"Then why did you plead guilty? Surely, you knew that you could have easily avoided going to prison."

"Yes, sir, I knew that. I also knew that I had taken a life, even by accident. I felt that I should be punished for breaking God's commandment."

"Who was the man you killed?"

"Walt Emerson. The defendant's son."

His reply caused a stir in the courtroom.

Max was dismissed and returned to his seat. As soon as he sat, Amanda smiled at him and patted him on his hand.

Next, the defense called Jerome Emerson.

As Max knew he would, he claimed he had ridden into Burden to rescue his daughters. He pointed at Max and called him 'that nefarious sex-crazed lecher' and implied that Max had his way with his daughters every day since he held them in his house.

Max almost laughed at the accusation, knowing he hadn't been with any woman, ever.

Then Mr. Burns took over, and it wasn't pretty.

"Mr. Emerson, who told you of these misdeeds by Mr. Wagner?"

"It's generally known."

"So, even though you were living alone in a farm four miles from town, you heard about it."

"I got friends."

"I'm sure you do."

"Now, on the day of the shooting, you said you shot Mr. Wagner as he was running toward you in an effort to get to your daughters. Is that right?"

"Darned right. I could see the sex-crazed look in his eyes, but I was gonna stop him."

"After you shot Mr. Wagner, what did you tell him when he had you by the shirt."

"I didn't say nothin'."

"Mr. Emerson, you just said you did say something. Did you mean to say that you said nothing?"

"That's what I said."

"Did you not, when he confronted you and asked if you had murdered his father, did you not say that you hadn't murdered his father but wanted to kill him?"

That flustered Jerome as he remembered saying it but didn't think it would come out.

"I don't remember that. He's lying. He always lies. Ask anybody."

"On the contrary, Mr. Emerson. If a man is willing to go to prison for five years by being honest, I would think that his integrity is beyond question. Now, again I ask you. Did you say that you wanted to kill him?"

"Who knows what I said? He had me by the shirt and I was mad as a hornet's nest."

"So, you did say you wanted to kill him for what he did to your son. Did it make you angry that your son had died?"

Jerome lost all semblance of control and shouted, "You're damned right it made me mad! Five years ain't enough. He shoulda been hung for what he did!"

Mr. Burns calmly said, "No more questions."

Jerome didn't understand what he'd just done and scowled as he left the witness stand to take his seat next to his disbelieving attorney.

After Jerome was sitting down, Mr. Burns said, "Your honor, the prosecution would like to call a witness to rebut Mr. Emerson's claims about the treatment of his daughters."

"Go ahead."

He called Amanda to the stand, and the men in the jury were almost universally smitten by the pretty young woman.

"Mrs. Peters, you live at Mr. Wagner's home with Colleen and Patty Emerson. Is that correct?"

"I do."

"Why were you living there? You have a house in town."

"My late husband, Johann, abused me and I was afraid to go back. When my husband got into some trouble in town, he ran and hid. The marshal and Mr. Wagner came to my house to find him, and they could see I was in a bad way, so Mr. Wagner asked if I felt safe. When I told him I didn't, he offered to let me stay at his house with Colleen and Patty Emerson. He said that we could help each other, and we have."

"Does Mr. Wagner sleep in the house?"

"Oh, no. In fact, he's rarely there. We were commenting on it just yesterday that we'd never seen him for more than ten minutes. It's his house, yet he still knocks at the door. He never enters on his own because he said he didn't want to risk embarrassing us."

"Why were the Emerson sisters there?"

"Patty Emerson's husband, Joe Endicott, had beaten her so severely that she needed medical attention. Doctor McKenna, who examined her, said she needed a few days of rest away from her husband, so Mr. Wagner offered his house as a refuge. Her sister, Colleen Emerson, stayed to look after her, and I arrived the next day."

"Has Mr. Wagner ever made any advances to any of you?"

"He's never even touched us."

"No more questions."

MAX

Mr. Severson had been debating all along whether it was worthwhile to cross-examine Amanda. He could really antagonize the jury, but he had to try because her testimony had just convicted his client.

He rose and slowly approached Amanda, then asked, "Mrs. Peters, since you've been there, has Mr. Wagner given you or the other women gifts?"

"Yes."

"What kinds of gifts?"

"Clothes, horses, food, and all sorts of small things."

"He's given you all horses?"

"Yes."

"Why? To ingratiate himself? To win affection?"

"No. He said it would give each of us the freedom to go where we wanted to go when we wanted to go."

"What other gifts has he given you?"

"Things that no man had given any of us."

"Such as?"

"Compassion, security, and concern."

"It sounds like you're in love with Mr. Wagner. Is that true?"

"We all are. I think half of Burden's women are, including the married ones. The other half probably just haven't seen him yet."

The jury laughed, prompting a warning from the judge. The sad thing was that even the men on the jury could see the truth behind her response.

Mr. Severson knew he had lost when the jury laughed and said dejectedly, "Defense has no more questions."

Both sides presented their closing arguments and the trial went to the jury. They were out longer than the prosecutor expected, seventeen minutes, but when they did return, they found Jerome Emerson guilty of attempted murder. The judge sentenced him to twenty-five years in the Kansas State Prison.

As they were leaving, Max asked Mr. Burns if the farm could be deeded over to the sisters. He said he'd meet with the judge shortly and to come and see him in two hours.

Max escorted Amanda from the courtroom. She was clutching his right arm as they descended the courtroom steps.

Max smiled at her and said, "Amanda, you were magnificent. You had that jury eating out of your hand. How about if I treat for lunch?"

Amanda was practically glowing. She knew she had done well and was more than pleased by Max's praise as he escorted her to the diner, which was two steps up from Sunny's.

They had prime rib for lunch. It was perfect, and Amanda was still bouncing when, an hour later, they reentered the courthouse. When they met with Mr. Burns, he handed Max a court order, giving ownership of the Emerson farm to Colleen Emerson and Patty Endicott.

"Just have them take this to the land office and they'll take care of it."

"Thanks, Mr. Burns. You did a great job in there. By the way, just out of curiosity, what happened to your predecessor, Mr. Price?"

"He's in the state legislature now."

"Just wondering. Thanks again, Mr. Burns."

"Thank Mrs. Peters. She saved our bacon."

Amanda was still beaming when they finally stepped up on their horses and headed back to Burden.

———

They arrived a little later than expected, but it was worth the delay to await the judge's order that he had in his pocket.

They stepped down in the front of the house and tied the horses. Because Amanda was with him, she was able to just enter without knocking and Max followed her inside.

Colleen and Patty were in the parlor where they had been waiting anxiously since just after lunch and could tell by Amanda's grin that it was good news.

"Max? What happened?" asked Patty.

"Your father is on his way to the Kansas State Prison for the next twenty-five years and you have Amanda to thank. She personally blew up the defense's case against me. I could tell that a few of the jurors were buying Jerome's lies until Amanda shot them full of holes. She was incredible."

The sisters hugged Amanda and thanked her as Max took out the judge's order and said, "And you, Colleen and Patty, are now the owners of the Emerson farm."

Both sisters whipped around and looked at Max's smiling face as he held the order out to them.

Colleen was closest, so she took it and read the order.

"What does this mean?" she asked.

"You both need to go to the land office and show them that paper. They'll change the deed to both your names, then you are free to sell it."

"We can?" asked Patty.

"You can."

"When can we do this?"

"You could do it right now if you want to."

"Let's do it, Colleen. We might lose the paper." Patty said excitedly.

"Max, can you come along?" asked Colleen.

"I'd be honored."

"I'll wait here," said Amanda, feeling a little tired from all the excitement and the ride.

Max held the door for the sisters as they stepped outside. Once he closed the door and they reached the ground something happened that he couldn't have expected.

Patty reached over and took his left arm, which didn't surprise him, but when Colleen suddenly took his right arm, he was almost shocked. It took him a few seconds to start breathing again as he felt the pressure of her arm on his and didn't say a word but just enjoyed having her so close.

Colleen, on his right side, was more than enjoying it, she was thrilled. She was holding onto Max's arm and loving it. The strength and warmth she felt were like soothing blankets and wondered how in blazes she had ever avoided it before.

They arrived at the tiny land office ten minutes later. It was only slightly larger than the Western Union office and most of its space was for land files. Max held the door for the two women, then followed them inside.

"Good afternoon, Max. What can I do for you?"

"George, Colleen Emerson and Patty Endicott have just been given possession of the Emerson farm by Judge Adams. They need to have the title changed."

Patty handed the judicial order to the land clerk, which didn't faze him at all. He found the deed, made some entries, then notarized the change, handed them a copy, and told them to run a copy to the county courthouse when they had the opportunity.

"George, what's the status of taxes on the place?" Max asked.

"Glad you asked, Max. The taxes are overdue. Another four months and it'd be in default."

"How much is due?"

"$76.22"

Max pulled a wad of bills from his pocket and paid the taxes. After George wrote out a receipt and annotated the records, the trio left the office to return to the house.

Patty hung onto the deed as they left the office, and said, "Thank you for doing that, Max. We couldn't pay that."

"I know, Patty. I'd hate for you to lose the place after all you had to go through to get it."

"How do we sell it?" she asked.

"The bank has an officer who handles real estate, so I figure that you and Amanda can go over there tomorrow and put your places up for sale. Patty, you're going to have to wait until Joe passes."

"Where is he, anyway? Surely, he's not still at Doctor McKenna's any longer."

"I'll go ask. Why don't you both go home, and I'll swing by shortly?"

Patty replied, "Okay," as the sisters angled toward the house while Max headed for the doctor's office.

But before he left, Max smiled at Colleen who returned his smile and Max melted a bit. He wasn't sure how she would react to any serious contact, but at least she's made huge strides already, even though he didn't understand why.

Patty had noticed the sudden change as well and was ecstatic for her younger sister. She thought of the idea of being the 'old' sister as somewhat humorous. She had turned twenty, just two months earlier. Amanda was the oldest of the three and was almost Max's age at twenty-four.

Max popped up to the boardwalk in front of Doctor McKenna's and walked into his office, then sat down, knowing that the good doctor would know he had someone in his office. He showed up thirty seconds later.

"You haven't been shot or stabbed, have you? No cannonballs taking off your head yet?" Doctor McKenna asked.

"No, sir. Not today. I'm just curious as to the location of Joe Endicott. Patty was asking."

"Oh, I'm sorry. I should have told her. But for some reason, I've been busy. Joe passed away last night. I guess his injuries were even more severe than I expected. Johann must have damaged something else. He was buried this morning. I had the distinct impression that there would be no mourners."

"With reason, Doc."

"I understand completely. Are you going to tell her?"

"I think she'll be relieved."

"I would expect so. Is she going to sell the ranch, do you think?"

"I'm sure she is."

"Do you know how much she'd be asking?"

"My guess is that with the cattle, around five thousand dollars."

"How many head are on there?"

"She said around two hundred or so."

"That's a really good price, Max. The cattle alone would fetch four thousand."

"If they were all first-class animals, branded and castrated you'd be right. But the herd would probably only fetch about twenty-five hundred."

"That's still a great price. If I offered her five thousand in cash, do you think she'd sell?"

"Don't you want to go out and look at the place first, Doc?"

"I already have. It needs a little work, but I've been looking for a ranch that's close to town, and this is the first one that's come up. I know my Geraldine is anxious about having a bigger place and we'd like some privacy now that the children are on their own."

Max smiled, then asked, "Are you sure it's just privacy that you want? You're not thinking of giving up the scalpel and raising cattle, Doc?"

"No, sir. My beloved wife doesn't care for the smelly critters much either. I'll sell the cattle off, then we'll fix it up and just enjoy the free space and yes, the privacy. I don't think I'd enjoy castrating those big beasts, even with a scalpel."

Max laughed, then said, "I'll ask her then come back and let you know."

"Thanks, Max. Your next gunshot wound is on the house," he said as he smiled.

"You Irishmen have nasty, but funny streaks," he said as he grinned back.

He left the office and returned quickly to the house, knocked and Patty answered.

"Come on in, Max. Did you find out where he is?" she asked as she preceded Max into the parlor.

"I did. And you are not properly attired, Mrs. Endicott."

Patty looked down at her dress and asked, "What's wrong with it?"

"It's red, and it should be black. Your husband passed away last night and was buried this morning."

Patty was horrified by her own reaction. The man she married was dead and she wanted to jump for joy.

"Why didn't anyone tell us?" she asked.

"I've been keeping the doc busy lately."

"Oh. It's all right, though. I was expecting it."

"I also have some other news that you may not have been expecting."

"I hate to ask," Patty said as she looked at Max.

"You've just been offered five thousand dollars cash for your ranch."

Patty was stunned by that announcement and blinked twice before asking, "Say that again?"

"Doctor McKenna just asked me if you'd accept five thousand dollars for your ranch."

"He did? Really?"

"Yes, ma'am. He said if you accepted his offer, I needed to come back and tell him. What is your reply, Mrs. Endicott?"

"I think I'll accept his offer."

"A wise decision. Do you want to come over with me or go over later?"

"I'll come with you. I can't believe this! In one week, in just a few days, I've gone through so many wonderful changes."

"And you deserve all of them, Patty. Come along."

He offered Patty his arm and she hugged it closely as they left the house as Patty glanced back, giving one grinning look at her smiling sister.

"Is he going to raise cattle, Max?" she asked as they left the house.

"No, ma'am. He's going to sell the cattle and live there. He's going to fix it up, too."

"Wonderful. I didn't think those cattle were worth it."

"He's already looked the place over, so don't worry. He knows what he's getting."

"That's good."

There was still enough time in the day for Max to escort Patty and a jubilant Irish doctor to the land office, where he gave Patty a five-thousand-dollar draft, and the deed was transferred to Doctor Patrick J. and Geraldine M. McKenna.

Instead of going straight back, Max and Patty went to the bank. Joe had no account, so Patty opened an account and deposited the draft. She was now an independently wealthy woman. While there, they met with the real estate officer and told him that the Peters house and the Emerson farm were on the market as well. He told them that the farm would move quickly because it was so close to town. The house would probably sell for about nine hundred dollars. Patty signed the contract for the sale of the farm and Colleen would have to sign it as well. Amanda would stop by tomorrow for the contract on the sale of the house.

MAX

Max walked back with a floating Patty on his arm. She couldn't talk she was so rapturous. *She had five thousand dollars in the bank!* She no longer had a drunk, wife-beating husband to torture her, and she was staying in a beautiful house with her sister and a friend under the protection of the best man in the state.

They reached the house and Max held the door open for Patty and felt that this was private time for her and Colleen, so he closed the door and went back to his shop.

Inside the house, Patty walked in with a giant grin on her face as she said, "Colleen! It's gone! I have five thousand dollars in the bank. Isn't it wonderful?"

Colleen half-laughed and half-squealed as she embraced her sister.

"Colleen, we need to go to the bank, so you can sign a contract for the sale of the farm. Amanda, you need to come, too. You can sign one for the sale of the house."

"Then what will we do after the farm and house are sold?" asked Amanda.

The room suddenly went silent.

After almost thirty seconds, Patty finally replied, "I don't know."

———

Max reached the shop and then realized he had left the two horses at the house, so he pivoted and retraced his steps. When he reached the house, he found the two horses looking at him.

"Sorry. I forgot. Stupid human," he said as he unhitched the horses and led them away.

When he reached the corral, he found two bundles of hay and a large bag of oats waiting. He tied the horses and brought the hay and oats into the barn, then he brought the horses in and stripped and brushed them both. He gave them all some oats and spread some additional hay.

He walked back into his shop, took off his hat, and sat on his bed. It had been one hell of a day.

———

In Wichita, Mary Jones was making her preparations for tomorrow's trip to Burden. She wouldn't pack as much as she normally would, only taking a single travel bag with a spare dress and undergarments as well as a nightdress. She didn't bother taking any protection. She had a derringer but decided to leave it. Her best weapons for the battle she planned on waging had been present for quite some time and decided to use Carl as a backup.

After she found him, she told Carl she would be needing a ride to the train station tomorrow and told him that she would be arriving in Burden in the late morning and would go and see Max Wagner that afternoon in his shop. It wouldn't be good for him to be seen on the train with her, so she suggested he leave on his horse a little earlier. She'd check into the hotel to give him time to arrive before she described his shop and how to get around the back.

Carl smiled. This was a lot better than that fiasco with Stud Smith, and she would owe him. She would owe him a lot.

To Mary, it was a risk, but if it all worked out, it was a risk worth taking.

CHAPTER 10

Max slept in a bit the next morning, meaning he didn't get up at the crack of dawn. He was dressed by six-thirty, but there still wasn't any food in the place, so he walked down to Sunny's and had breakfast.

He was debating about getting more food when he got back to the shop as he swung the front doors wide. He may as well do something constructive, and with no outside repair orders, he decided to repair something of his own that had no useful purpose at all.

He had an old miniature model steam engine that he had been tinkering with before his interruption to do some heavy labor with the state. He pulled the toy from the shelf and did a quick inspection. It was in good condition, as it was made of brass, so he set it on his work bench and began to disassemble the working parts.

He felt good to be working on something, even if it was a toy. He had been doing nothing productive since he returned.

He leaned back and looked outside to get a read on the weather. It was going to be a warm one, bordering on hot. He wondered if he could ever just do what he enjoyed doing. With the sale of the ranch and the probable sale of the farm and house, the women were set financially. All the threats to them had been removed, so he was done with all of those issues.

As he worked on the little steam engine, he felt he had been more useful in prison than in Burden. He had fixed dozens if not hundreds of things. Since he'd returned, he hadn't fixed anything. He had broken a few things, though, including himself, and had another few days to wait before he got those sutures removed.

Then there was the Mary situation which added impetus to his decision to leave. If he wasn't here, she couldn't find him. Maybe she had given up after the aborted assassination attempt. It was a stupid reason to have him killed anyway.

There was no money or power involved in her motive. It was just pride, nothing more. Yet she failed to realize that sooner or later, something else would cause her ruination in society because of her determination to stay among those who judged others so harshly.

He sighed and returned to work.

———

Mary was waiting for Carl to pull the carriage around. Her train left in an hour and ten minutes, and the ride would only take ten minutes, but she didn't like to cut it close.

She heard the carriage and Carl stopped in front of the house. He clambered down from the driver's seat, picked up her travel bag, and opened the door for her to enter. Once she was in, he put the travel bag on the floor, closed the door, then climbed into his driver's perch and got the team moving.

Ten minutes later, he dropped her off at the station, carrying her travel bag for her. After getting her first-class ticket and leaving the travel bag with the agent, she went into the hotel restaurant to have some tea while Carl returned to the carriage and drove back to the house. He put the carriage away and climbed on his sorrel, which he'd saddled before leaving for the train station. He had his Winchester in the scabbard as he rode out of the large estate. It was forty-two miles to Burden and he could make it in six hours without a problem.

_____

Mary boarded the train and took her seat in first class. When the train pulled out on time at 10:20, Carl had already been on the road for almost an hour.

_____

Amanda, Colleen, and Patty had gone to the bank to take care of the paperwork, and after Colleen and Amanda signed the contracts, all three decided to visit Max in his shop and could see his open shop doors from the bank.

Max was hunched over the recently reassembled steam engine and was about to fire it up when the ladies arrived.

"Working hard, Mr. Wagner?" asked Patty, startling him.

He looked up into the bright light and said, "What are you three beautiful young ladies doing in a town like this? Shouldn't you all be in New York, Chicago, or St. Louis?"

"They don't have nice horses there. We thought we'd take a ride in a little while."

"They're your horses. You can take them wherever you want whenever you want."

"Will you come with us?" asked Colleen.

"I will, but I need to clean up some and none of you seem to be outfitted for riding."

"We'll go change while you clean up. What are you working on, anyway?" Colleen asked.

"A model steam engine. It should work now."

"What are you going to do with it?"

"Give it away, I guess."

"Could I have it?" asked Colleen, which surprised Max.

"I could never deny you anything, Colleen. I'll polish the brass a bit after I test it. So, off you go to get changed and I'll make myself presentable."

"You're always presentable, Max," smiled Amanda, as the women all started walking east.

Max set aside the toy and closed his front doors, then went to the living area where he washed and changed his shirt. He still needed to do his laundry.

He went outside and began saddling horses. It took him almost forty minutes, and his timing was pretty good as he saw the three young ladies walking down the alley towards him. Colleen was smiling, and he was glad that she seemed to be making progress. He still didn't know if she really wanted him as anything more than just a friend, so he wasn't going to force the issue. Besides, he'd be leaving soon.

"Your steeds await, my ladies," he announced when they were close.

They all mounted and decided to avoid the roads and travel cross country heading north. They were five miles out of town when the train arrived.

Mary stepped from the train onto the platform carrying her travel bag, then headed for the hotel.

Carl was still sixteen miles out when Mary checked in, then went to her room and changed out of her nice dress to a more comfortable riding outfit, even though she hadn't planned on doing any riding.

Max and the ladies had turned around and were heading back to town, and Colleen was riding next to Max, as she had on the way out as well. They had talked of many different things, from steam engines to the sale of the farm. She had laughed at many of his stories and Max enjoyed having her near and making her happy, but still had that now deeply instilled concern about getting too familiar.

They returned to the shop shortly before one o'clock and Max offered to handle the horses, but they all insisted on taking care of their own animals and Max was glad to hear it. After they had all brushed their horses down, the ladies were going to head home for lunch.

"Max, why don't you come and join us?" asked Amanda.

"I want to finish the steam engine for Colleen. You go ahead."

Colleen smiled at Max as she left. He returned her smile, then blew out his breath after she walked away with her sister and Amanda.

"Colleen," he thought as he watched her leave, "what am I going to do about you?"

He returned to his shop and began to polish the brass on the tiny steam engine.

———

Mary had gone to lunch at Sunny's, and no one recognized her. She was happy about it, too, but felt decidedly odd to be back in her hometown. She wasn't as uncomfortable as she thought she'd be, though. She was just appalled that she had lived in such plebian surroundings.

She left Sunny's, walked back to the hotel, and as she approached Max's shop, she noticed that the doors were open. *Should she approach him now? Why not?* Carl should be close to arrival now.

Max was still polishing the little engine when Mary looked in, and like all of the other women who saw him, she was stunned. *Was that really him?* He had changed immensely. He was still extremely handsome, but less boyish, and he was so much bigger. She felt flushed just looking at him and was almost ashamed of what she was going to do, but not enough to change her mind.

"Max, is that you?" she asked.

Max looked up and had no doubt who was talking to him, which put him immediately on guard.

"Hello, Mary. Come in and have a seat," he said calmly.

She stepped inside and sat in the chair on the other side of the workbench, then asked, "Max, can I close the doors? It's too bright."

Max stood and closed the doors, wondering about Mary's true reason for asking. He knew if she wanted to be alone with him, it wasn't for anything good, but he didn't think she'd be foolish enough to try and shoot him.

"I was going to come up and see you, Mary," he said as he resumed his seat.

"Why?"

MAX

"Having someone try and kill you is a good reason. I wanted to know why you felt it necessary to have me assassinated. I never told anyone about that night, Mary, except my mother, and she's dead now."

Mary was stunned that he knew she had been involved in the assassination attempt but managed to hide her shock.

"I didn't do that on purpose, Max. I really didn't. I told my driver, Carl, that you could cause me trouble, and he took it on his own. I'm sorry it happened. Really."

"Well, I'm willing to let that go, Mary. I always was. I just want to get on with my life and not have to worry about someone drygulching me. How did you know I was back, anyway?"

He suspected it was Johann but wanted to hear it from her.

"Johann Peters wired me. He and I had an affair about a year after he married Amanda. He's been trying to get me back into his bed ever since."

The admission surprised Max before he said, "Well, Johann is dead. I shot him as he sat in that corner waiting to drygulch me. I'm getting tired of being shot, Mary."

"That won't happen because of me, Max."

"Then we have no problem, Mary."

"Max, what do you do now?"

"Nothing much. I just got out of prison less than two weeks ago."

"Was it bad, Max?"

"Not for me. I signed up for hard labor and I worked every day except Sundays. I also fixed a lot of things."

"I should never have done that to you, Max. Can you forgive me?"

"I will, Mary. I don't hold grudges. Let me rephrase that. I don't hold grudges against people that cause injury to non-innocents. Hurt someone who is an innocent, and I won't forgive."

"Who are innocents?"

"Children, most women, and some men."

"You don't consider yourself an innocent?"

"No."

"Max, you may be the most innocent man I've ever known."

"I've killed four men, Mary. How can that be innocent?"

"Four?"

"Walt Emerson, who was a perverted bastard, his even more perverse father, your assassin, Stud Smith, and Johann Peters."

"Why do you say that about Walt?"

"He spied on his sisters and even began groping them when he could."

"If I had known that, I never would have tried him."

"Why did you do that, Mary? Walt Emerson was nothing. You could have had anyone."

She sighed and answered, "He was always available. It was pretty stupid, I guess."

"Are you happy now, Mary?"

"Honestly? I'm not sure. I'm pretty sure my husband is having an affair with his secretary, Clara Crenshaw."

"Is he stupid or just blind?"

She laughed and said, "Maybe both. She is cute, though."

"If all he wants is cute, why doesn't he get a puppy?"

Mary really laughed, then asked, "Max, are you married?"

"No."

"Girlfriend?"

"Good question. Yes and no."

"That's a very cryptic answer."

"It's a very puzzling situation."

"Want to talk about it?"

"Not really. I can't even explain it to myself."

"So, what are you going to do? Are you staying here?"

"I don't think so. I don't feel like I have anything here anymore. My parents are dead."

"I didn't know that."

"So, Mary, what will you be doing?" he asked.

"I'll go back to Wichita and my husband and I will pretend to be happily married and we'll go to parties and the opera."

"It sounds like the life that you always wanted, Mary."

"It does, doesn't it. I have so many nice dresses and gowns and I don't have to cook or do any housework. It's just so empty. I don't get any satisfaction from anything. I feel like my friends aren't really friends, they're just people that I know."

"It is funny that way, isn't it, Mary? We make one or two wrong decisions early in our lives and we can never go back and change them."

"You pled guilty to manslaughter instead of telling anyone that I was there. Why didn't you at least ask for a trial?"

"I was guilty, Mary. I killed Walt Emerson. I paid my penalty and that part of my life is over. I don't regret that decision."

"I should have asked you, Max."

"Asked me what?"

"To satisfy me. If I had offered myself to you, would you have accepted?"

He looked at her for a second before replying, "Yes."

"Would you accept the offer now?" she asked as she slid her hand to his thigh.

"No."

"What's changed, Max. Am I not attractive enough anymore?"

"You're more than attractive enough. It's just that things have changed."

"I heard you have three young women in your house. Is that why?"

"Partly, but not for the reason you think."

"What reason do you think I have?"

"You think I'm bedding one or all of them?"

"Aren't you?"

"If I told you the answer, you'd probably laugh yourself silly."

"No, I wouldn't. Really, Max, I wouldn't laugh."

"I've never been with a woman before."

She didn't laugh, but she was stunned.

"Max, you can't be serious. A man like you? The girls were ready to jump into your bed in school."

"I was too naïve, Mary. I thought you only did that with a girl you really loved. By the time I found out differently, I was in prison. I've only been out for a couple of weeks and those women in the house have all been abused by men they trusted. I've never done anything to make them uncomfortable."

Mary simply didn't know how to respond, so after a few seconds of silence, Max asked, "How long are you going to be in town, Mary?"

"Just a day or two. I need to give my husband warning if I'm coming back so he can hide Miss Crenshaw."

"Are you staying at the hotel?"

"Room #3. What are you working on?"

"A toy steam engine. I'm just getting ready to fire it up and test it."

"That sounds like fun. Can I watch?"

Max smiled, knowing she had to stretch this out for some reason, he just didn't know why. His nerves were already on edge as he tried to fathom her reason.

"Sure. Let me add some water. It uses kerosene to heat up the water."

"Does it have a steam whistle like a train?"

"Yes, ma'am."

Surprisingly, Mary was enjoying herself with Max but wondered where Carl was. She stood up and walked to his side of the table as he poured the water into the tank and closed it off. Then he added some kerosene to the small firebox and set it on fire.

"Now we wait until the steam builds up," he said as he smiled at her.

"This is fun, Max. I'm actually having fun."

"Good."

Mary shouldn't have worried about Carl as he rode into town just as the steam engine was building up pressure. Carl spotted Max's shop and turned between the buildings to access the alley behind his shop. He saw the corral, tied his horse to the top rail, and stepped down, then pulled his Colt and cocked the hammer before pulling the back door open slowly.

Inside the shop, the little engine began turning and Mary giggled at the sight. Max went to the street side of the table to adjust the steam pressure just as Carl stepped into the room.

As soon as Max saw him, he understood the reason for Mary's delaying tactics and now had a bigger problem than he could have expected as he saw the cocked hammer on Carl's pistol.

When Mary saw Carl approaching with his Colt, she relaxed and then winked at him to let him know the show was on.

"Carl, what are you doing here?" she demanded in apparent shock.

"Keeping you from making a fool of yourself with this bastard. Get away from him, Mary."

"You do not order me around, Carl. Put away your gun. Mr. Wagner is not a threat. Get on your horse and leave."

"You don't tell me what to do, Mary. I'm telling you to get out of the way."

Mary moved slowly to her left, away from Max.

"You're a dead man, Wagner. Me and Mary get along. Do you understand?"

"You've got to be kidding, Carl. You have to be an idiot. You probably don't even know what this is all about, do you?" Max replied as he put his hands on opposite sides of the little chugging steam engine.

"What's what all about?"

"The reason why Mary wants you to kill me. I already killed your friend Stud Smith, which you have to admit was a silly name for such a tiny man."

Carl wanted to know why Mary thought Wagner might cause her trouble, so he asked, "What do you think it is?"

Max said, "The reason is…", then suddenly grabbed the steam engine and tossed it into the air at Carl, who instinctively reached with his bare hand to either deflect or catch the steaming missile, but as he was swiping at the heavy toy, Max was reaching into his pocket and pulling out his Remington derringer.

Carl caught the steam engine to knock it away, but it was a lot heavier than he expected and he just knocked it into his thigh, then his finger jerked the trigger and fired as the steam spewed boiling water scalding his chest and leg as it dropped. Max fired just a second later with his small pistol. Carl's .44 caught Max in the left thigh, but Max's .41 caliber round hit Carl just to the left center of his chest before both men collapsed to the ground.

Down the street, Emil bolted from his chair in his office and raced outside. Mary just stood, backing away as she watched.

Max stood, his leg bleeding heavily, as he swung the outer doors open again just as Emil arrived.

Emil saw Max with his left leg bleeding heavily, and Carl on the ground with a bullet to his chest. He hadn't noticed Mary standing off to the side in the darkened workshop.

"Max, what happened?"

"He drew a gun on me and had the hammer cocked, so I tossed the steam engine at him and he fired. I had my derringer out and fired a little while later. I caught his round in my left thigh. I'm not sure where I hit him."

"You stay here. I'll go and get the doc."

Emil trotted down away to Dr. McKenna's office and Mary stepped out of the shadows once he was gone and walked up to Max, ignoring her lifeless driver.

"Max, what can I do to help?" she asked.

"Nothing much, really. The doc's going to have to dig the slug out."

"Max, I hate to ask," she began.

Max interrupted, saying, "You weren't here, Mary. Go back to your hotel room. Use the alley through the shop, then get out of town."

"Thank you, Max," she said, before scurrying back through the shop and disappearing out the back.

All her playacting had come in handy, Mary thought as she hurried along the alleyway, not realizing that Max had known all along.

"Max, you wonderful, handsome, but incredibly naïve man," she whispered to herself.

———

Doctor McKenna came running down the street with his black bag. Emil was with him and they both looked at Carl first.

"No use spending time with this one, Doc."

Doctor McKenna turned to Max and asked, "Where's this one, Max?"

"Left thigh. This one isn't as easy as the others, Doc."

"Let me take a look," he said as he ripped away Max's pants and began examining the wound.

Max looked over toward Carl, but not at Carl, then said, "Emil, be careful with that steam engine. It's really hot. Use a cloth to put it flat on the ground and then you can pick it up by the wooden base."

The marshal looked for a cloth but wound up using Carl's Stetson to set it back to its base, then picked it up and returned it to Max's worktable.

"How's it look, Doc?" asked the marshal.

"Like a .44 caliber gunshot wound to the thigh. The good news is that it didn't hit the femoral artery. It passed through the outside of the muscle, so I'll have to sew up both entrance and exit wounds."

"Whatever you think is right, Doc. You want to do it here?"

"Why not?" he replied as he picked up his black bag.

Max lay on the workshop table next to the still hot steam engine as Dr. McKenna removed some alcohol from his bag and cleaned the wound. Max ground his teeth, knowing better than to complain. He would only be wounded further by the Irishman's wit.

As the doctor began suturing the wound, he said, "I think this is a record, Max. You've been shot three times now in about a week. Was this just to take advantage of my offer for free services for your next gunshot wound?"

"It was an offer I couldn't refuse, Doc."

The doctor held off for a second to laugh, then he resumed suturing.

"This is going to be really sore for a while, Max."

"I know."

"Who was he, Max?" asked Emil.

"He's Mary's driver, Carl something-or-other. She's in the hotel. She stopped by to warn me about him. I think he's got an obsession with her. She came in on the train and he rode in from Wichita on that roan you can see through the back door."

"What is Mary doing here?" he asked.

"She came to apologize. It seems that she just mentioned that she was worried about me to Carl, and he sent Stud Smith after me without her knowledge."

"That's good to hear. I hate to think Mary would do that."

The doctor finished his suturing and Max asked, "Can I walk on this thing, Doc?"

"If you can put up with the pain."

"I need to go and tell Mary that I shot her driver. I don't know if she'll be mad at me or him."

"Better you than me," said Emil.

The doctor closed his bag, stood up, and said, "No more, Max."

"Trust me, Doc, I really don't want this to happen anymore either."

"Who's paying for this burial, Max?"

"I'll pay for it if he doesn't have enough cash on him. Tell John to see me. I should be back at my shop by then."

"Okay, Max. Do you want the horse?"

"No. I'll ask Mary what she wants to do with it."

"Let me know."

"I will, Emil. Thanks for getting here so fast. You too, Doc."

The marshal headed to Lambert's Mortuary to tell John about another new customer in the street in front of Max's shop and to see Max for payment if necessary. As it turned out, Carl had more than enough to cover his own burial and Doctor McKenna returned to his normally docile practice.

Max started walking to the hotel, his leg much more than stiff. It throbbed pretty badly but he made it to the hotel and headed for room three and tapped on the door.

Mary opened it, saw Max, and waved him in, closing the door behind him.

"How's Carl?"

"He's dead, Mary."

"I suppose I should be upset, but I'm not. He was getting scary."

"What I told the marshal was that you had arrived in town to apologize to me for Carl taking what you said out of context and dispatching Stud Smith on his own. I also said that you had warned me about Carl because he had become obsessive about you. It helped that Carl rode in while you took the train. So, you're in the clear. Let's not make this a habit, Mary."

"How are you, Max?"

"I'll live. I'd better head back. Oh. Before I go, I need to know what you want to do with his horse."

"I don't want it."

"Alright, I'll see who has a use for it."

"How much to bury him, Max?"

"Don't worry about it."

Max opened the door, shuffled out, then headed back out through the lobby and down the street to his shop and noticed that John had already removed the body. The horse was still there, though, so he limped over to the horse and rubbed his neck.

"Boy, you had one screwed-up owner. Let's see if we can do better for you."

He took the horse's reins and walked him into his corral. It would be overcrowded for a day, but they would have to live with it.

He unsaddled the roan and got him into the corral with some effort. Lugging the saddle into the barn wasn't a treat, either.

He finally returned to his shop. The doors were still wide open, so he walked out front and intended to close the doors, but instead sat at his worktable to finish Colleen's steam engine. It hadn't been damaged at all, but it had to be cleaned and polished again.

He was working on the steam engine as he reviewed the situation with Mary. There was no doubt that Carl was acting on her orders. She'd delayed him enough to let Carl get there. He surely wouldn't have found his shop without asking around. As soon as he saw Carl, he knew that Mary was behind it. He'd behaved like she was innocent because he knew that with Carl dead, she'd be able to pass the same story to a jury that she'd tried to use on him.

If he was going to stop Mary and pay her back for two attempts on his life, he had to do it using her own type of weapons, and that would mean that trip to Wichita would be even more urgent.

He finished the steam engine and closed the doors, then walked into his living area and closed the back door. He removed his pants and shirt and looked at himself. Sutures everywhere. *He was safer in the damned prison!*

He pulled on a new pair of pants and a new shirt, taking the cash out of his ruined pants pocket and stuffing it into his new pants pocket. He hobbled into the workroom and wrote a note and put it next to the steam engine, then turned and picked up his canteen before going back outside and saddled Mars. He made sure his bedroll was in place before he climbed up awkwardly. Once he was in the saddle, he turned Mars and rode north across the rolling hills. His leg still throbbed, but he was moving, and he needed to get away.

He rode for over an hour and found a small hill, then carefully stepped down, led Mars to a small stream, then after he'd had enough to drink, hitched him to a good-sized bush, laid out his bedroll, then carefully lowered himself to its soft surface.

———

Mary wasn't sure about what to do. Carl had almost killed Max, but Max had survived, and Carl hadn't. She couldn't believe that Max had just covered for her again. He may be a hell of a man, but he still trusted people too much.

She needed to get out of here, but the next train to Wichita wasn't till morning, so she would stay in her room till then.

———

Word finally filtered to the ladies about the shooting two hours later and they quickly bustled from the house together to see how Max was. When they arrived, they found his shop doors closed, but not locked and Amanda pulled the door open.

"Max?" she asked as she stared into the quiet darkness.

As Patty and Amanda walked back to his living area, Colleen walked up to his workbench and found the shining steam engine and the note.

Colleen:

Your steam engine is done. I wish I could fix other things so easily.

Max

Colleen clutched the note to her chest as she looked down at the small machine that was much more than a toy now.

"Look at this," said Patty as she held up his damaged and bloody pants.

"Where did he go?" asked Amanda.

"He shouldn't have gone anywhere with that wound," answered Patty.

They walked outside and saw the new roan but the absence of Mars.

"Let's go and talk to the marshal again," said Amanda.

The three women walked out the double doors and headed to Marshal Becker's office.

———

Emil was just getting settled down when the door opened, and the three women entered.

"Emil, what happened? We know that Max has been shot, but we don't know what happened."

Emil sighed and said, "Mary Preston showed up to apologize for the assassination attempt and warned him about her driver. Some guy named Carl. Anyway, the man shows up and draws on Max while he was running that little steam engine. Max threw the engine at him as he fired, and Max drew his derringer and shot him. Carl's shot got him in the left thigh."

"And he's riding around with another bullet wound?" asked a startled Amanda.

Emil was surprised and asked, "Where did he go?"

"We don't know. That's why we came here."

"Well, I don't know, either."

"Where is Mary?" Colleen asked.

"She's in the hotel."

Without another word, the three women left the marshal's office, marched across the street to the hotel, and strode up to the desk.

"Katie, we need to see Mary Preston. She just got in this afternoon."

"She's in room three," Katie replied.

They turned in formation, stepped smartly to room three and Amanda tapped on the door.

Mary made a minor mistake when, as she opened the door, said, "Max?"

"No. Hello, Mary," said Amanda as she glared at her.

"Oh. Hello, Amanda. Come in, please."

They walked in and turned as Mary closed the door.

Amanda said, "What the hell is going on, Mary? We just talked to the marshal and he gave us some nonsense about you coming down here to apologize to Max and your driver just deciding to shoot Max on his own."

"I did come to apologize to Max. I really did. Carl followed on his horse and threatened Max. The only real difference was that I was there when Carl shot him. I didn't even have to ask Max to cover for me. He just did."

Each of the women was stunned that Max had fallen for her lies so readily again, but their anger was for Mary, not Max.

"So, why did he leave?" Patty asked.

"He's gone?"

"His horse is gone and he's not around, so I'd say so."

"Then there's nothing we can do about anything," Mary said.

Amanda said, "We'll go back to the house. Maybe he'll stop by."

Without a word to Mary, Amanda, Patty, and Colleen, turned, left the room, then the hotel, and returned to the house.

————

Max was stretched out on his bedroll. After lying there for almost an hour he finally knew exactly how he could manage to finally stop Mary, and ironically, it had been Mary who had given him the answer.

He stood awkwardly, rolled up his sleeping bag and set it in place, and tied it down, then unhitched Mars and mounted, but instead of heading south back to Burden, he rode north. He estimated he was only thirty miles from Wichita or about four hours at a good pace, and that would put him in the city around nine o'clock tonight. He'd get something to eat and then a room. He'd get a shave and a haircut in the morning, and then he'd find Charles Jones, the banker, who he hoped really was enamored of his secretary as Mary had claimed.

————

His timing wasn't off by much. He hit the streets of Wichita a little after nine o'clock, stopped at a café, had something to eat, and checked into the Railway Hotel, leaving Mars with the hotel's livery.

MAX

He went to his room, cleaned up, and after undressing, he laid down on the bed and fell asleep easily, despite the pain from all his recent wounds, even his throbbing thigh. His plan for revenge was set in his mind and that peace made the pain less noticeable.

CHAPTER 11

Max woke up to a throbbing left thigh and didn't have to recall why it hurt. He got out of bed and limped to the washroom, and then opened the door and gimped his way to the bathroom at the end of the hallway where he took care of his morning needs. After he was clean, he put on his gunbelt and left the room, stopped at the hotel restaurant, and had breakfast before checking out. He picked up Mars and rode the streets in search of a barber shop, finding a nice establishment just two blocks away. He was their first customer of the day and was soon looking presentable, meaning that it was time to find Charles Jones. He didn't know which of the four banks was his, so he first went to the largest bank in town, the First National.

After entering the bank, he stepped up to a clerk and said, "Excuse me, but I need to speak to Charles Jones."

"Mr. Jones' office is on the second floor."

"Thank you."

As he gimped up the stairs to the second floor, Max couldn't believe his luck in finding him so quickly. Mr. Jones' office was also easy to find, as his name was painted on the window. He opened the door and saw Miss Crenshaw, the young woman that Mary had told him was having an affair with her husband. He could understand it, too. There was no nameplate on her desk, so he had an advantage.

"Can I help you, sir?" she asked with a big smile on her face.

For once, Max appreciated it, as he asked, "Miss Crenshaw, I believe?"

She held the giant smile, "Why, yes. Do I know you? I'm sure if I'd met you, I'd remember."

"No, I haven't had the honor, miss. My name is Max Wagner. I was wondering if I could take a few minutes of Mr. Jones' time. It concerns his wife, who is down in Burden at the moment."

"Let me go and ask him. Have a seat, please."

"Thank you."

She smiled once more and entered the prestigious office of Mr. Charles Jones, then returned a few seconds later.

"Go right in, Mr. Wagner."

"Thank you, Clara," he answered, sending a shiver down her spine.

Charles Jones was standing when Max entered and didn't seem flustered by the two pistols Max was wearing. High society or not, Charles Jones had sand, Max thought.

He shook Max's hand and offered him a seat.

Max sat, and Mr. Jones asked, "Miss Crenshaw said that you needed to talk to me about my wife."

"Yes, sir. I've known your wife, Mary for quite some time, and you and I both share something in common. She has played us both for a fool. The time she did it to me resulted in my spending five years in the Kansas State Prison. She tried a second time yesterday while she was in Burden, which resulted in my taking a .44 caliber slug in my left thigh and shooting your driver, Carl, who died as a result. Mary skated through the first event unscathed, and I have no doubt that she believes that she has this time as well. She'll probably be returning on the train in a couple of hours."

Charles Jones sat there completely shocked. He knew Mary had secrets, *but this?* The odd thing was that the man seemed totally believable.

"Aside from your story, do you have any evidence?"

"Other than the fresh bullet wounds in my leg, none whatsoever. One thing she did tell me yesterday is that she thinks you're having an affair with Clara Crenshaw."

Another shocking revelation, and one that changed his view of the stranger sitting before him.

"Is this an attempt at blackmail?" he asked.

"No, sir. If you want proof, just ask Mary how her trip went. Look into her eyes. She's a good liar, but she wouldn't suspect that you have any idea what happened. If you ask her where Carl is, she'll lie. She was standing there as we exchanged gunfire. I went to her hotel room and told her about his death, and she didn't bat an eye."

"Why would she do such a thing?" he asked, still astonished at the news.

"To keep me quiet. She married you so she could fulfill her dream of living in the upper crust of society. Five years ago, she was involved in an incident that she knew if I told anyone, would be her ruin. Now, I have no intention of telling anyone other than you, so if you decide to let it go, then so be it."

"What was the story?"

Max told him about the stagecoach office episode as he listened attentively and didn't interrupt.

When Max finished, Mr. Jones leaned back and said, "When I first met her, I was smitten by her looks and figure. She invited me to her bed and then a month later, said she was with child. So, despite my parents' objections, we were married. A month later, she said she had made a mistake and she had just missed her monthly. I wondered if she had just set me up, and now it's all making sense. Do you mind if I call you Max?"

"Not at all."

"Call me Charlie, then. No one calls me that, not even Mary. She says it's degrading, but I like it myself. I'm going to take your advice. I'm going to very casually ask about her trip and then about what happened to Carl. This whole thing would cause an enormous scandal in the family, though."

"I'll tell you something else. She offered herself to me yesterday. I don't know if it was just part of her act to get me to trust her or not. Carl made it sound like he had been with her, and I imagine you know some lawyers of some quality. If you find what I say to be true, I'd confront her and tell her you will divorce her for adultery with Carl.

"If she agrees to a quiet divorce, you could settle for some cash to make her go away. Have her sign a non-disclosure agreement. If she refuses, and she may threaten to expose the whole sordid tale to try to get you to leave the status quo, tell her that I know what she did and I'm not happy with her. Imply that if she doesn't agree, you'll give me free rein."

Charlie smiled as he said, "So, a double-pronged threat that would give her no options. If I allowed her to stay, she'd be afraid of what you would do. If she agrees to the divorce, at least she'll get something."

"There you go."

A grinning banker asked, "Are you staying in town?"

"I can, at least for a day."

"Where are you staying?"

"I was at the Railway Hotel last night."

"Hold on."

He stood, walked to the door, and opened it.

"Miss Crenshaw, could you let the Metropolitan know that Mr. Wagner will be staying in my suite tonight?"

"Yes, Mr. Jones."

"Thank you, Clara."

He closed the door and returned to his seat.

"Just go to the Metropolitan and tell the desk clerk your name. He'll set you up in my suite."

"I appreciate it."

"I'll drop by the hotel as soon as I find out what her reaction is," Charlie said.

"I'll look forward to your arrival," Max said as he rose, and they shook hands.

Max left the office and smiled at Miss Crenshaw as he passed while she beamed back at him. Mary had been right about one thing; Miss Clara Crenshaw was most assuredly cute.

MAX

He left the bank and saw the Metropolitan across the street, but first decided to get some more clothes while he was here.

He stepped up on Mars and rode around until he found a men's clothing store, then slowly dismounted, tied Mars, and walked inside. Their selection was vast, so he had no problem finding four new shirts and three more pairs of pants. He bought a new belt and some new underpants as well, then added a new jacket and two more vests. After paying for his order, he took the bag outside and rode to a leather shop where he bought a nice leather travel bag. Then, he went to the one store he had wanted to visit first…the gun shop.

He was mesmerized by the weapons on display, but he wanted one that was a bit more common. He found a Webley Bulldog and a matching shoulder holster and had to buy another box of .44 cartridges as his ammunition was all back at the shop. He could have used the rounds on his gun belt but didn't like using the emergency cartridges.

He took his gun purchases, left the shop, put them into his saddlebags, and rode to the Metropolitan. He left his horse and Winchester with the livery and walked into the fancy hotel. The clerk looked at the large man sporting two pistols, a set of saddlebags, and two shopping bags with some misgivings, but when he gave his name, his attitude changed dramatically as he gave him the key to room 410, Mr. Jones' suite.

Max got there with some difficulty. Four flights on a leg that had been sutured a day earlier wasn't a good idea. He found the room, if one could call it that, and opened the door. It was a bit much for Max to take in as he closed the door behind him. It was enormous, with a large bed, a full sitting area, and even a full bathroom with a bath with hot and cold running water, so Max figured it was time to get cleaned up.

———

Mary stepped off the train as Max was stepping into the room. She had no driver, so she had to hire a carriage to take her home. She was emotionally drained as she walked into the house. It had been such a close call. If Max hadn't covered for her, there would have been questions, too many questions, but the naïve child had been fooled again. She smiled until she opened the door and found Charles walking toward her. *What was he doing home so early?*

"Welcome home, sweetheart. How was your trip?" he asked.

She smiled at him and replied, "Fine. I took care of the issue faster than I thought. I just had to sign two papers and it was dealt with."

"Wonderful. I just wanted to let you know that we have been asked to a special afternoon luncheon with the governor, and I was hoping you'd make it back in time."

"The governor? Really?" she replied, excited by the prospect.

"Yes, my love. I've been looking for Carl to drive us there, but I can't find him anywhere. He didn't go with you to Burden, did he? That makes no sense because the carriage is still here."

"No, of course, he didn't. There would be no reason for him to be there."

"That's what I thought. Some marshal down in Burden wired and asked if we had an employee by that name working for us. It seems that the Carl he was asking about was involved in a gunfight with a local man. I was going to wire him back and tell him that there was no reason for his being there, but then I went looking for him to be sure, and I couldn't find him anywhere."

Mary was desperately searching for a plausible reason, then said, "I wonder if he followed me. You know, I didn't want to bring this up, but he's been getting a bit obsessive about me lately and I was beginning to fear for my safety."

"We can't have that. I'll just have to let him go, assuming we can find him."

Mary then tentatively asked, "Did the marshal say anything else about the man down in Burden?"

"Yes, he did. He said the man had been shot in the shootout."

"That's horrible. I didn't hear any shooting while I was down there."

"No one was talking about it at all?"

"Not a soul."

"That's odd. Someone reported that you were seen nearby. That's why the marshal asked about his being an employee."

"It must have been someone else."

"Most likely. Max was probably mistaken," he said, watching for her reaction.

And Mary most assuredly did have a reaction, and it wasn't a good one.

Mary was rendered momentarily speechless as her eyes darted to the floor, and she said, "Max? I have never heard the name before."

"But you grew up there. Surely, you've heard the story of Max Wagner. It's very well known in legal circles."

Mary felt trapped, but said, "Oh. Yes. I had forgotten about him. That was years ago, after all."

"He seemed to be a strange young man. Imagine serving five years in prison for saving some young woman's virtue."

Now, Mary was panicking inside as she asked, "Where did you hear that story?"

"It's common knowledge. The marshal found a note in the dead man's shirt pocket arranging a rendezvous and there was a lilac scent in the room when the doctor arrived. It's a fascinating story."

She didn't know about the note. *What an idiot Walt was!*

"It sounds like it. I need to go and rest, Charles. It's been a long day."

"Aren't you coming to the governor's banquet? I'm sure he'd like to meet you."

"Normally, I wouldn't trade it for the world, but right now I'm tired and not feeling well."

"The guest of honor is going to be none other than Max Wagner himself. He just arrived this morning," Charlie said using each word as a dagger.

Mary almost fainted, then thought that maybe it would have been better if she had.

She asked nervously, "Why would he be the guest of honor? He's a convicted killer."

"That's just it. He was never convicted, he pled guilty and was never tried. Once the story got out about the attempted rape, his honorable behavior came to the attention of the governor who gave him a pardon."

"But he can't be here! He was shot yesterday!" she exclaimed.

Oops.

"How do you know that, Mary?" Charlie asked as he stared at his wife.

"I heard someone talking about it," she said, fumbling desperately for a way out of her self-created trap.

"But you just said you didn't even hear about the shooting."

"I...I..., never mind. I just heard. Now, I'm going upstairs," she said as she began to turn.

Charlie stopped her by grabbing her shoulders and saying, "No, Mary, you are not. You are coming with me into the sitting room. We are going to talk about what happened while you were in Burden. Both before we were married and yesterday."

Mary knew she was done. *How had he found out?*

She quietly followed Charles into the sitting room where his attorney, Francis Masterson, was waiting.

They sat and discussed the terms of a divorce and Charles never had to bring up Max's secondary offer. Mary had been beaten at her own game and simply accepted the offer of a five-thousand-dollar settlement and signed a non-disclosure agreement. She agreed to be the adulterer in the divorce, as long as it was sealed, which suited them both.

She was allowed to keep all of her clothing, but none of her jewelry. She was given a draft for the money and could stay in the house for another week until the divorce was final. Where she went after that was up to her.

She retired to her bedroom. She didn't cry, but she was emotionally drained. But as she lay down, she made plans to go to Kansas City. Five thousand dollars was a good amount of money, she still had plenty of nice clothes and could probably find some nice young heir. She smiled. She was still young and pretty, so it should be easy.

After she went upstairs, Charles shook hands with his attorney, then went outside had his groom saddle his horse, and rode to the Metropolitan.

Max had bathed and shaved. His wound was looking acceptable, as far as day-old .44 caliber wounds went, and the hot bath seemed to help with his mobility.

As pleased as he was with his recovery, he was much more pleased with the meeting with Charlie Jones and wondered how his meeting with Mary had gone.

He had dressed in some new underwear, pants, shirt, and a vest and had even donned the now-loaded Webley and shoulder holster before he put on his jacket. He hadn't had clothes that fit this well in years, certainly not in the past five years.

He was getting ready to go out and buy a book to read when there was a knock on the door.

After hobbling to the door, he opened it and found a grinning Charlie Jones and waved him inside, knowing that Mary had acquiesced.

As soon as Charlie entered, Max closed the door.

Charlie exclaimed, "She caved in, Max! Everything you said was true. You should have seen her face!"

"I wish I had. It would almost have been worth spending five years in prison."

"We were both fools, Max. At least I didn't have to get shot as a result. Speaking of which, my attorney said that you could sue us for what Carl did."

"I would never do that, Charlie. I don't play games."

"I didn't say you would. I'm just saying that my attorney is worried about a possible lawsuit and a lot of this coming out. So, he suggested that we get a written non-disclosure agreement from you, including a waiver of all claims."

"I'll sign it to keep the lawyer happy, Charlie, but I wouldn't have said anything anyway."

"Here's the agreement."

Max signed it without reading and blew in it until it was dry before handing it back to Charlie.

"And here's your settlement," he said, holding out a bank draft.

"For what?" Max asked.

"Didn't you read that agreement? It said that in consideration of payment of ten thousand dollars, you would agree not to talk about what happened or sue us."

"*What?*" he asked incredulously, before saying, "No, Charlie, that's unnecessary. You keep your money."

"It's just business, Max. Trust me, the money isn't important to me at all. Being free of Mary is. I wonder how long before she thought she could just bump me off and be the rich widow."

Max then accepted the draft and slid it into his jacket pocket before saying, "Don't underestimate her, Charlie. But unless I miss my guess, she'll head off and find some other rich man to swindle."

"That's his problem. By the way, Clara was very impressed with you. She said if she wasn't already smitten with me, she'd be setting her cap for you."

"I'm already taken, Charlie. Sort of."

"I'd love to hear the story, Max, but I'm off to see Clara and give her the good news."

"Congratulations to you both, Charlie."

He shook Max's hand and closed the door as he left. Max pulled out the draft and stared at it. It was a very unexpected benefit.

He left the room and went down to the hotel restaurant and had a very expensive lunch. Two dollars. *Who spends two dollars for a lunch?*

He did go and buy a book to spend the rest of the afternoon and evening. Then, he stopped in a jewelry store, found what he wanted, and paid for his order before he returned and had dinner.

He was getting physically and emotionally exhausted when he undressed and climbed into the massive bed. The mattress was a bit too soft, but he survived.

———

The next morning, he dressed and put on his three pistols. His new jacket covered the two pistols mostly, so he didn't seem overly armed. He went downstairs, checked out, had his breakfast, and when he finished, took Mars out of the livery and rode him to the train station.

By ten o'clock, he was on his way back to Burden.

———

The women were all sitting in the sitting area. Amanda had been delegated to go and see if Max had returned and came back with no good news. Max and Mars were both still missing.

"Where do you think he went? His things are still there," asked Amanda.

Colleen was absent-mindedly spinning a wheel on her steam engine that was now sitting on the table.

"I hope he's not gone for good. Is this all my fault?" she asked quietly.

"No, Colleen. It's not. This was Mary's fault, and no one else's. She made him look foolish again and he knows it."

"But I was the one who made him want to leave, Patty. I've pushed him away too often, and now he might not come back because of me."

"He'll come back. He has to. He's left too many things unsettled. You'll see."

The train whistle sounded in the distance, but none of them paid any attention. Max would be riding in, not taking the train.

The train pulled into the station and Max waited until it was stopped. He wasn't that spry yet. He stepped down carefully, walked across the platform to the stock corral and picked up

Mars, then put his new leather travel bag's strap over the saddle horn and carefully mounted. He headed to the bank to get rid of the massive draft, and after arriving, stepped down, tied off Mars, and walked inside. He just moseyed up to the teller window and said he needed to make a deposit and slid the draft to the cashier.

The man almost got away with being nonchalant about a ten-thousand-dollar draft, but when he tried to say, "Let me give you a receipt and new balance', it came out, "Let me give you a balance and a new receipt."

Max didn't comment, but he took the receipt and his new balance sheet of $19,647.55.

He left the bank and slowly stepped up on Mars. He needed to see the ladies, so he set Mars to a medium trot and arrived outside the house a minute later.

Amanda heard a horse, looked out the window, and shouted, "It's Max!"

He tied up Mars and was walking up the stairs and was bowled over by all three women. Even Colleen had a grip on him.

"Ladies, if you'll let me come in the house, I'll explain where I've been in the last day or so."

It was Amanda and Colleen who clutched his arms as he was escorted into the house where they sat him down on the couch before Colleen plopped down next to him. She was a lot closer than he expected, not that he minded.

"Max, before you begin, I have to tell you, you look amazing in those clothes," said Amanda.

"Thank you, Amanda. It was nice to find clothes that fit. Before I forget, I want to let you know that Johann had been sending telegrams to Mary. She said that she had an affair with him the first year after you were married."

"It never stops, does it?" she asked before she sighed.

"It does now. Anyway, as you probably know, I was kind of upset about what happened, but not about getting shot again. I'm almost getting used to it, although I'd rather it ends with that one. I needed to stop Mary from ever doing something like this again and I had to use her own weapons against her. I needed to get away from distractions and didn't want to be in town with her nearby, so I rode Mars north and laid down for a while wondering what I should do. I decided around five o'clock and by nine I was in Wichita."

"You went to Wichita? But Mary was still here," Patty said.

"I know, Patty. That was why I rode to Wichita when I did, so I could get there before she left Burden. I met her husband, Charles Jones, the next morning and we had a nice chat. He waited for Mary to come home and confronted her with the information I provided to him and she finally gave it up. She agreed to a divorce settlement, and she can't say anything about what happened, but she received a five-thousand-dollar divorce settlement and got to keep her clothes. My guess is she'll go off somewhere and find some other rich victim to marry."

"Good for you, Max!" exclaimed Patty.

"I had to sign a non-disclosure agreement as well, so they would be sure I wouldn't say anything or sue them for Carl shooting me."

"But you wouldn't have said anything, Max," Colleen said.

"You're right, Colleen. But his lawyer got involved, so I had to sign the agreement."

"It probably doesn't matter anyway," Amanda replied.

"Normally, Amanda, I'd agree with you. But signing the agreement did make a difference. If I signed the agreement, the attorney recommended a settlement."

"How much did they give you?" asked Patty.

"Ten thousand dollars," he said without the least bit of fanfare.

There was stunned silence before Colleen started laughing.

"You finally get Mary to pay some measure for what she did, and if that wasn't satisfaction enough, you get ten thousand dollars for your effort. That's wonderful, Max!"

"What are you going to do now, Max?" asked Patty.

"You know, I still have no real idea. I want to fix up my shop to make it nicer, but I'd really like to do something nice for each of you. You've become very special to me."

"We don't need anything more, Max. You've given us much more than just things. You've made our lives worth living," said Patty.

"I've never told you how proud I am of each one of you. You've all come through terrible situations and have persevered. You've kept your dignity and your basic goodness. I'm lucky to know each of you."

"Max, it's not like we don't know that. Now that everything is settled, will you spend more time in the house?" asked Amanda.

"I'll still sleep in my shop. Especially after I fix it up. But I think I'm more relaxed now about all the things that have been going on. Let's face it, getting shot every other day can play havoc with your good moods."

They all laughed as Max was getting more conscious of Colleen sitting next to him.

"Now, I know that none of you would ever ask for anything, but when I was in Wichita, I wanted to find something for each of you. They're slightly different, but basically the same."

He reached into his jacket pocket and brought out three boxes and handed one to each lady.

They opened the boxes and Max could tell they were all pleased, even Colleen.

"Max, these are wonderful," said Patty.

"Thank you, Max. It's so useful, too," said Colleen, much to Max's relief.

"Are they set to the right time?" asked Amanda.

"They are. They're the same as my watch, so we can all be at some place at the correct time."

"But yours is so much plainer than ours."

"That's because I am a male of the species. If I were to carry an ornate watch, my fellow males would cast dispersions upon my manhood."

They all were tickled by the comment.

"I'm sure they'd all think you were on our side of the playing field," joked Amanda.

"I'd have a hard time finding a corset to fit, though."

They all started giggling at that image and Max noticed that Colleen had her hand on his shoulder as she laughed. Maybe.

"Now that we're all aware of the time, can I treat you ladies to lunch?" Max asked.

"Absolutely not, Mr. Wagner. You will allow us to make your lunch and dinner for you. You have never let us do that, and we are going to spoil you," said Colleen.

Max smiled, and not just because of what was said, but who had said it. It sounded as if she was coming out of her shell, but he wasn't about to press the issue. He wanted Colleen to be as comfortable as possible.

"Then, I'll accept your generous offer. I'll come out with you and we can talk while you're all trying to fatten me up."

Colleen still had her hand on his shoulder. and he didn't want to get up.

"Max, how is your leg?" asked Colleen.

"I know it's there."

"Does it hurt?"

"It's worse than the other two, but it'll get better. By the way, at the risk of making you all jealous, when I was in Wichita, Charlie Jones put me up in his suite at the Metropolitan Hotel. It had a full bathroom with hot and cold running water. I took a nice hot bath and whenever the water started cooling off, I just turned on the hot water valve again."

"Well, you're just going to have to take us all there, then," said Amanda.

"I will if you'd like to. We could take the train to Wichita, stay in the Metropolitan Hotel, then you could all go shopping and we could take the train back."

"You're serious, aren't you?" asked Patty.

"Of course, I'm serious. It would be a nice two-day trip. Listen, I have all that money sitting in the bank, so I may as well spend some on my favorite people."

Patty turned to Colleen and said, "That does sound like fun."

"I'd like to go," said Amanda.

"So, would I," said Colleen.

Now Max was really wondering what miraculous change had occurred in the past twenty-four hours and what had precipitated it.

"Let's plan on going in three days. Hopefully, Mary will already be gone. If she's not, I'll be prepared."

"How so?" asked Patty.

Max pulled back his jacket and showed them the Webley.

"Oh, my! You are prepared," she said.

"When we go to Wichita, I'll leave my Russians here."

"Let's go and get lunch going," said Amanda as she stood.

Amanda and Colleen both rose and Max waited for them all to pass him before he stood and walked behind them. As he followed, he wondered what he would do with all that money. The trip to Wichita, even if the ladies went crazy shopping, which he didn't think likely, wouldn't cost three hundred dollars.

Max sat at the kitchen table and watched the women as they prepared the food. He was trying not to concentrate on Colleen, but it was difficult.

"Did you know we talked to Mary that night?" asked Amanda.

"I hate to ask what she told you," Max replied.

"Just what you told her," she replied.

Max was a bit worried now. *Just how much had Mary said?*

"What exactly did she tell you?" he asked.

"She said that you covered for her."

"Which I really didn't, but I needed her to think that, but she said nothing else of a, um, sexual nature?"

"No. Why? What did you two talk about?"

Now, Max realized he had talked himself into a corner, but replied, "She basically thought I was bedding all of you."

"You told her the truth, didn't you?" asked Patty.

"Of course, I did. I was kind of annoyed that she brought it up."

He was blushing, so Amanda thought he was hiding something and asked, "Alright, Max, what did you tell her that is so embarrassing?"

"I'd rather not tell you. It's kind of personal and has nothing to do with any of you or Mary, either."

Now all the women had their curiosity nerves tingling, and it was Patty who guessed it first but didn't say anything. Amanda was not so circumspect.

"Never?" she asked loudly.

Max turned six shades of scarlet as Colleen finally caught on and felt sorry for Max. Not because he was a virgin, but because he was so embarrassed by it.

Max exhaled and said, "You have to understand. I was just a naïve kid who thought that you only did that with someone you loved. By the time I found out differently, I was in prison."

"Well, I for one, am proud of you, Max," said Patty.

"You're not the only one," said Colleen quietly, not thinking anyone had heard but was wrong.

"Well, we'll just have to lock you two in a bedroom," joked Amanda.

It was a bad choice to try to lighten the conversation, as a flushed Colleen ran from the kitchen into her room and closed the door.

Max thought that all the positive changes Colleen had made were just thrown away, but he couldn't blame Amanda, although Patty seemed to be going that way.

"I'm sorry. I didn't mean to get Colleen upset," Amanda said.

"I know, Amanda. It's just a sensitive subject to those of us with that situation," he said, knowing that Colleen's problems had less to do with her unsullied condition than her memories.

"I think maybe I should leave. Colleen will do better if I'm not here," Max said.

"Max, it's not your fault," said Patty.

"I know that, but it's my presence that's causing the problem. That's why I've been staying away so much. I really do understand Colleen and I wish I could help, but there's nothing I can do. I'll get something at Sunny's."

Max stood and walked out the back door, then headed around to the front and mounted Mars, feeling as if he was right back where he was before Mary's arrival. He rode back through the alley, arrived at the corral, and found the extra horse still there, Carl's horse. He had to get rid of the animal, so he left Mars saddled, mounted, and just looped a trail rope around the roan and led him out of the corral and down the street to the livery, where he dismounted and led the horse into the barn.

"Bob!" he shouted as he walked inside.

Bob popped out of the small living area he had on the right side of the barn and asked, "Max, what do you have there?"

"A gift, Bob. Do you want him?"

"Sure. What's the catch?"

"No catch. He belonged to that goofball that tried to kill me a couple of days ago."

"Oh, that one. So many have been trying to kill you these days, it's hard to keep up."

"You know, that would be funny if it weren't true."

He handed the trail rope to Bob and returned to Mars but didn't bother getting in the saddle. It was less painful to walk than it was to mount and dismount again. After reaching the corral, he returned Mars to join the three mares and unsaddled him before returning to his shop.

———

Colleen had been terrified by the implication when Amanda had said that. Yet, as she lay on her bed, she held Max's note about the steam engine in her hands. She kept reading that simple line and remembered how wonderful she had felt when she sat next to him on the couch and rested her hand on his shoulder, and she was disgusted with herself. *Why can't she be like other women?*

There was a gentle knock on the door, and she hoped it wasn't Max.

"Colleen?"

Colleen relaxed and said, "Come in, Patty."

Patty opened the door and stepped inside, closing it behind her.

"Are you all right, Colleen?" she asked as she sat on the edge of the bed.

"I'm fine. I was just startled by what Amanda said."

"She didn't mean for it to come out that way."

"I know. It's not Amanda, Patty. It's me."

"Colleen, I know what that bastard that called himself our father did to me or tried to. But I kicked and scratched, so he left me alone. You were too afraid to do that, and he took advantage of you. I can't imagine the horror of living with that every night for a year.

"All I can tell you is that it isn't the same when you're married. I didn't even love Joe, but I didn't mind it at all. I enjoyed it sometimes and would have enjoyed it immensely if I had been in love with Joe and he had loved me back. A man like Max is so rare. He loves you so much he's willing to give up what he wants to do just to make you happy. He'll leave Burden rather than make you feel uncomfortable."

Colleen looked quickly at her sister and asked, "Why would he leave? This is his house."

"Because he thinks you see him as a threat."

"That's not true, Patty. I just wish he could fix me like he did that steam engine. I'm so broken."

"He can fix you, Colleen, but you have to want him to fix you. If your watch stopped working and it needed to be repaired, wishing it would be fixed doesn't get it working again. You have to take the watch to the watchmaker, so he can work on it.

"When I was broken, I got married. Because I didn't love Joe, it took longer for me to be fixed than if I had a repairman who knew what he was doing. Max loves you, Colleen. He wants to help fix you, but you have to go to him and let him know you need his help."

"Do you think that would really work?" she asked quietly.

"How did you feel when you sat next to him today and rested your hand on his shoulder?"

"Wonderful," she admitted.

"Now, how would you feel if he held you close and kissed you?"

"I don't know."

"I do. You'd melt, Colleen. You'd know that he loves you and you would feel it flow through you."

"How do you know?"

"There have been moments, Colleen. Not with Joe, but with boys that I thought I loved. They were just summer romances, but it would curl my toes. I can't imagine how extraordinary it would be with a man like Max who loves you as much as he does."

She thought for a few seconds before quietly asking, "Where is Max?"

"He returned to his shop."

"He didn't stay for lunch?"

"No. He said he felt his presence was making you uncomfortable."

"It wasn't him. It was the thought. It took me by surprise."

"I know, Colleen. Come on out and have some lunch."

She followed her sister out to the kitchen and received a heartfelt apology from Amanda.

———

Max wound up skipping lunch. He had his new leather travel bag still filled with his clothes from Wichita and wondered if it wouldn't be wiser to get out of town for a week or two and let things settle down.

He took off his new jacket and hung it on a peg, then walked into the shop and looked around for something to take his mind off Colleen. It wasn't easy. He didn't know if he could take the extreme swings in his mind. Colleen holds his arm and he's ecstatic. She gets upset and he drops into a morass. *Will it always be like this if he continued to care?*

He almost wished he could just turn it off, but he couldn't. He wanted to be able to help Colleen, but if he tried, she'd probably be worse off. It was a problem for which he saw no solution.

There was a knock on the big doors, and Max smiled. It was an odd time for his first customer since his return.

He stood, unlocked the door, and pushed it open slowly, seeing Colleen standing there with her steam engine.

"I need something fixed, Max," she asked softly.

"Come in, Colleen," he said as he stood aside.

Colleen walked in and set the steam engine on the table. Max sat down at the table to examine the toy as Colleen turned and pulled the door closed.

"What's wrong with it, Colleen?" he asked.

"Nothing, Max. That's not what's broken. I am."

Max looked back at her, and asked quietly, "Sit down, will you please, Colleen?"

MAX

Colleen sat down across the table from Max and said, "Max, I just don't know what to say."

"Colleen, I can't fix something if I don't know the symptoms or the cause. Could you talk to me about how you're broken?"

Colleen wanted to look down but found her eyes drawn to his and focused there instead while she spoke softly.

"It's my father. After Patty left, for a year, he would climb into my bed and pull up my nightdress. He'd lie against me and fondle me, and I can't tell you how terrified I was every night. I kept waiting for him to violate me, but he never did. I don't know if that was worse, expecting it every night or imagining the worst. All I know is that I'm now so frightened of being close to another man, even you, Max."

Max watched her eyes, saw the pain and the doubt before he replied so softly, it almost reached a whisper, "Colleen, I won't pretend to even have a tiny bit of understanding of just how horrible that must have been for you. For you to have even been able to function as normally as you have is remarkable. I imagine most young women put into a situation like that would have been reduced to a blubbering mess.

"But that doesn't mean you're free from troubles, because I know you aren't. But there is one thing you need to understand and that is that I love you, Colleen. I'll do anything I can to make you better and I would be willing to leave if I thought it would help, but now I know the best way I can help is to stay with you."

Colleen's eyes were misting as she replied, "Thank you, Max. I do love you, Max. Please believe me. It's just so difficult, the other part. Trust me in that."

"I do trust you. Thank you for telling me, Colleen. I was never sure that I'd hear you say what happened."

"Is it important?", she asked, her eyes still locked on his.

"For what I'm about to do, it is."

"What are you going to do, Max?" she whispered.

"I'm going to kiss you, Colleen."

Colleen looked at him, those warm, wonderful blue eyes, and saw nothing but compassion and something else. *Was love enough to beat back her demons?*

"Okay," she barely whispered.

Colleen stood after Max rose and walked close to her. He put his hands softly on her shoulders and leaned forward and gently placed his lips on hers.

Colleen felt her toes curl and a chill run down her back.

Max took his right hand from her shoulder and placed his fingers under her chin and lifted her head upward slightly and kissed her a little more passionately.

Colleen didn't know why she did, but she put her hands behind his head and pulled him closer. Max then wrapped his big arms around her and held her close. Now, Colleen understood. This was thrilling and not horrible at all.

Finally, Max ended the kiss and put his lips near her ear, and whispered, "I love you, Colleen."

Colleen couldn't answer as she began to cry.

Max at first thought he had upset her and was ready to release her, but she put her arms around him and pulled him closer, and held onto him as tightly as she could. Her tears washed away all her fears and terrors as unbridled ecstasy engulfed her entire being. This, very simply, was love. She felt her demons trying to fight back, but losing as she continued to cry, and Max let her as he held onto Colleen.

She cried for almost three minutes and then finally, she looked up into his eyes and with a sobbing laugh, asked, "What is your charge for fixing broken women?"

Max smiled as he looked at her face and replied, "I'm not sure. What do they charge for a marriage license?"

———

Two weeks later, Max stood across from Colleen at the altar. Their vows had been exchanged, their rings placed on their fingers, but before he kissed his new bride, Max reached into his pocket and took out a simple emerald necklace with a small diamond on each side.

Colleen gazed into his eyes as she held her auburn hair back, allowing Max to clasp the necklace around her throat. For five seconds, they looked into each other's eyes. The love was palpable in the church. Then, Max pulled his new bride to him and kissed her as Colleen Wagner.

EPILOGUE

Max watched as his son toddled across the main room floor.

"He's trying to escape, Colleen. He's heading your way."

Colleen laughed and trotted toward the main room and caught little Harry, then picked him up and turned him back toward his father.

Colleen walked over to Max and sat down next to him on the couch and curled up against him. Max automatically put his arm around his wife.

"Is she finally asleep?" he asked.

"She is. I don't remember Harry being as active as she is."

"He was. We just didn't have to spend all our time chasing another one around."

"No. You were too busy chasing me around," she said as she laughed.

"And you were letting me catch you, my love."

She kissed him and said, "That's when the fun starts."

He still remembered those first few days when they were both so new at this husband-and-wife routine that they wound up laughing at themselves half the time. But by the end of the week, they had all the details worked out.

They were best friends and still wanted to spend as much time together as possible. Of course, with Harry toddling around, and his little sister staying awake so much, a lot of that free time evaporated. But their children would never know a house without love. And when little Elsa would be standing at the altar in twenty years or so, she'd be wearing a familiar piece of jewelry that had first been worn by her namesake. But for now, it was worn by her mother; her happy, completely contented mother.

And on the table in the main room was a shiny little steam engine with a brass plaque that read:

Repaired by Max Wagner.
He can fix anything.

BOOK LIST

1	Rock Creek	12/26/2016
2	North of Denton	01/02/2017
3	Fort Selden	01/07/2017
4	Scotts Bluff	01/14/2017
5	South of Denver	01/22/2017
6	Miles City	01/28/2017
7	Hopewell	02/04/2017
8	Nueva Luz	02/12/2017
9	The Witch of Dakota	02/19/2017
10	Baker City	03/13/2017
11	The Gun Smith	03/21/2017
12	Gus	03/24/2017
13	Wilmore	04/06/2017
14	Mister Thor	04/20/2017
15	Nora	04/26/2017
16	Max	05/09/2017
17	Hunting Pearl	05/14/2017
18	Bessie	05/25/2017
19	The Last Four	05/29/2017
20	Zack	06/12/2017
21	Finding Bucky	06/21/2017
22	The Debt	06/30/2017
23	The Scalawags	07/11/2017
24	The Stampede	08/23/2019
25	The Wake of the Bertrand	07/31/2017
26	Cole	08/09/2017
27	Luke	09/05/2017
28	The Eclipse	09/21/2017
29	A.J. Smith	10/03/2017
30	Slow John	11/05/2017
31	The Second Star	11/15/2017
32	Tate	12/03/2017
33	Virgil's Herd	12/14/2017
34	Marsh's Valley	01/01/2018
35	Alex Paine	01/18/2018
36	Ben Gray	02/05/2018
37	War Adams	03/05/2018

38	Mac's Cabin	03/21/2018
39	Will Scott	04/13/2018
40	Sheriff Joe	04/22/2018
41	Chance	05/17/2018
42	Doc Holt	06/17/2018
43	Ted Shepard	07/16/2018
44	Haven	07/30/2018
45	Sam's County	08/19/2018
46	Matt Dunne	09/07/2018
47	Conn Jackson	10/06/2018
48	Gabe Owens	10/27/2018
49	Abandoned	11/18/2018
50	Retribution	12/21/2018
51	Inevitable	02/04/2019
52	Scandal in Topeka	03/18/2019
53	Return to Hardeman County	04/10/2019
54	Deception	06/02.2019
55	The Silver Widows	06/27/2019
56	Hitch	08/22/2018
57	Dylan's Journey	10/10/2019
58	Bryn's War	11/05/2019
59	Huw's Legacy	11/30/2019
60	Lynn's Search	12/24/2019
61	Bethan's Choice	02/12/2020
62	Rhody Jones	03/11/2020
63	Alwen's Dream	06/14/2020
64	The Nothing Man	06/30/2020
65	Cy Page	07/19/2020
66	Tabby Hayes	09/04/2020
67	Dylan's Memories	09/20/2020
68	Letter for Gene	09/09/2020
69	Grip Taylor	10/10/2020
70	Garrett's Duty	11/09/2020
71	East of the Cascades	12/02/2020
72	The Iron Wolfe	12/23/2020
73	Wade Rivers	01/09/2021
74	Ghost Train	01/27/2021
75	The Inheritance	02/26/2021
76	Cap Tyler	03/26/2021

Made in United States
North Haven, CT
06 April 2023

35095668R00188